MR. WOLF'S CLASS

MYSTERY CLUB

ARON NELS STEINKE

AN IMPRINT OF
SCHOLASTIC

For my students

Library of Congress Control Number: 2017962944

ISBN 978-1-338-04774-5 (hardcover)
ISBN 978-1-338-04773-8 (paperback)

10 9 8 7 21 22 23

Printed in China 62
First edition, March 2019

Edited by Cassandra Pelham Fulton
Book design by Phil Falco
Creative Director: David Saylor

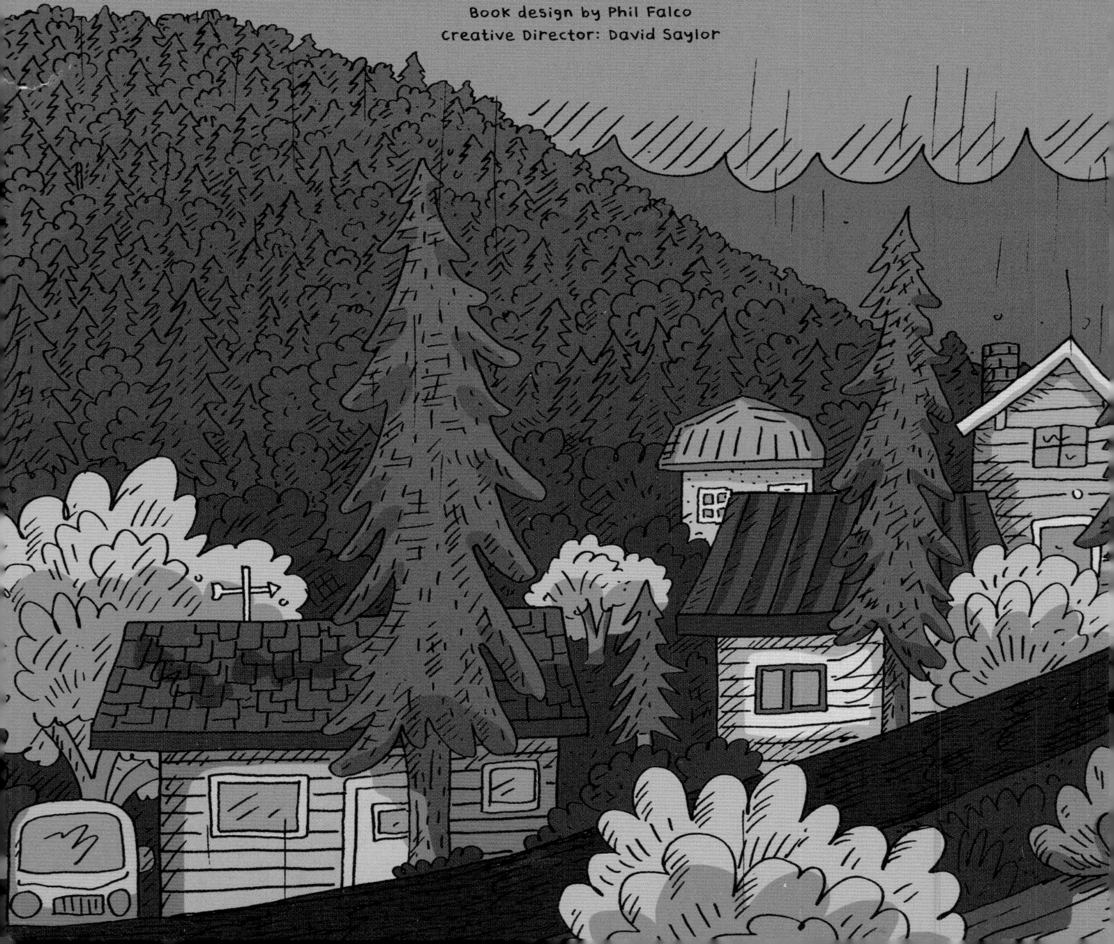

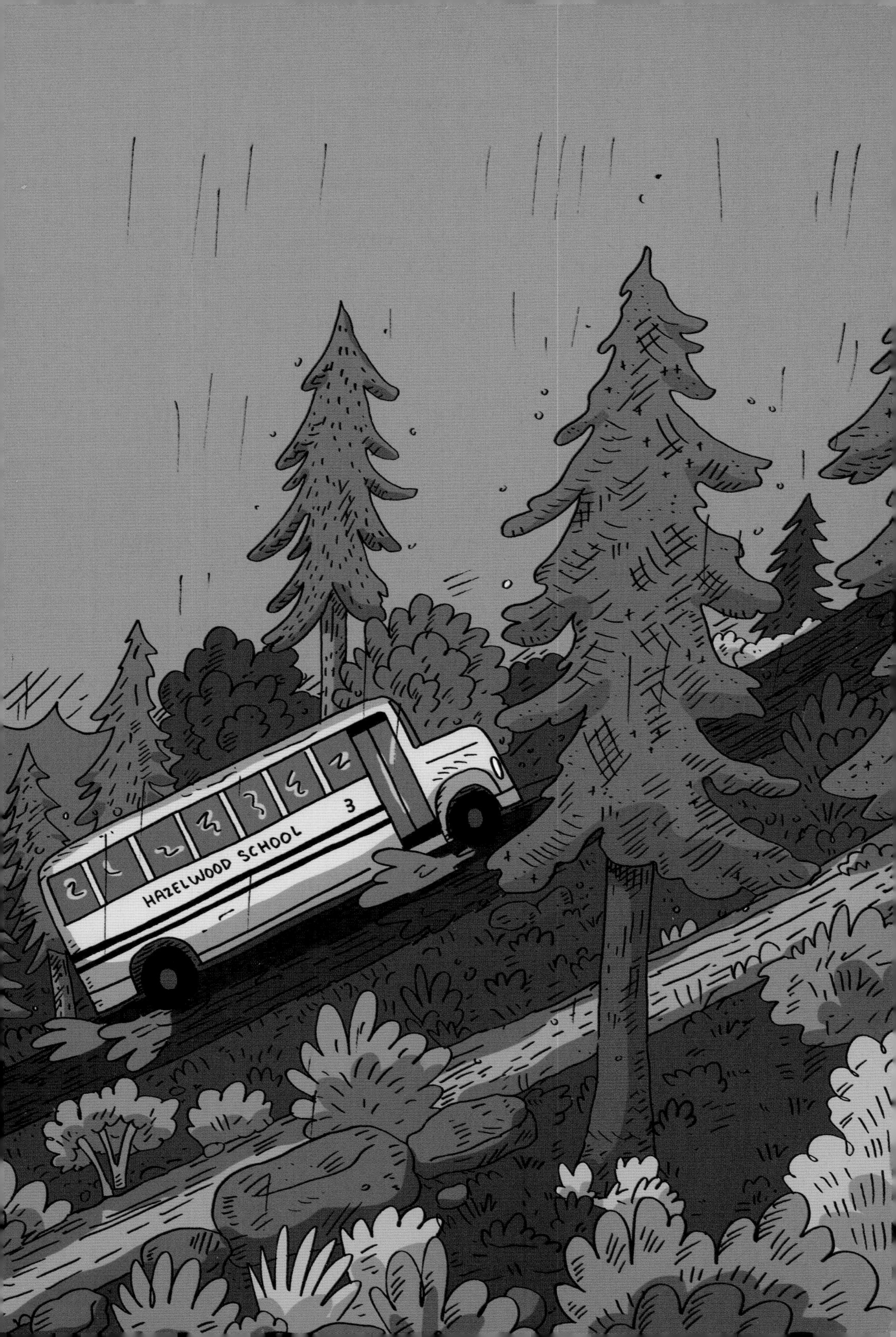
HAZELWOOD SCHOOL
3

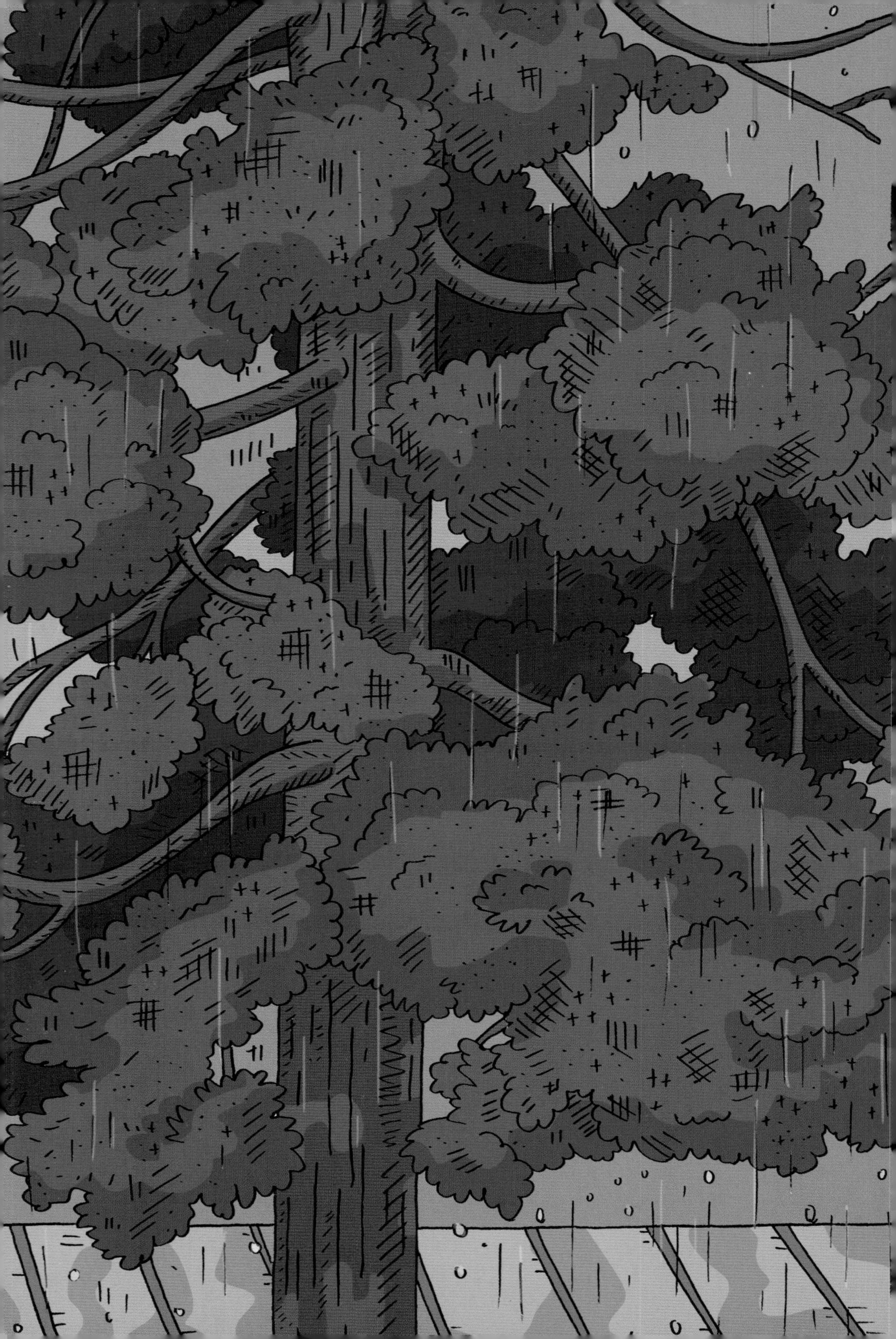

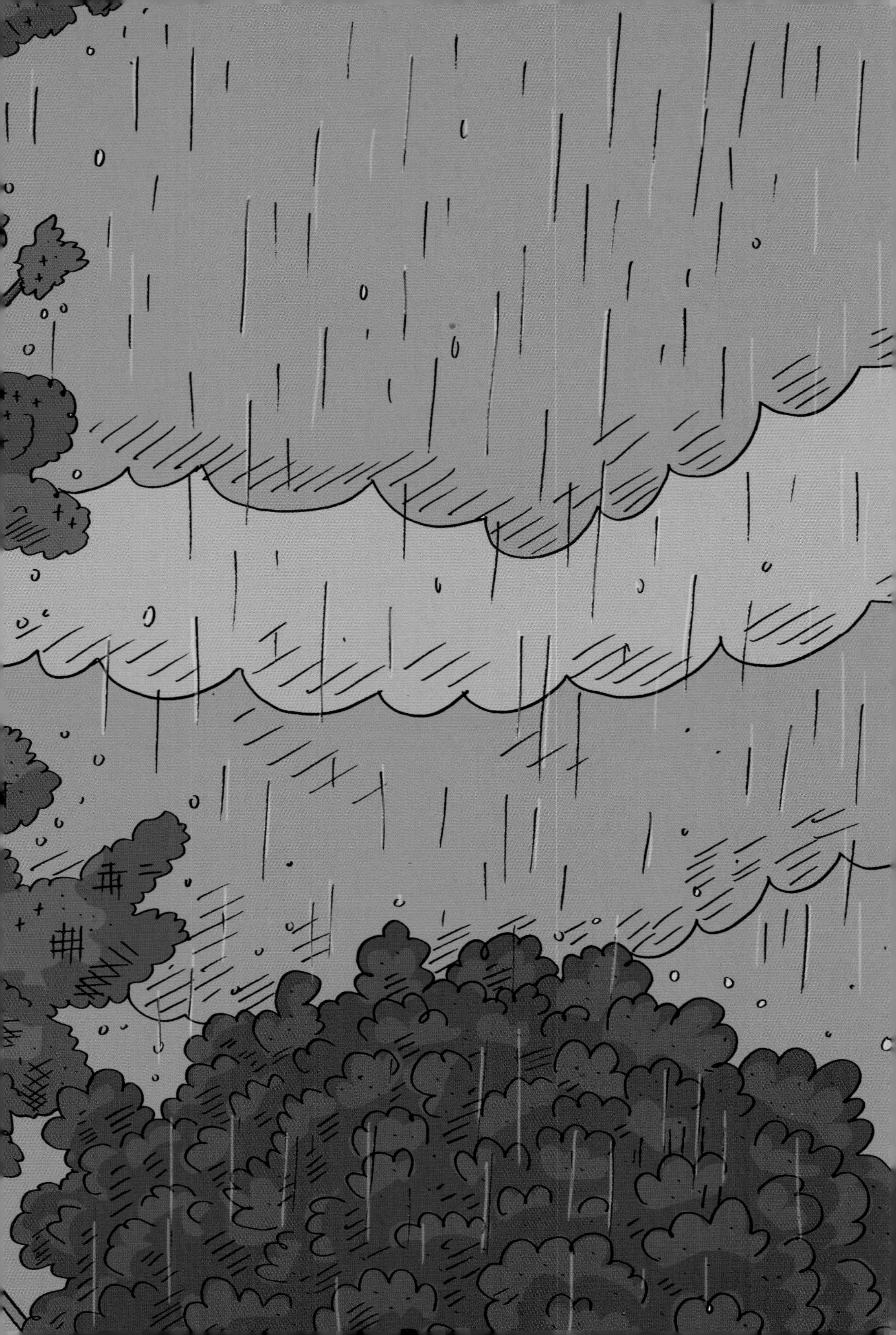

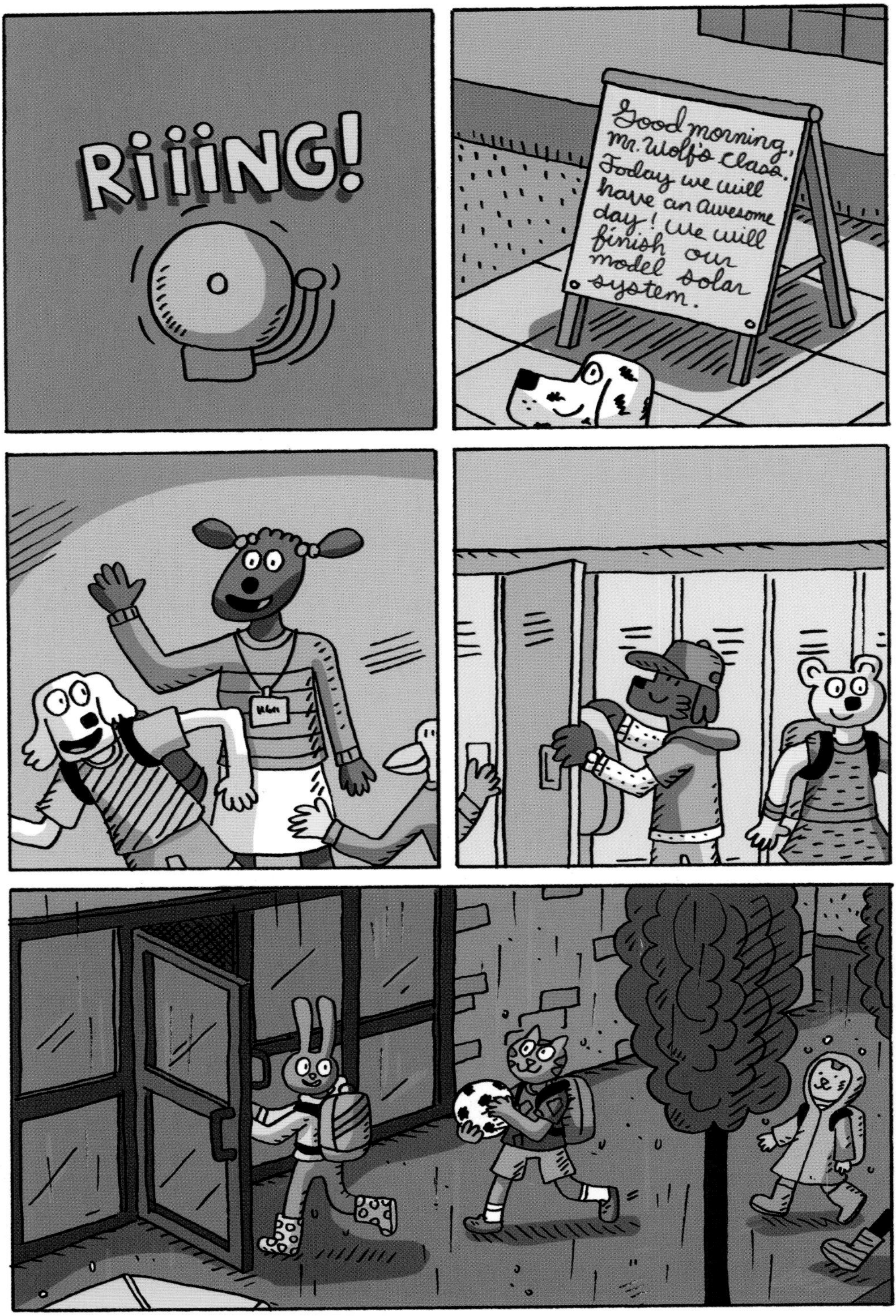
RIIING!
Good morning, Mr. Wolf's class. Today we will have an awesome day! We will finish our model solar system.

CHAPTER ONE

You're All Invited

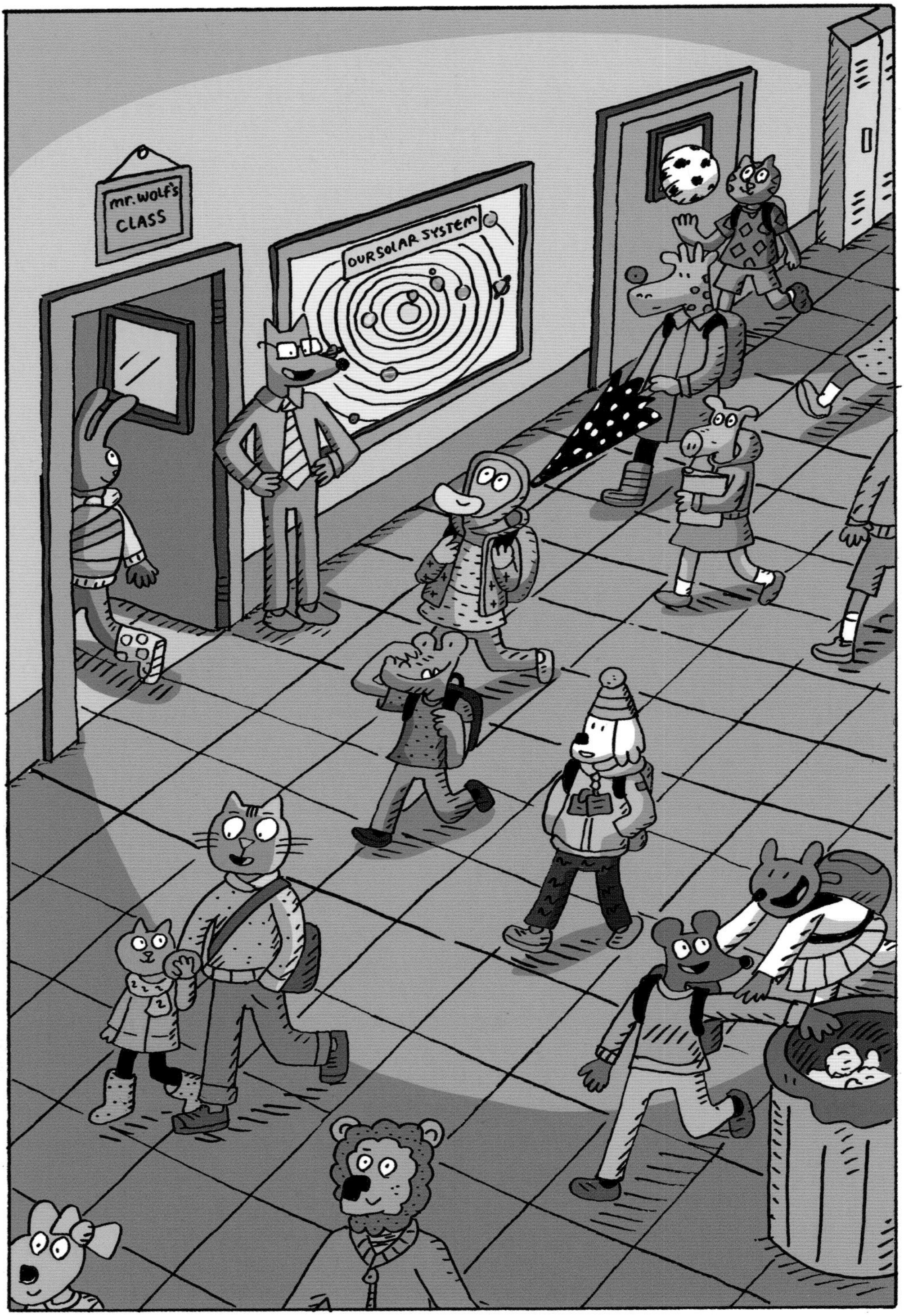
mr. wolf's CLASS
OUR SOLAR SYSTEM

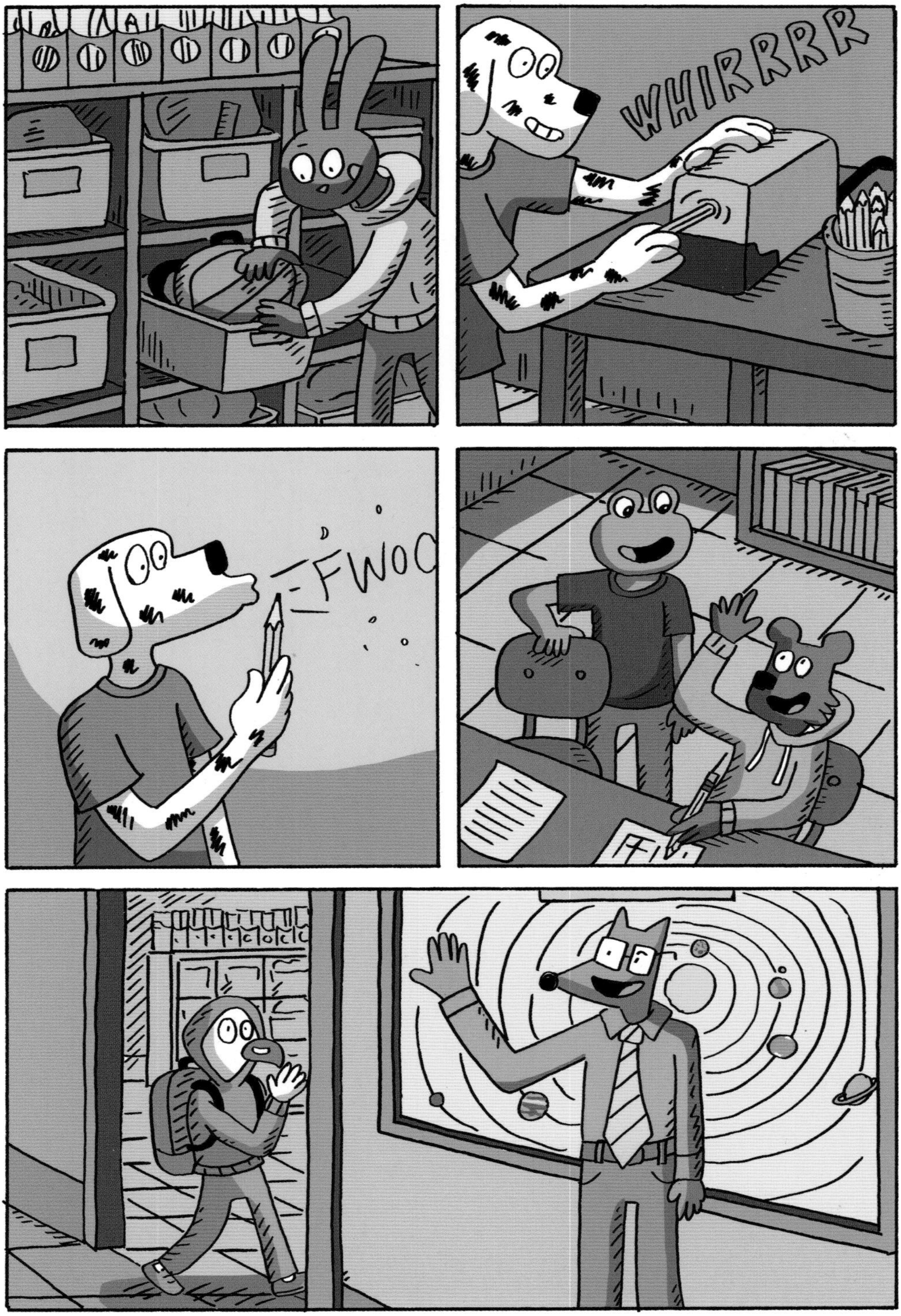
WHIRRRR
FWOC

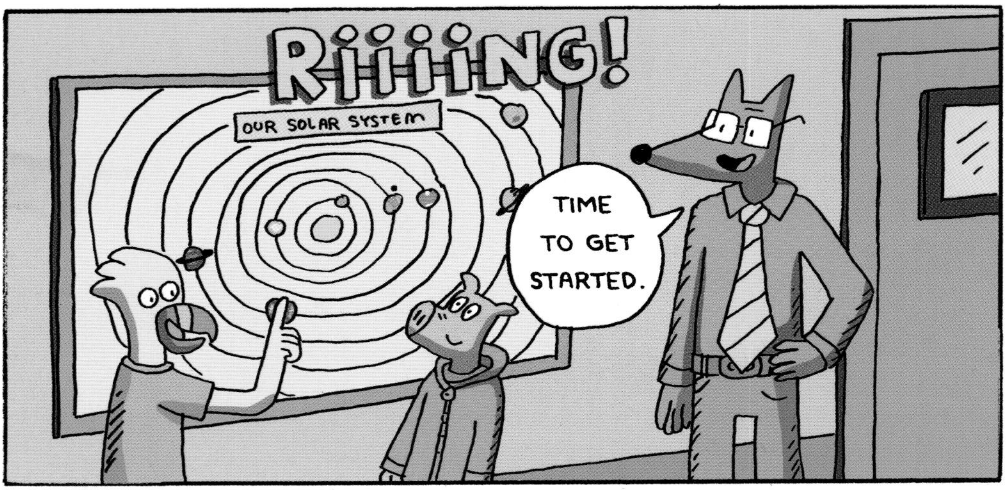
RIIIING!
OUR SOLAR SYSTEM
TIME TO GET STARTED.

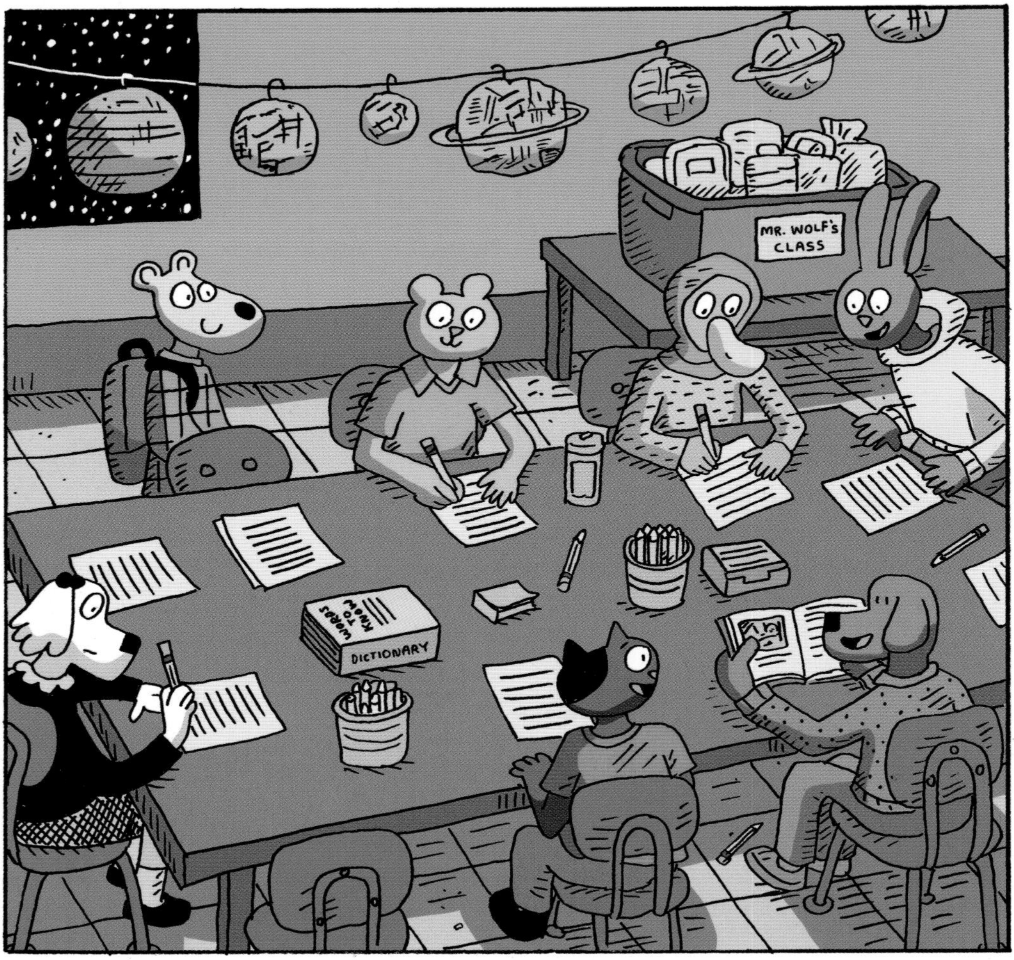
MR. WOLF'S CLASS
WORDS TO KNOW
DICTIONARY

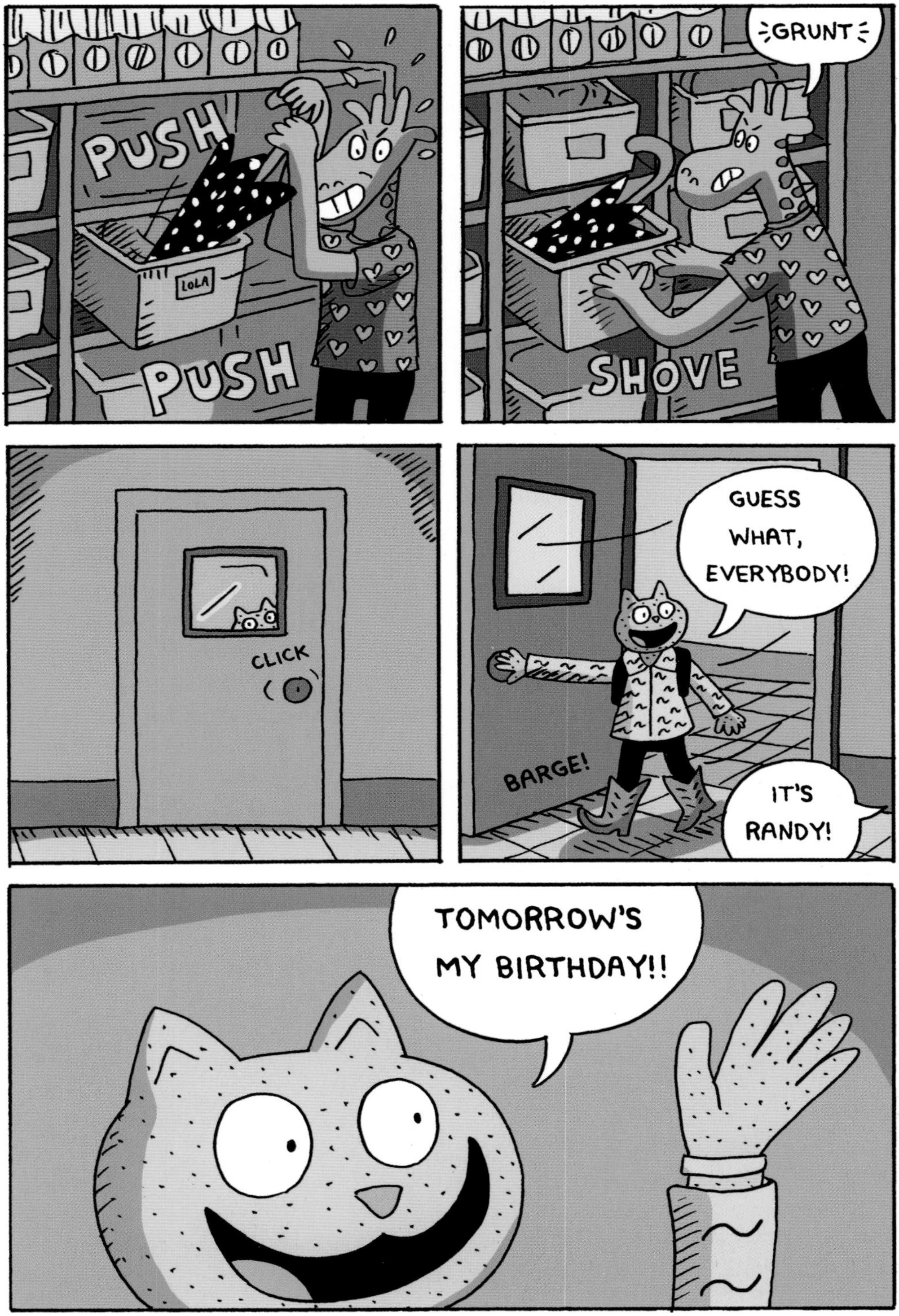
PUSH
LOLA
PUSH
GRUNT
SHOVE
CLICK
GUESS WHAT, EVERYBODY!
BARGE!
IT'S RANDY!
TOMORROW'S MY BIRTHDAY!!

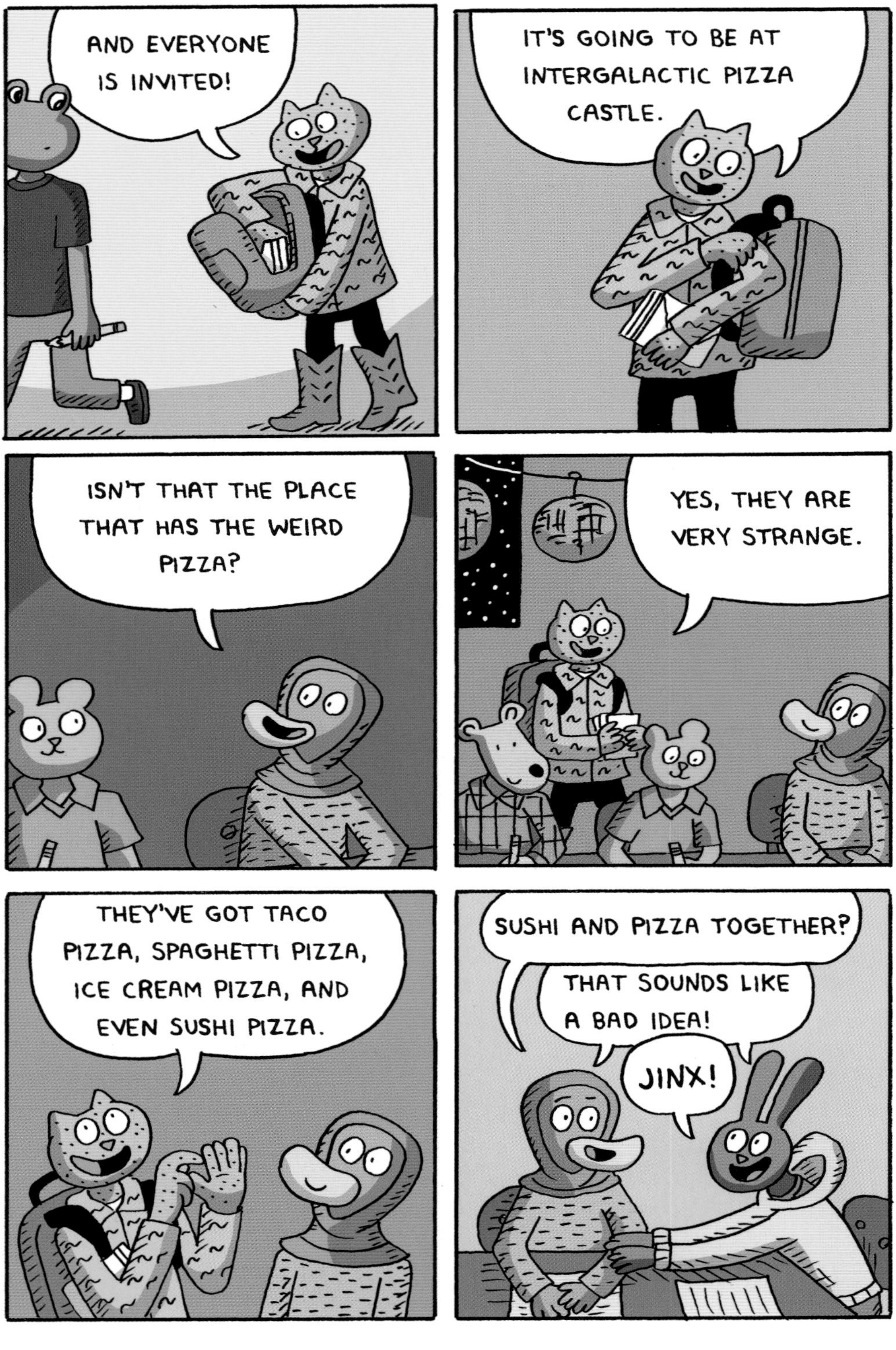
AND EVERYONE IS INVITED!
IT'S GOING TO BE AT INTERGALACTIC PIZZA CASTLE.
ISN'T THAT THE PLACE THAT HAS THE WEIRD PIZZA?
YES, THEY ARE VERY STRANGE.
THEY'VE GOT TACO PIZZA, SPAGHETTI PIZZA, ICE CREAM PIZZA, AND EVEN SUSHI PIZZA.
SUSHI AND PIZZA TOGETHER?
THAT SOUNDS LIKE A BAD IDEA!
JINX!

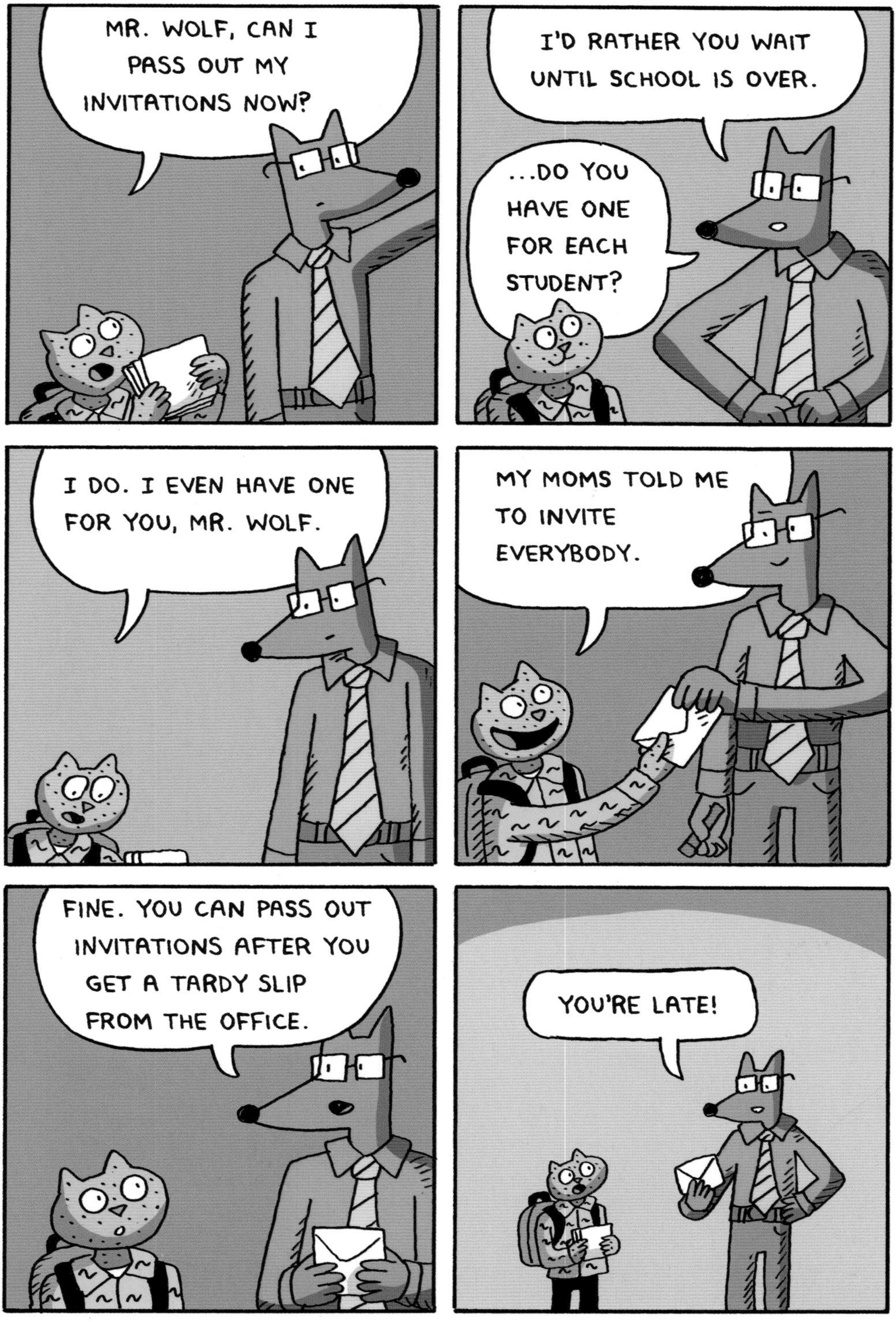
MR. WOLF, CAN I PASS OUT MY INVITATIONS NOW?
I'D RATHER YOU WAIT UNTIL SCHOOL IS OVER.
...DO YOU HAVE ONE FOR EACH STUDENT?
I DO. I EVEN HAVE ONE FOR YOU, MR. WOLF.
MY MOMS TOLD ME TO INVITE EVERYBODY.
FINE. YOU CAN PASS OUT INVITATIONS AFTER YOU GET A TARDY SLIP FROM THE OFFICE.
YOU'RE LATE!

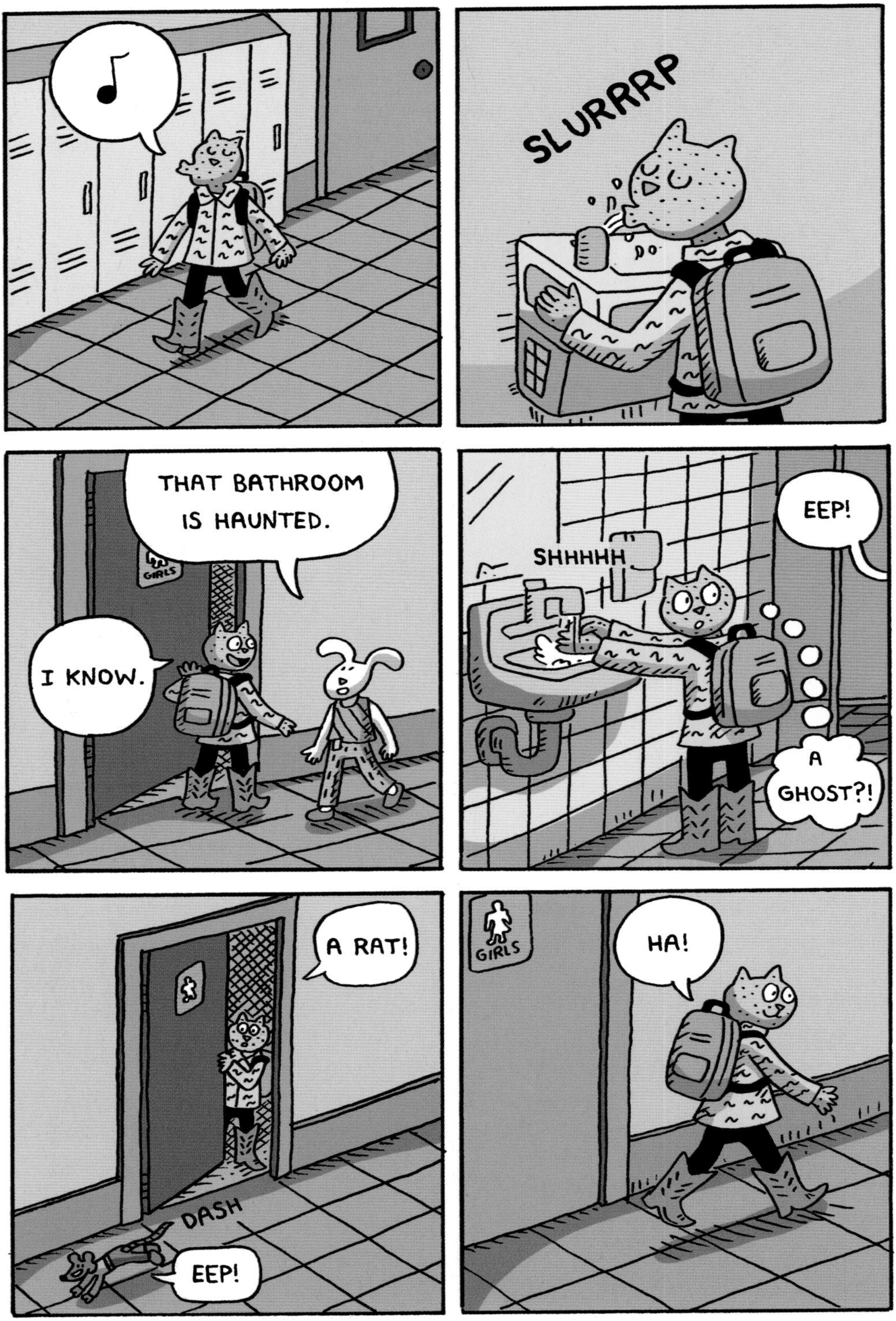

♪
SLURRRP
THAT BATHROOM IS HAUNTED.
I KNOW.
GIRLS
SHHHHH
EEP!
A GHOST?!
A RAT!
DASH
EEP!
GIRLS
HA!

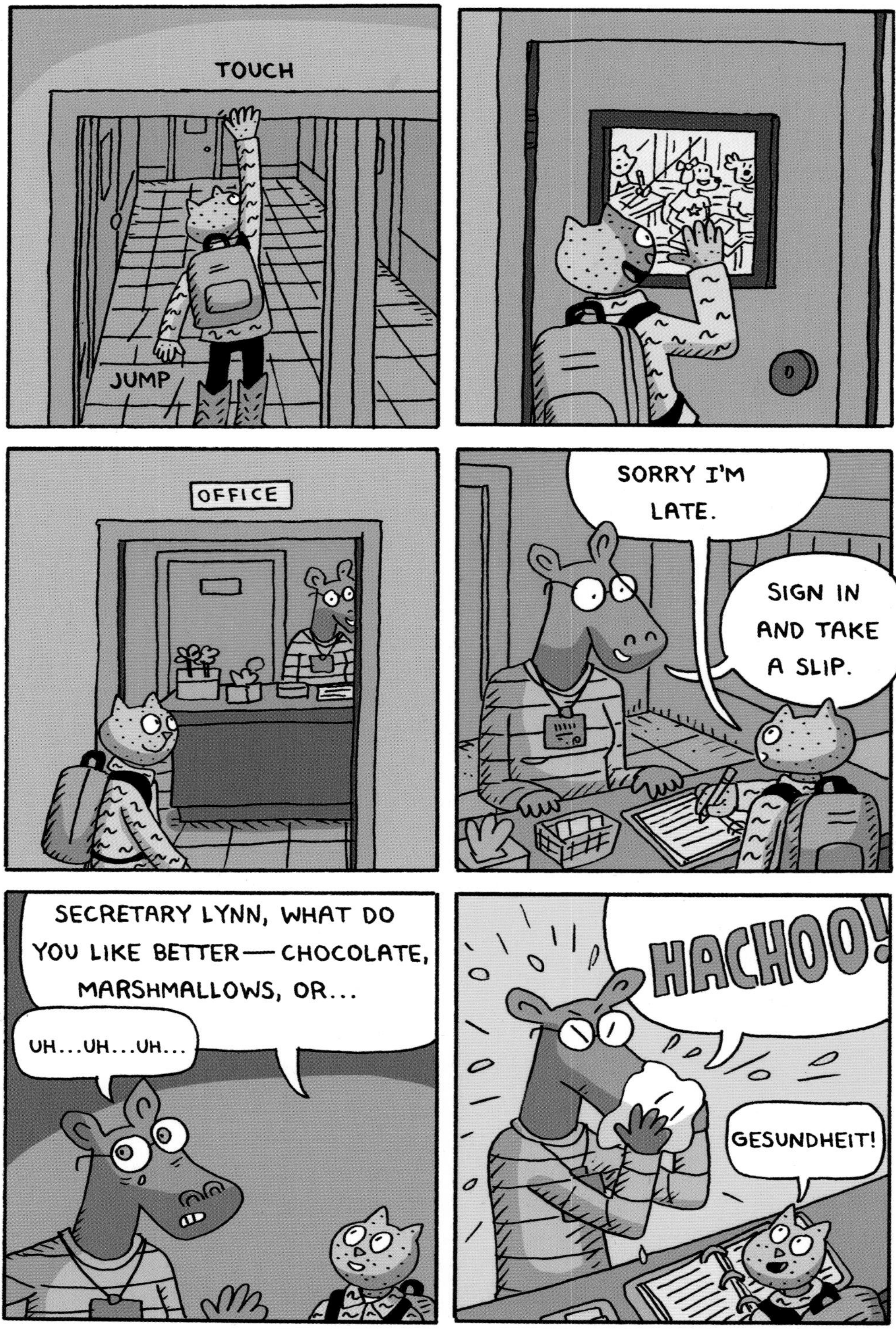
TOUCH
JUMP
OFFICE
SORRY I'M LATE.
SIGN IN AND TAKE A SLIP.
SECRETARY LYNN, WHAT DO YOU LIKE BETTER—CHOCOLATE, MARSHMALLOWS, OR...
UH...UH...UH...
HACHOO!
GESUNDHEIT!

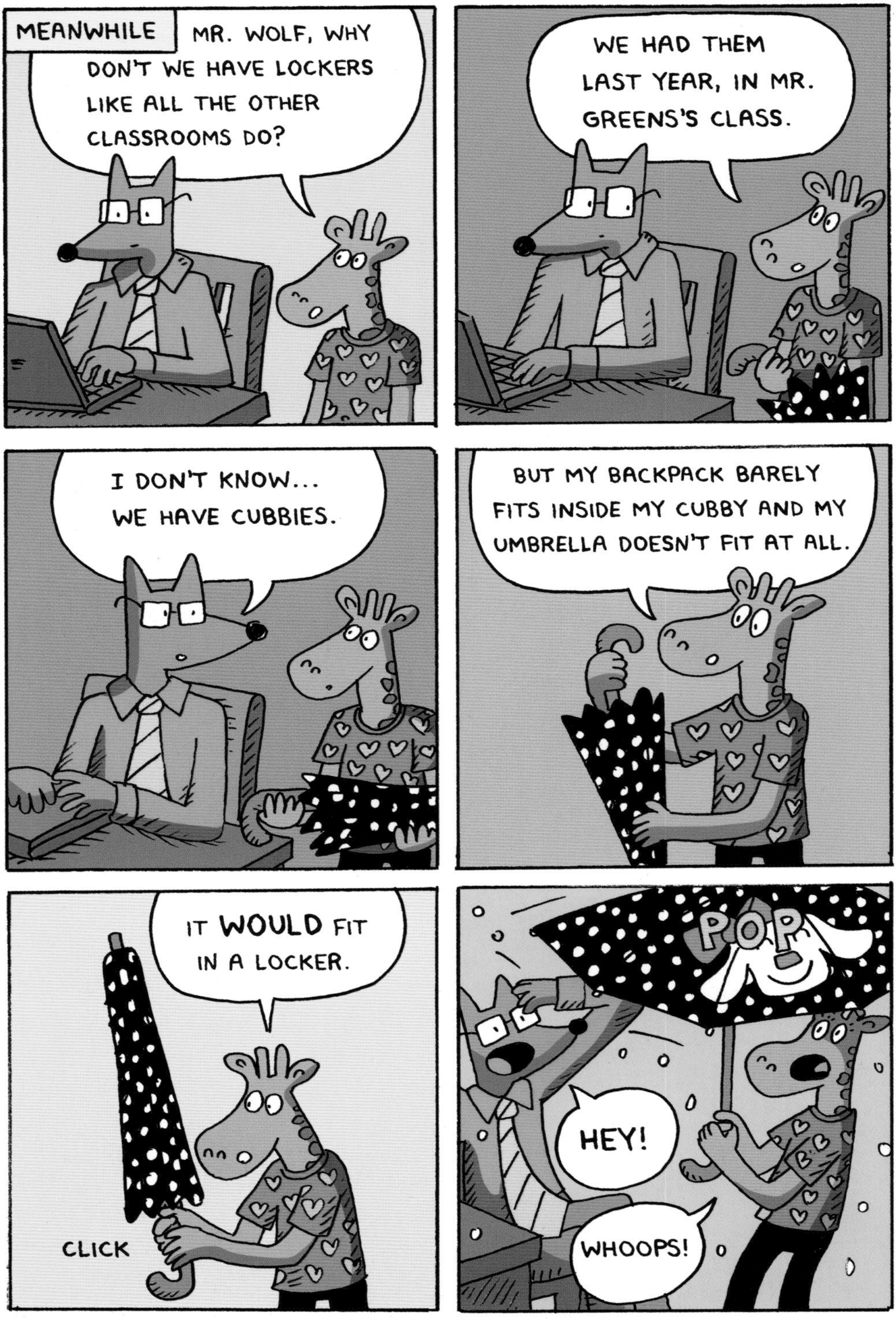
MEANWHILE
MR. WOLF, WHY DON'T WE HAVE LOCKERS LIKE ALL THE OTHER CLASSROOMS DO?
WE HAD THEM LAST YEAR, IN MR. GREENS'S CLASS.
I DON'T KNOW... WE HAVE CUBBIES.
BUT MY BACKPACK BARELY FITS INSIDE MY CUBBY AND MY UMBRELLA DOESN'T FIT AT ALL.
IT WOULD FIT IN A LOCKER.
CLICK
POP
HEY!
WHOOPS!

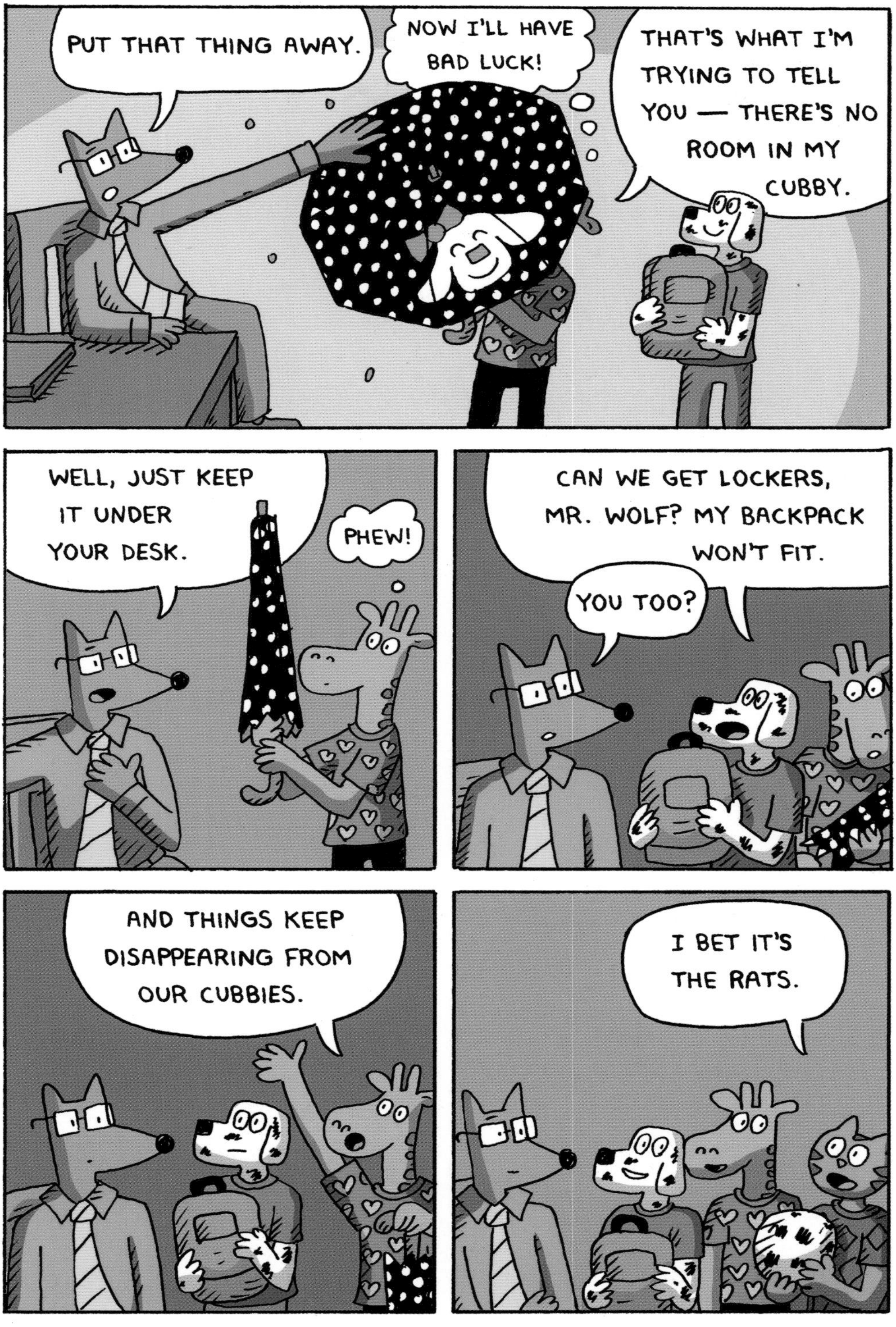
PUT THAT THING AWAY.
NOW I'LL HAVE BAD LUCK!
THAT'S WHAT I'M TRYING TO TELL YOU — THERE'S NO ROOM IN MY CUBBY.
WELL, JUST KEEP IT UNDER YOUR DESK.
PHEW!
CAN WE GET LOCKERS, MR. WOLF? MY BACKPACK WON'T FIT.
YOU TOO?
AND THINGS KEEP DISAPPEARING FROM OUR CUBBIES.
I BET IT'S THE RATS.

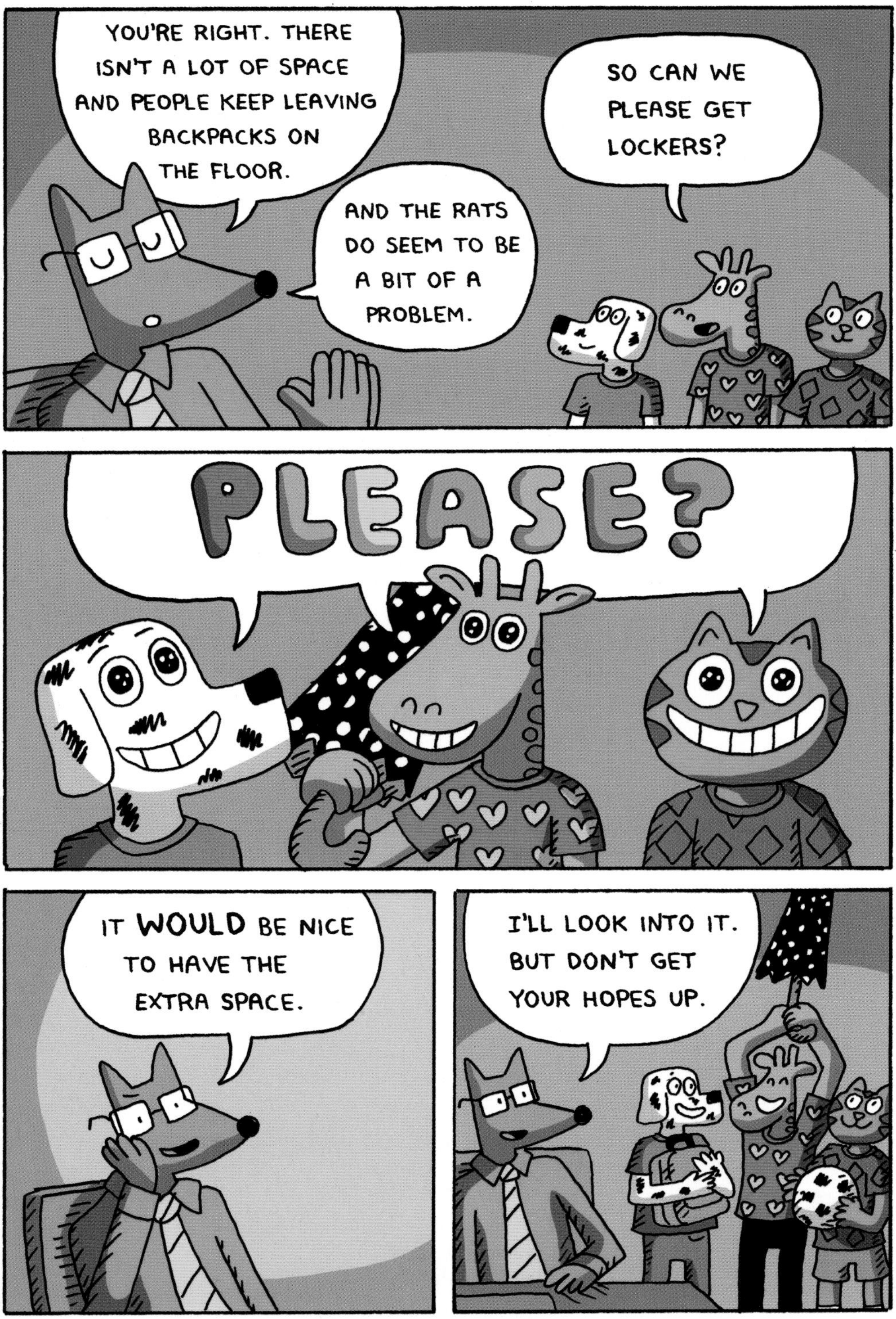
YOU'RE RIGHT. THERE ISN'T A LOT OF SPACE AND PEOPLE KEEP LEAVING BACKPACKS ON THE FLOOR.
AND THE RATS DO SEEM TO BE A BIT OF A PROBLEM.
SO CAN WE PLEASE GET LOCKERS?
PLEASE?
IT WOULD BE NICE TO HAVE THE EXTRA SPACE.
I'LL LOOK INTO IT. BUT DON'T GET YOUR HOPES UP.

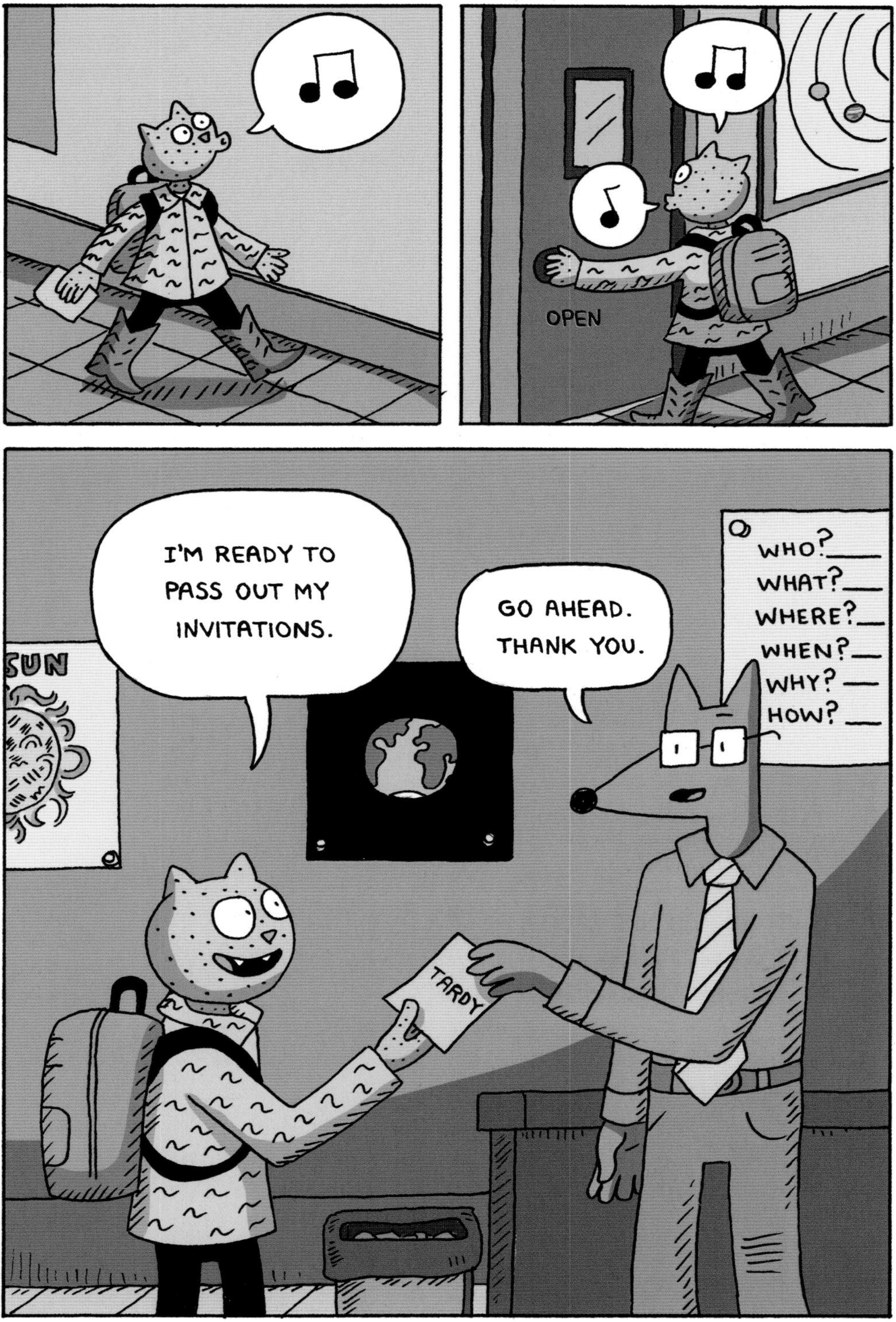
OPEN
I'M READY TO PASS OUT MY INVITATIONS.
SUN
GO AHEAD. THANK YOU.
WHO?
WHAT?
WHERE?
WHEN?
WHY?
HOW?
TARDY

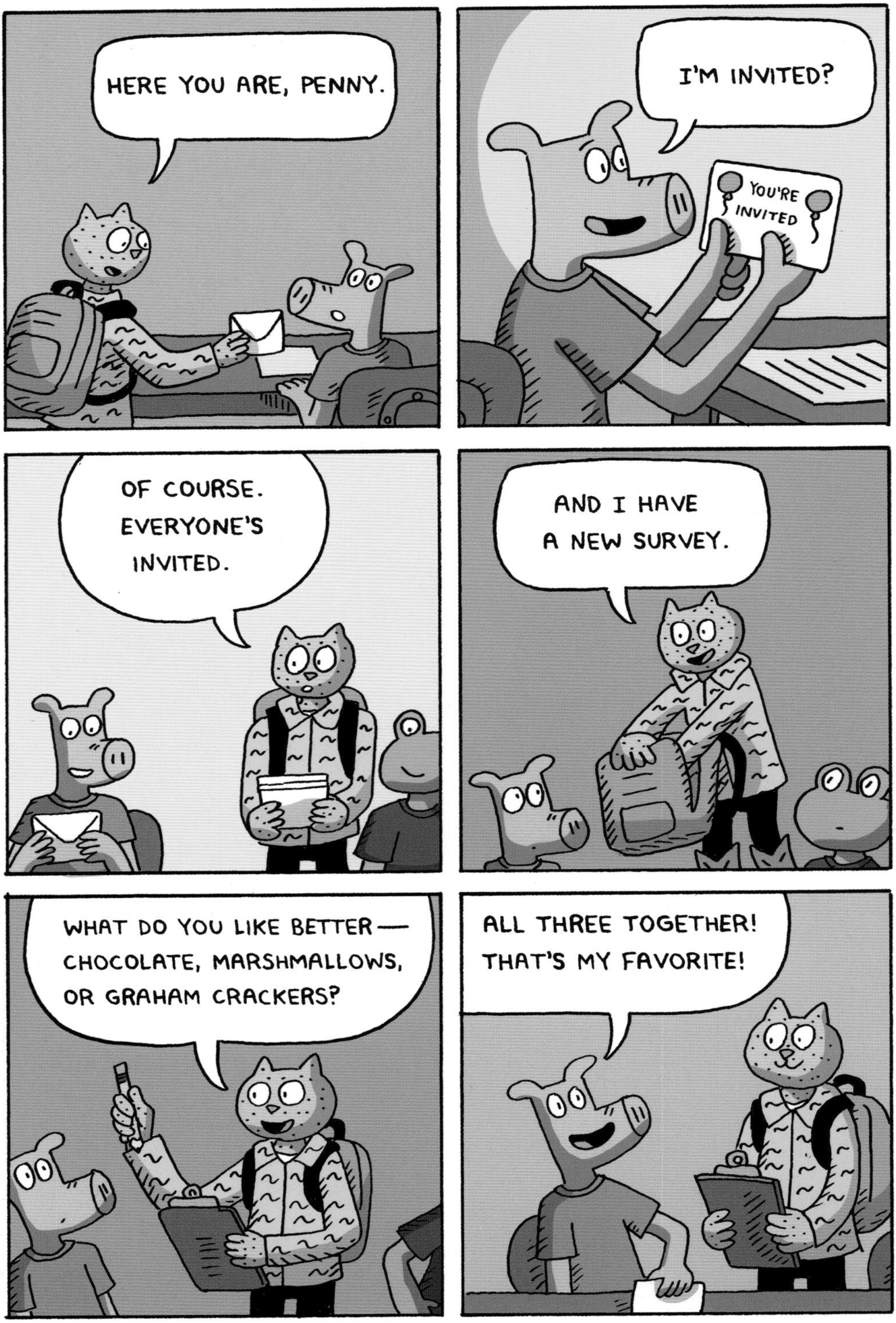
HERE YOU ARE, PENNY.
I'M INVITED?
YOU'RE INVITED
OF COURSE. EVERYONE'S INVITED.
AND I HAVE A NEW SURVEY.
WHAT DO YOU LIKE BETTER— CHOCOLATE, MARSHMALLOWS, OR GRAHAM CRACKERS?
ALL THREE TOGETHER! THAT'S MY FAVORITE!

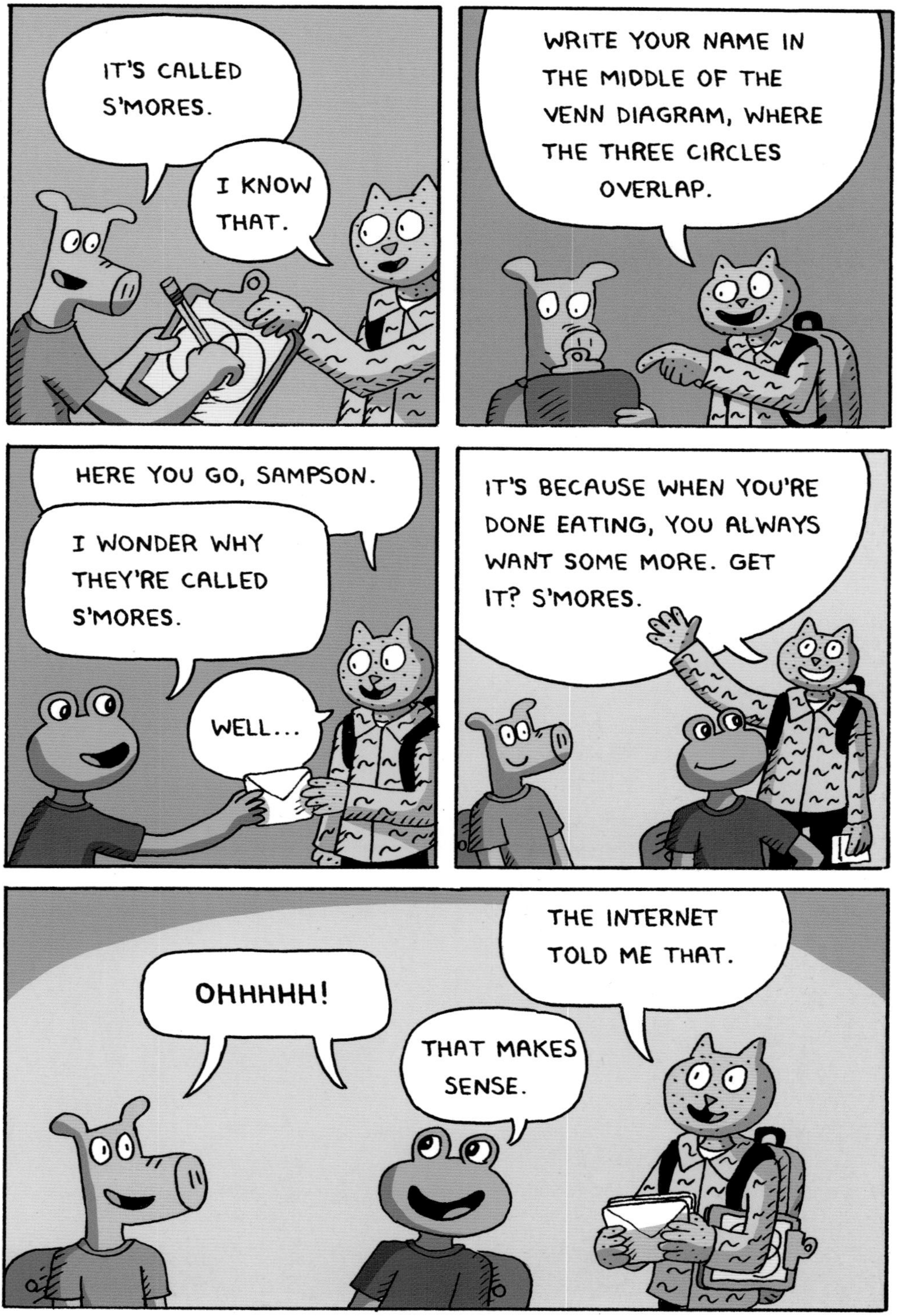
IT'S CALLED S'MORES.
I KNOW THAT.
WRITE YOUR NAME IN THE MIDDLE OF THE VENN DIAGRAM, WHERE THE THREE CIRCLES OVERLAP.
HERE YOU GO, SAMPSON.
I WONDER WHY THEY'RE CALLED S'MORES.
WELL...
IT'S BECAUSE WHEN YOU'RE DONE EATING, YOU ALWAYS WANT SOME MORE. GET IT? S'MORES.
OHHHHH!
THAT MAKES SENSE.
THE INTERNET TOLD ME THAT.

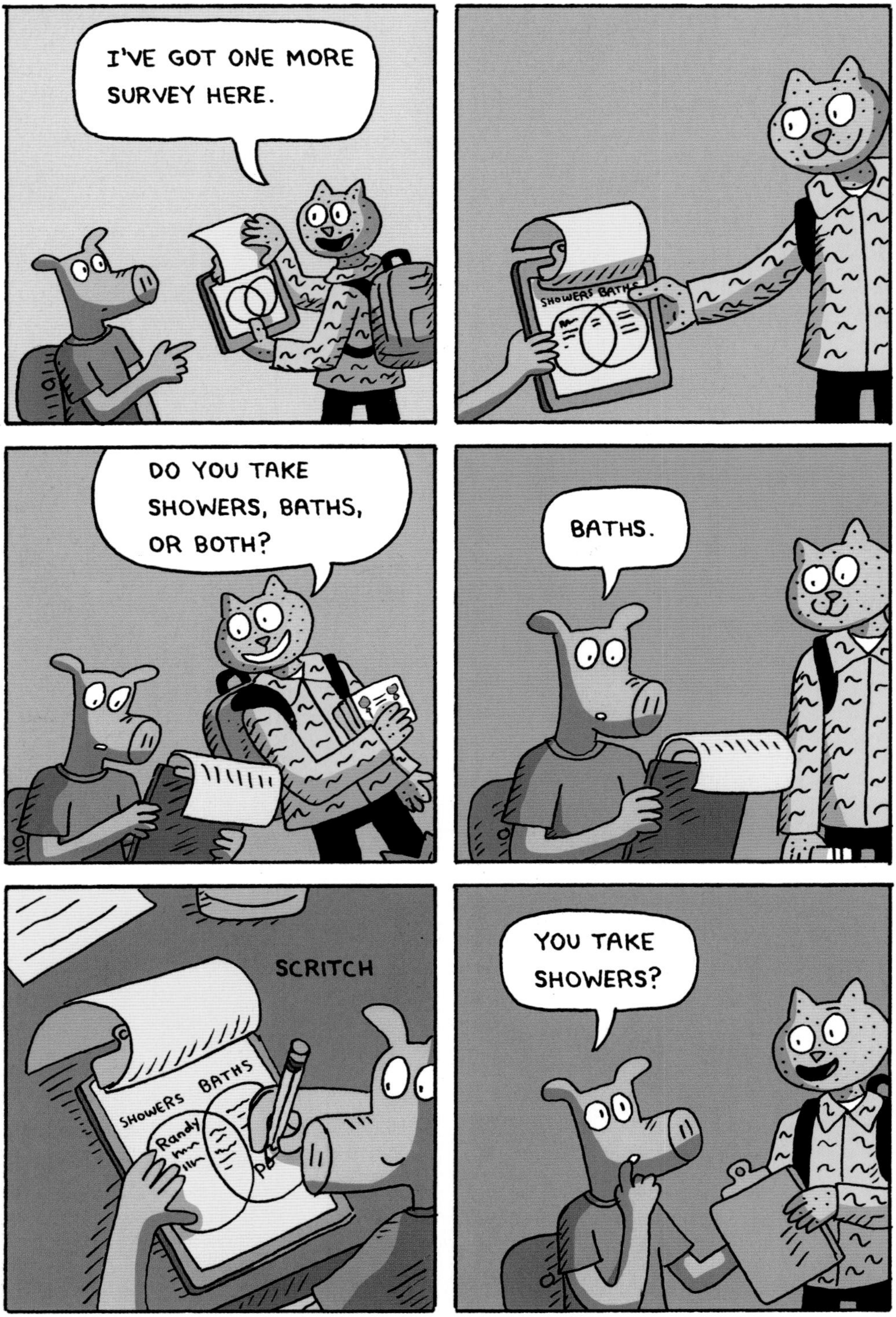
I'VE GOT ONE MORE SURVEY HERE.
DO YOU TAKE SHOWERS, BATHS, OR BOTH?
BATHS.
SCRITCH
SHOWERS
BATHS
Randy
YOU TAKE SHOWERS?

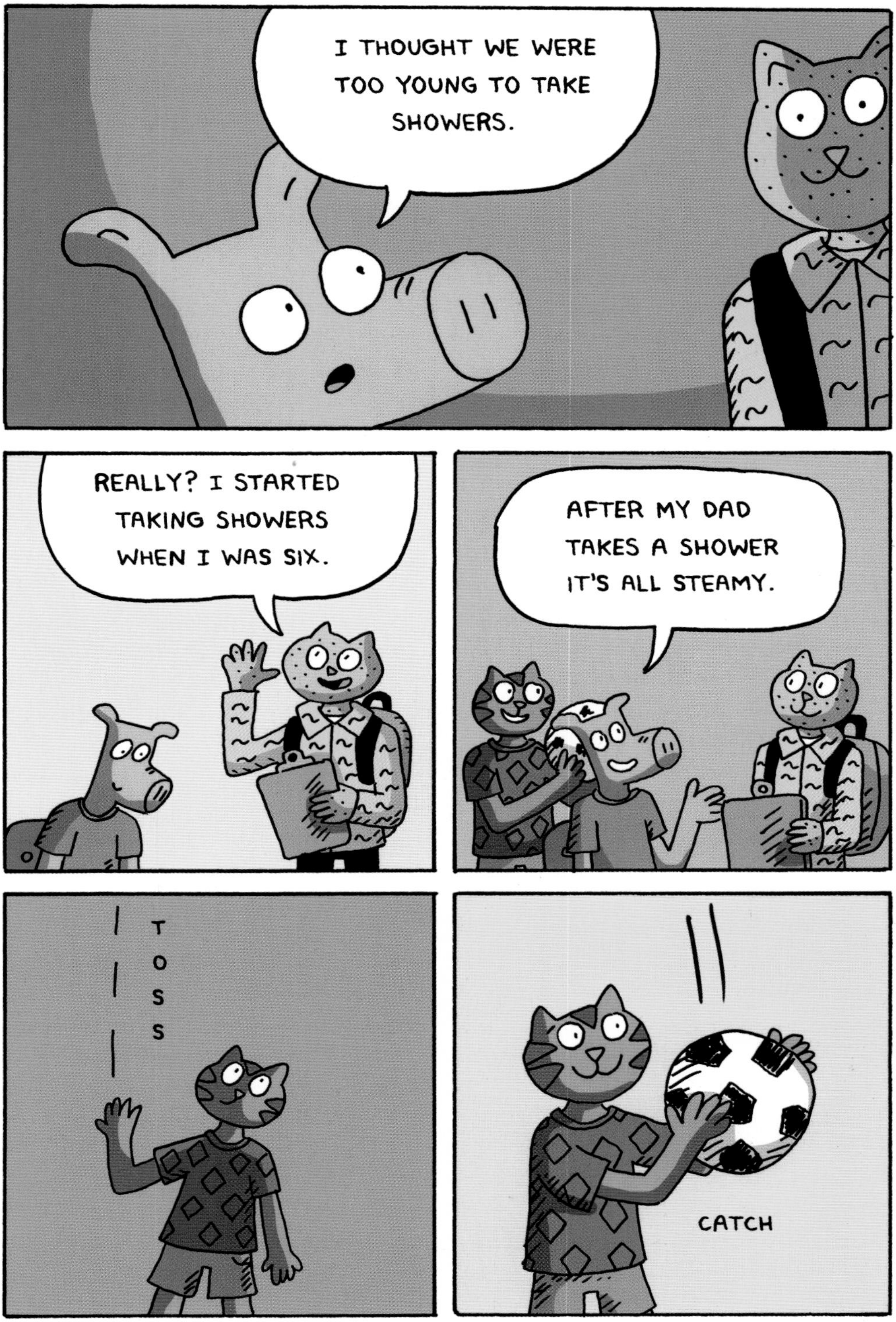
I THOUGHT WE WERE TOO YOUNG TO TAKE SHOWERS.
REALLY? I STARTED TAKING SHOWERS WHEN I WAS SIX.
AFTER MY DAD TAKES A SHOWER IT'S ALL STEAMY.
TOSS
CATCH

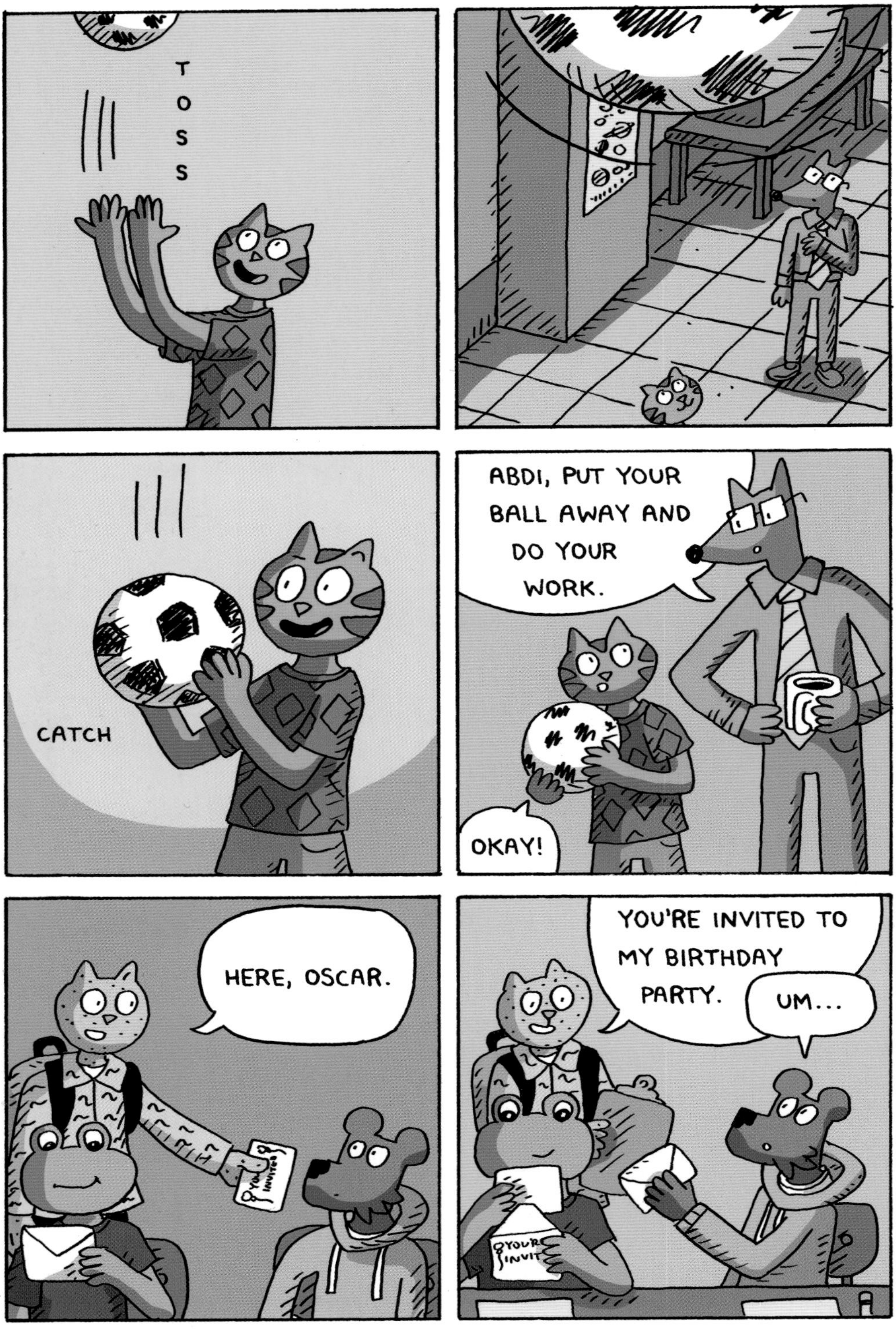
TOSS
CATCH
ABDI, PUT YOUR BALL AWAY AND DO YOUR WORK.
OKAY!
HERE, OSCAR.
YOU'RE INVITED TO MY BIRTHDAY PARTY.
UM...

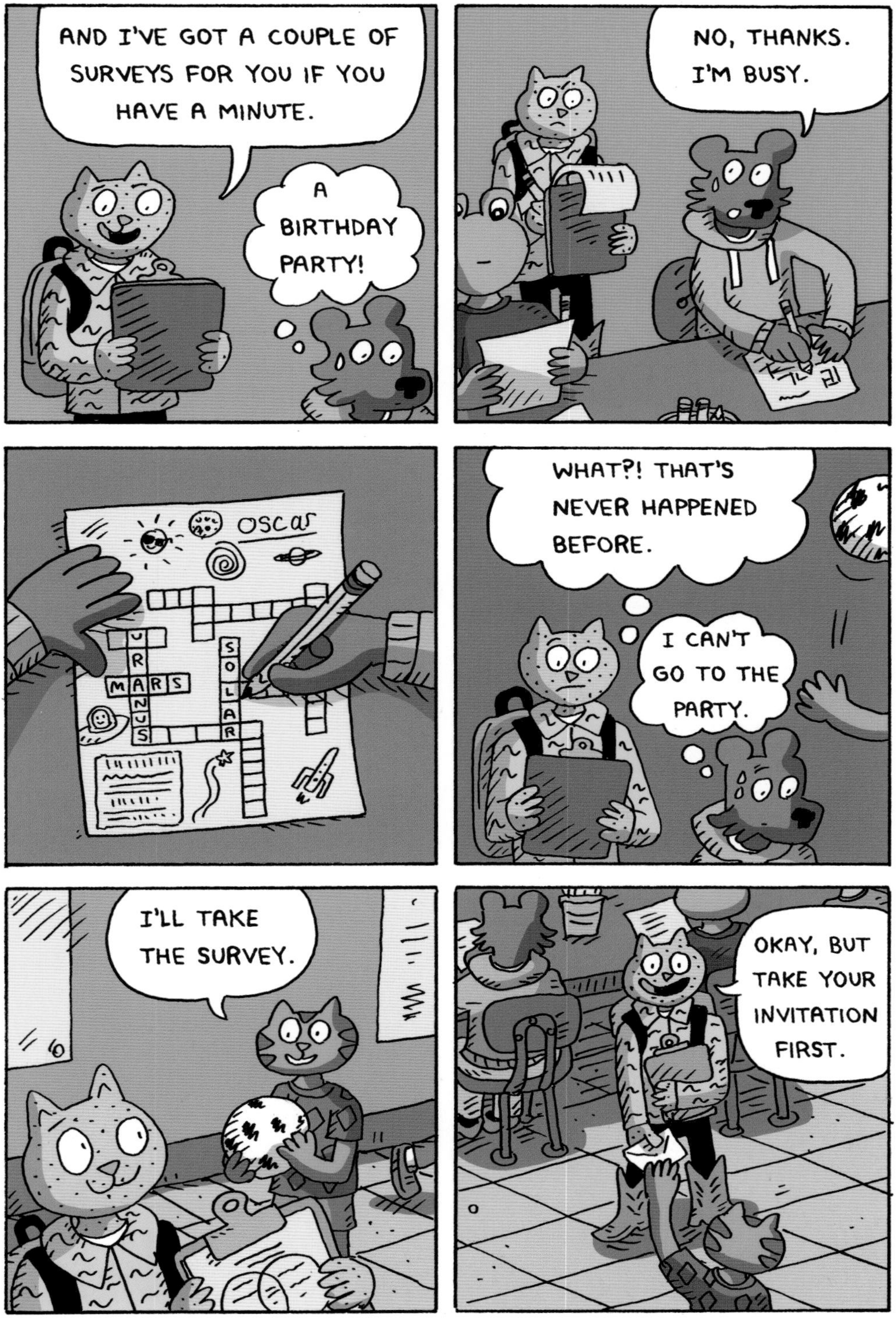
AND I'VE GOT A COUPLE OF SURVEYS FOR YOU IF YOU HAVE A MINUTE.
A BIRTHDAY PARTY!
NO, THANKS. I'M BUSY.
OSCAR
U
R
MARS
N
U
S
SOLAR
WHAT?! THAT'S NEVER HAPPENED BEFORE.
I CAN'T GO TO THE PARTY.
I'LL TAKE THE SURVEY.
OKAY, BUT TAKE YOUR INVITATION FIRST.

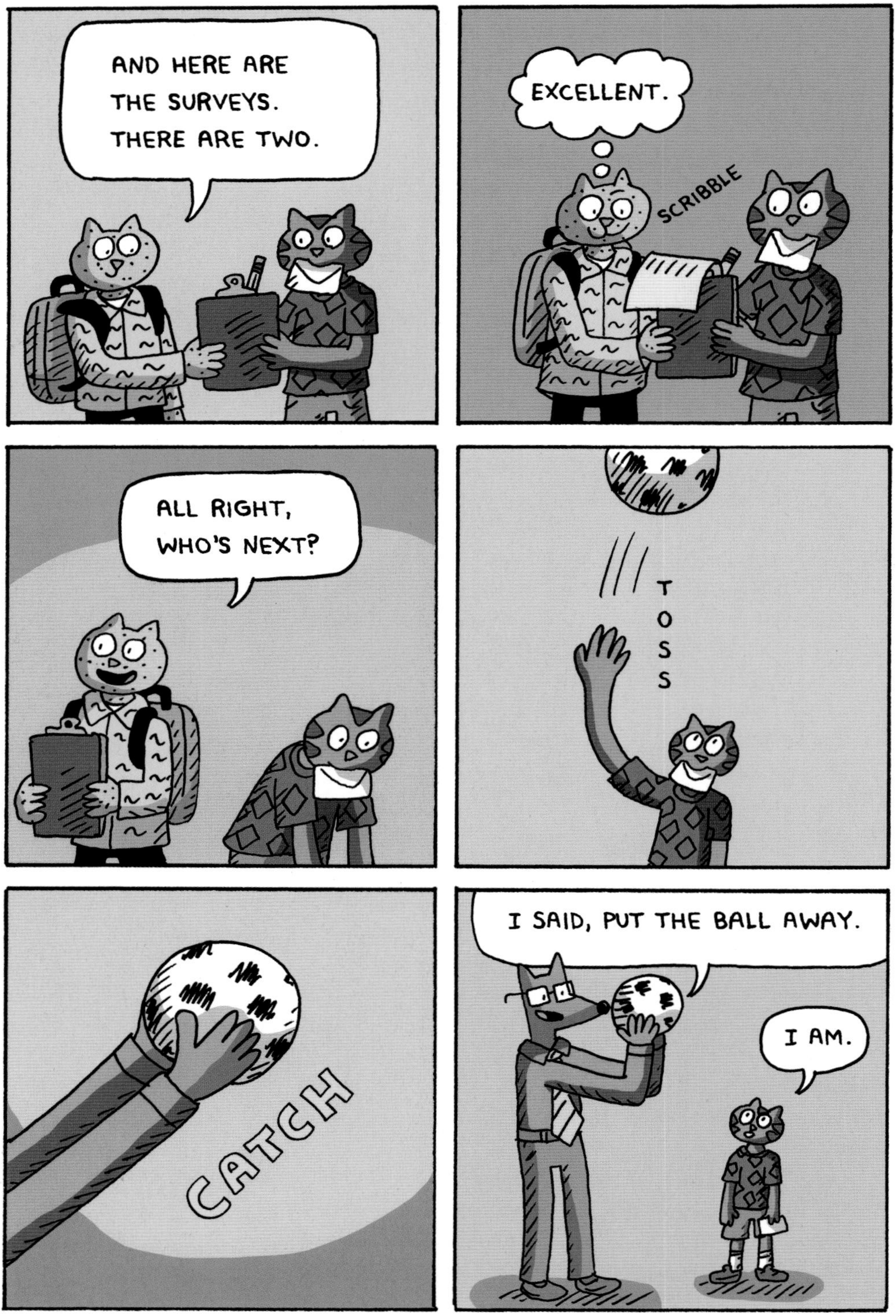
AND HERE ARE THE SURVEYS. THERE ARE TWO.
EXCELLENT.
SCRIBBLE
ALL RIGHT, WHO'S NEXT?
TOSS
CATCH
I SAID, PUT THE BALL AWAY.
I AM.

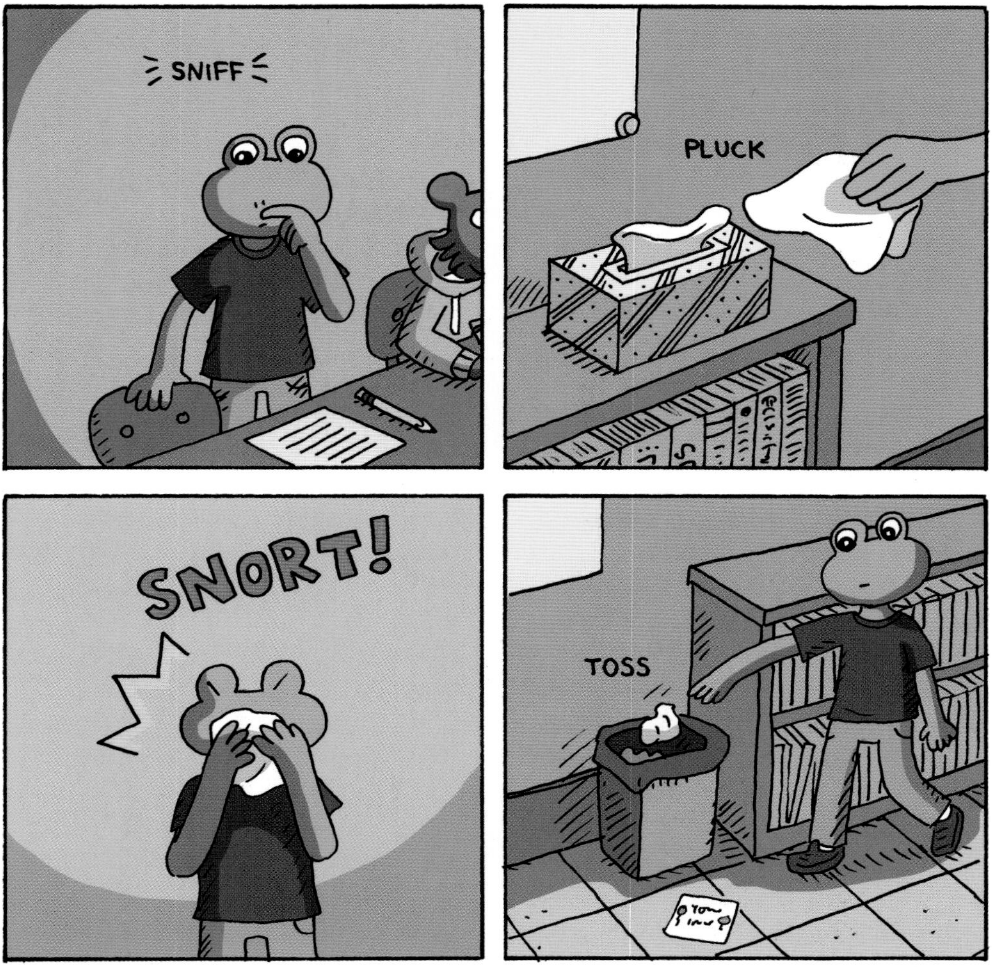
SNIFF
PLUCK
SNORT!
TOSS
YOU'RE INVITED
OSCAR'S INVITATION?

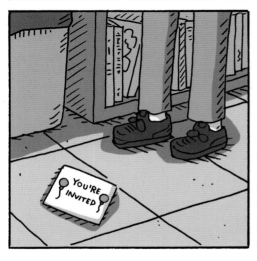

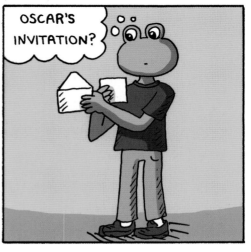

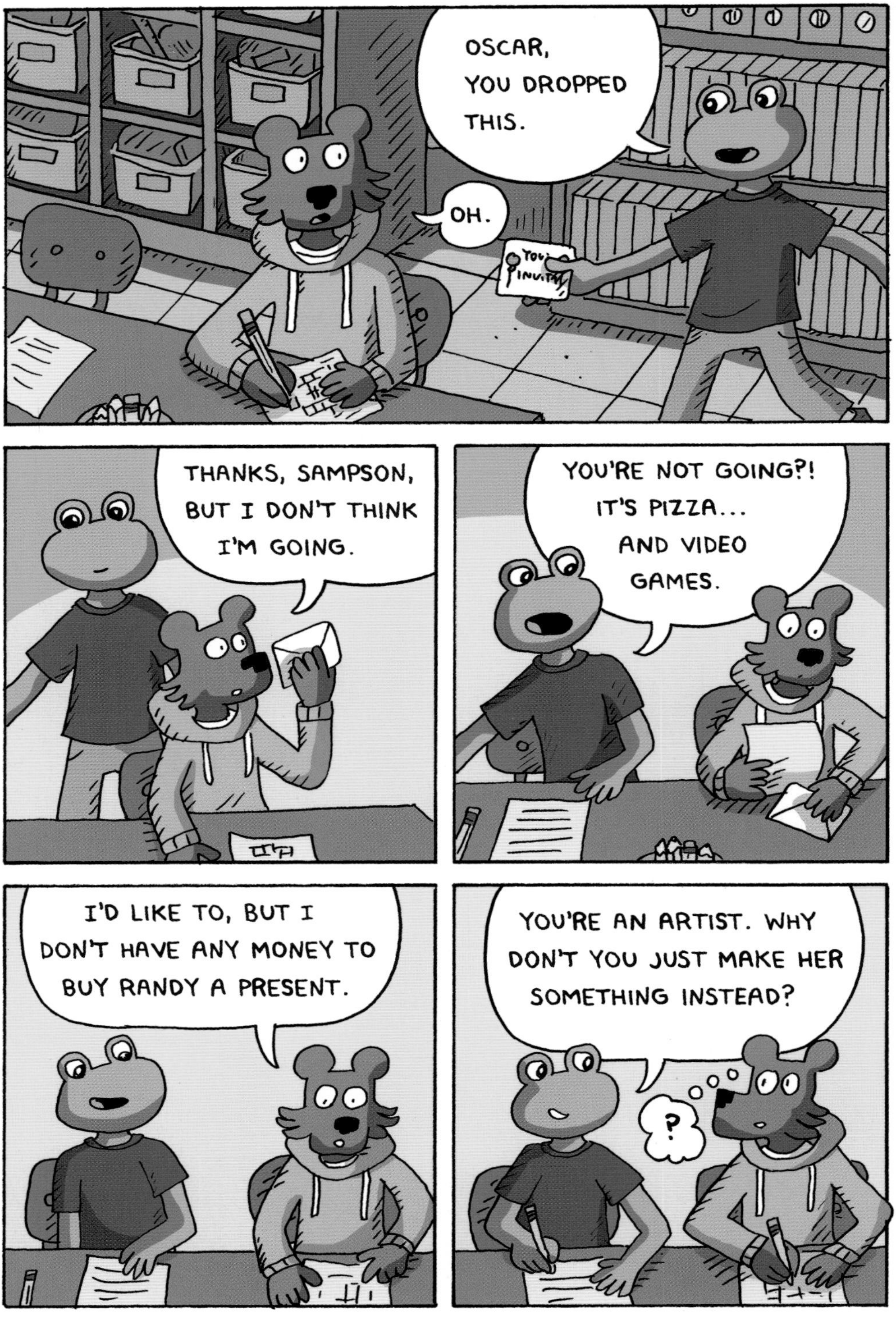
OSCAR, YOU DROPPED THIS.
OH.
THANKS, SAMPSON, BUT I DON'T THINK I'M GOING.
YOU'RE NOT GOING?! IT'S PIZZA... AND VIDEO GAMES.
I'D LIKE TO, BUT I DON'T HAVE ANY MONEY TO BUY RANDY A PRESENT.
YOU'RE AN ARTIST. WHY DON'T YOU JUST MAKE HER SOMETHING INSTEAD?
?

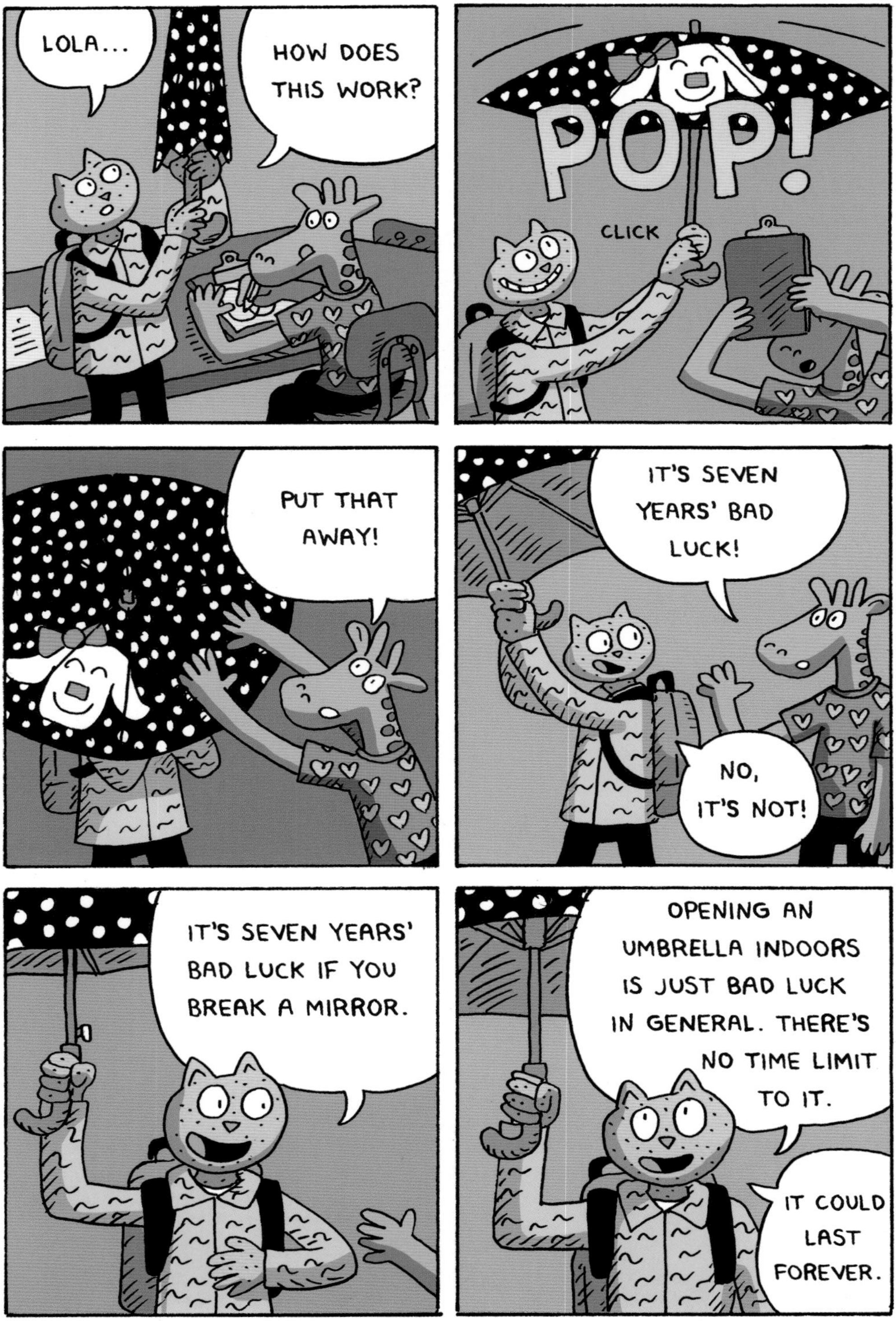
LOLA...
HOW DOES THIS WORK?
POP!
CLICK
PUT THAT AWAY!
IT'S SEVEN YEARS' BAD LUCK!
NO, IT'S NOT!
IT'S SEVEN YEARS' BAD LUCK IF YOU BREAK A MIRROR.
OPENING AN UMBRELLA INDOORS IS JUST BAD LUCK IN GENERAL. THERE'S NO TIME LIMIT TO IT.
IT COULD LAST FOREVER.

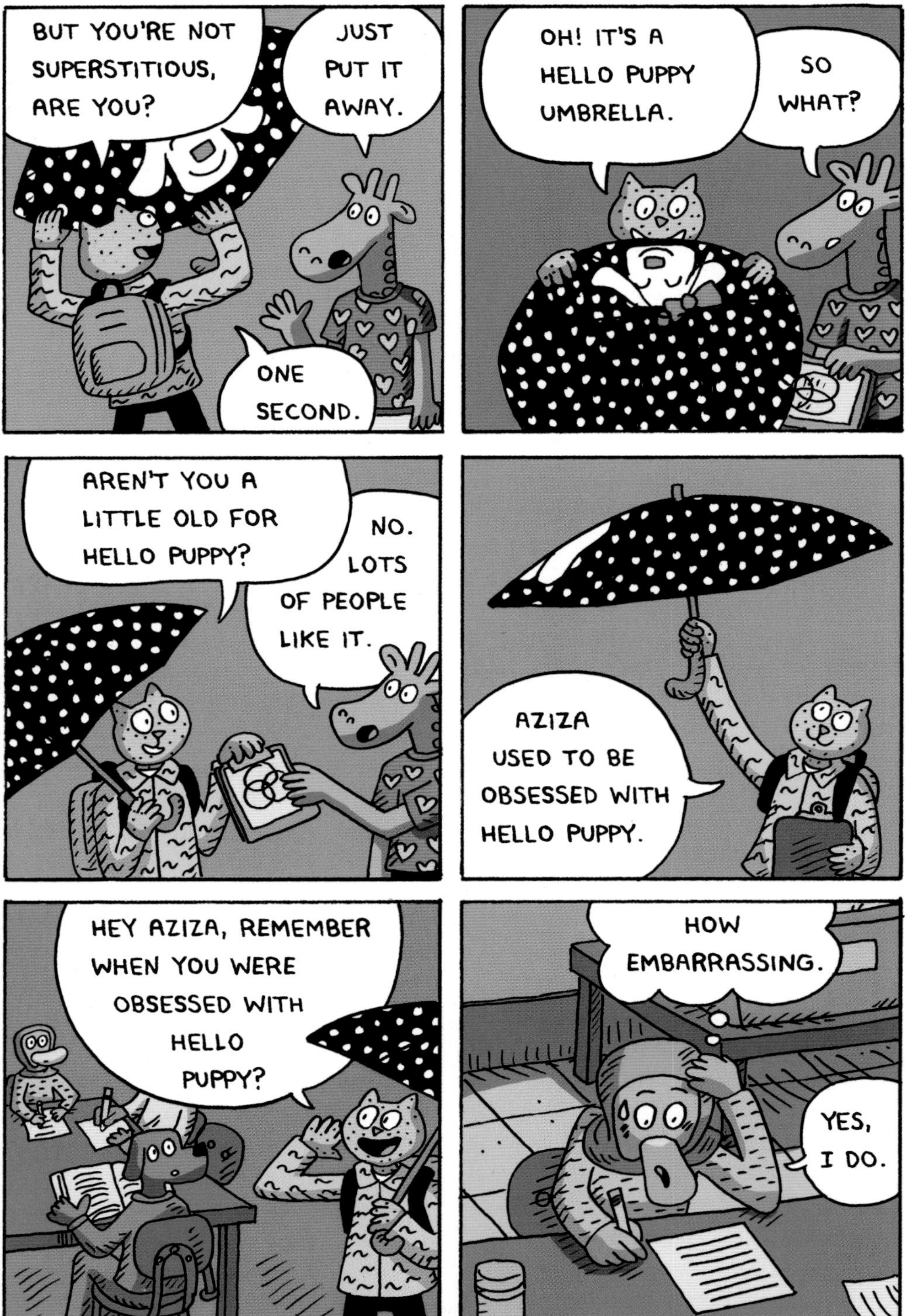
BUT YOU'RE NOT SUPERSTITIOUS, ARE YOU?
JUST PUT IT AWAY.
ONE SECOND.
OH! IT'S A HELLO PUPPY UMBRELLA.
SO WHAT?
AREN'T YOU A LITTLE OLD FOR HELLO PUPPY?
NO. LOTS OF PEOPLE LIKE IT.
AZIZA USED TO BE OBSESSED WITH HELLO PUPPY.
HEY AZIZA, REMEMBER WHEN YOU WERE OBSESSED WITH HELLO PUPPY?
HOW EMBARRASSING.
YES, I DO.

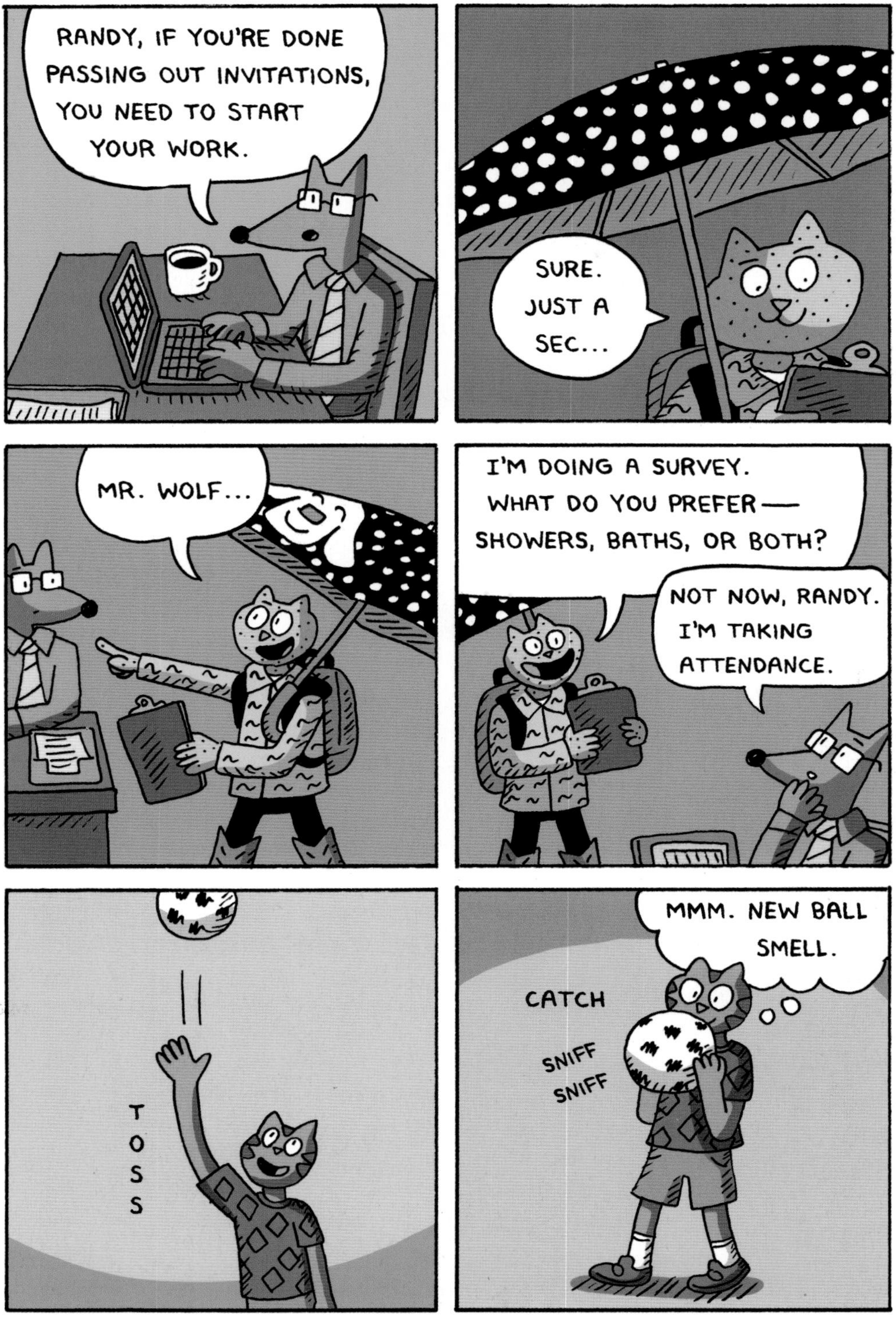
RANDY, IF YOU'RE DONE PASSING OUT INVITATIONS, YOU NEED TO START YOUR WORK.
SURE. JUST A SEC...
MR. WOLF...
I'M DOING A SURVEY. WHAT DO YOU PREFER— SHOWERS, BATHS, OR BOTH?
NOT NOW, RANDY. I'M TAKING ATTENDANCE.
TOSS
MMM. NEW BALL SMELL.
CATCH
SNIFF
SNIFF

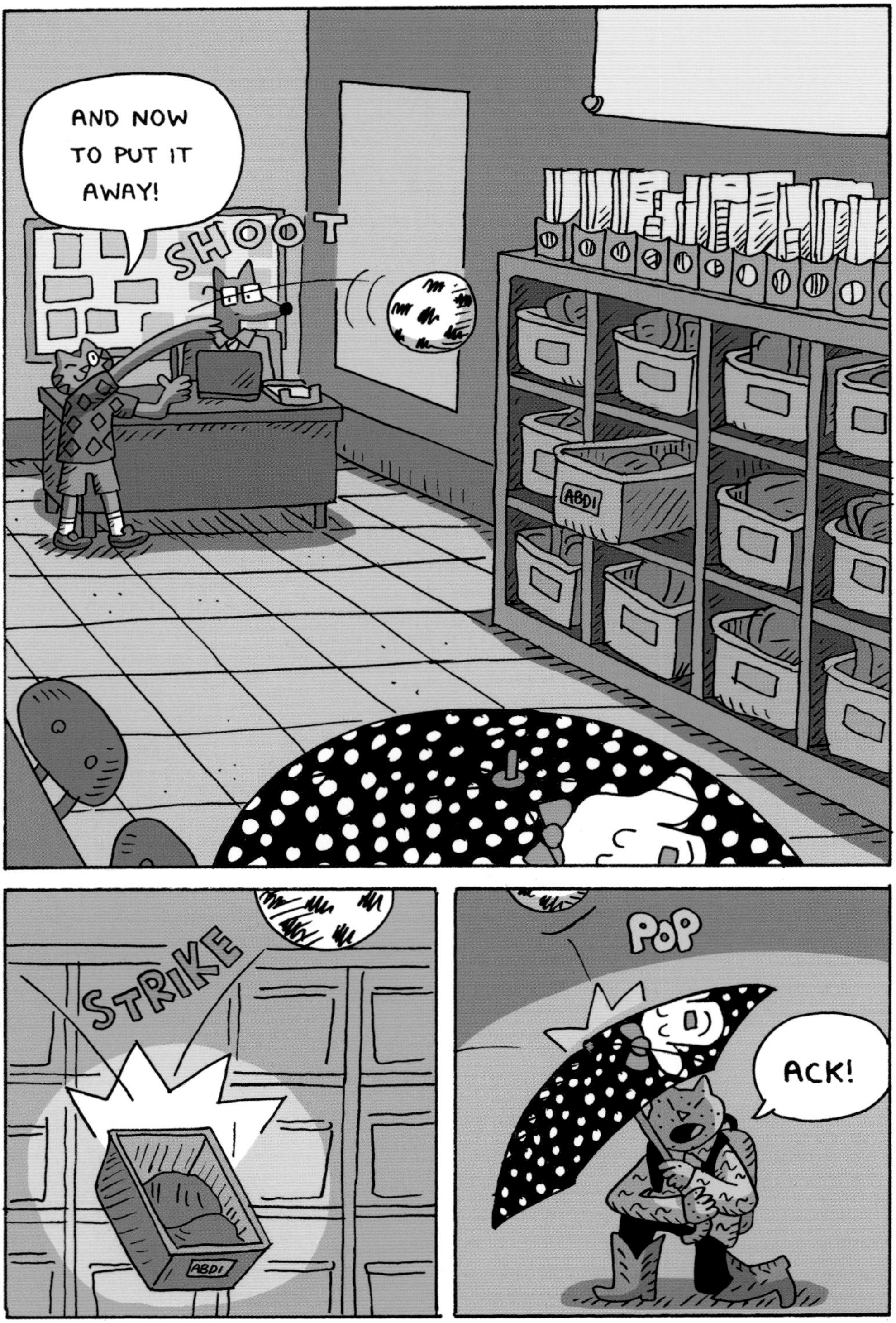
AND NOW TO PUT IT AWAY!
SHOOT
ABDI
STRIKE
ABDI
POP
ACK!

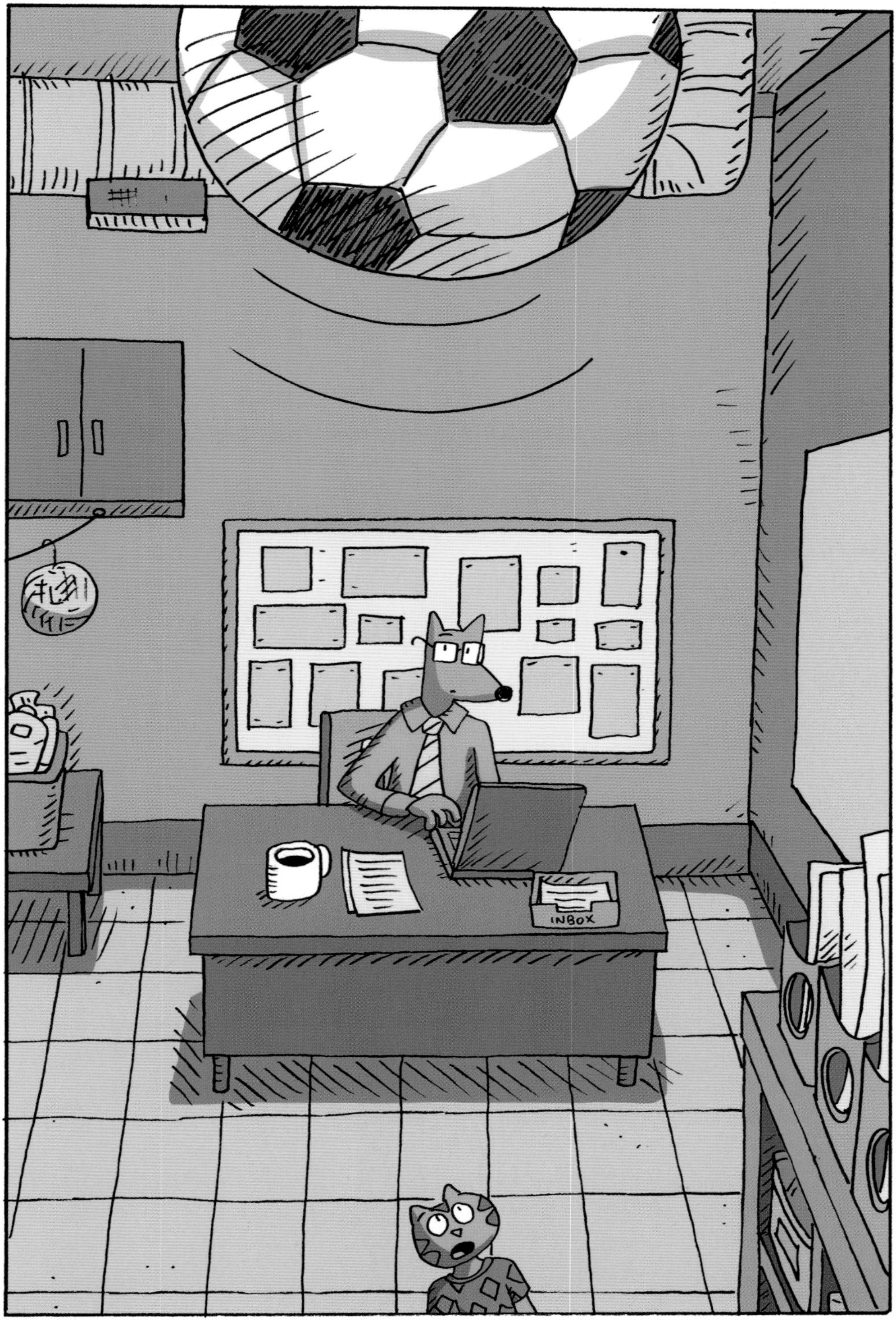
INBOX

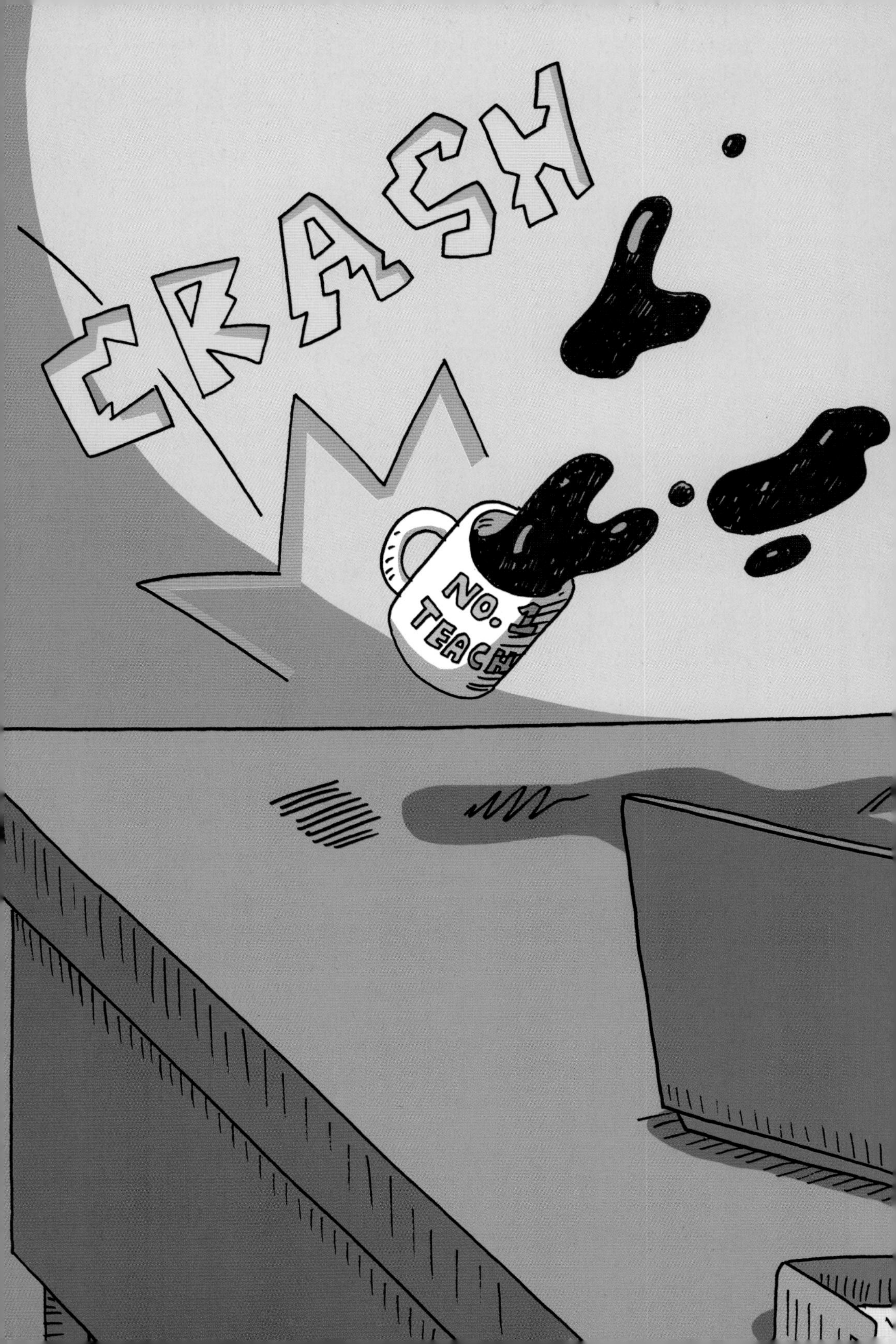
CRASH
NO. 1
TEACH

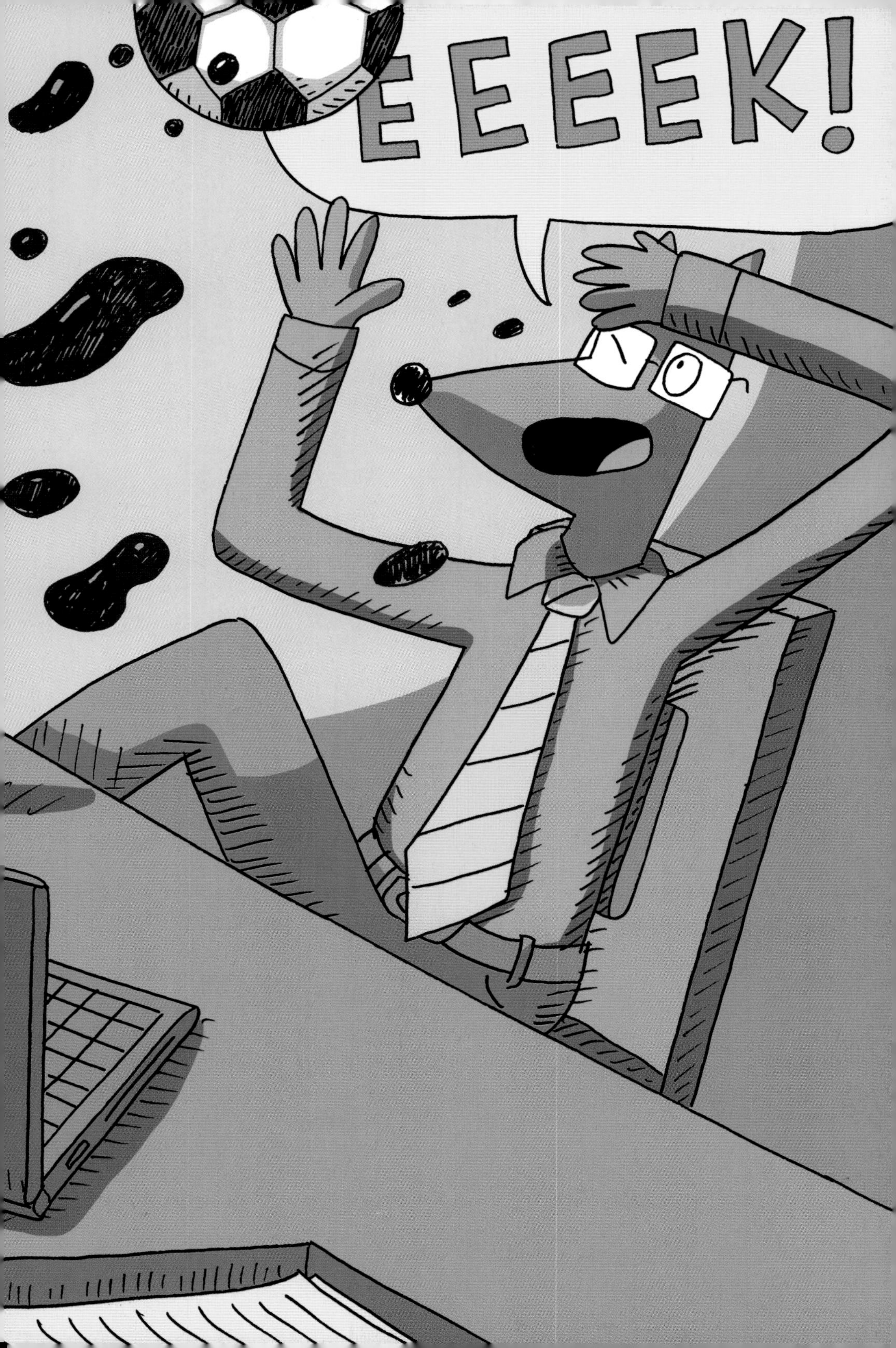
EEEEK!

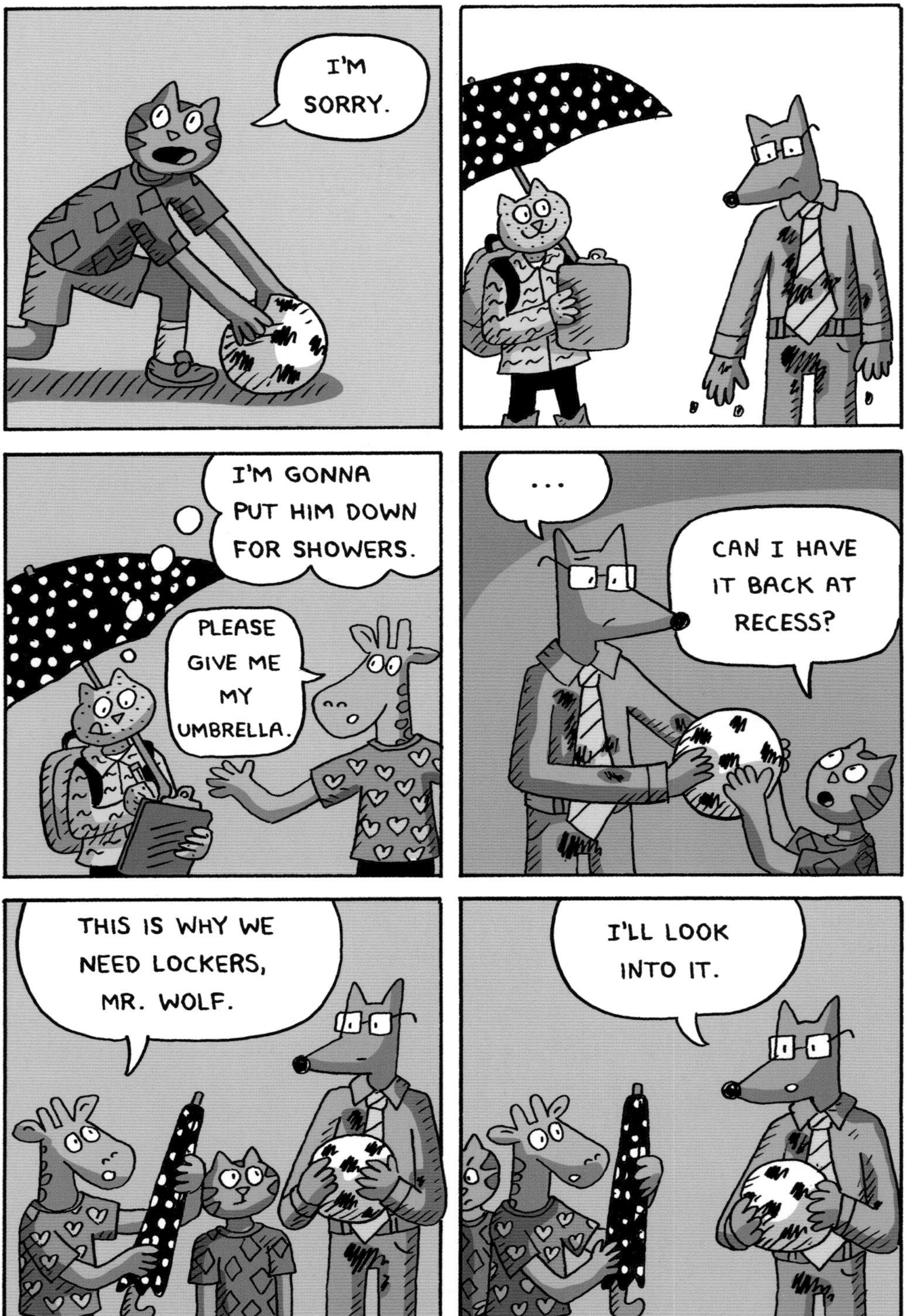
I'M SORRY.
I'M GONNA PUT HIM DOWN FOR SHOWERS.
PLEASE GIVE ME MY UMBRELLA.
...
CAN I HAVE IT BACK AT RECESS?
THIS IS WHY WE NEED LOCKERS, MR. WOLF.
I'LL LOOK INTO IT.

CHAPTER TWO
Mystery Club

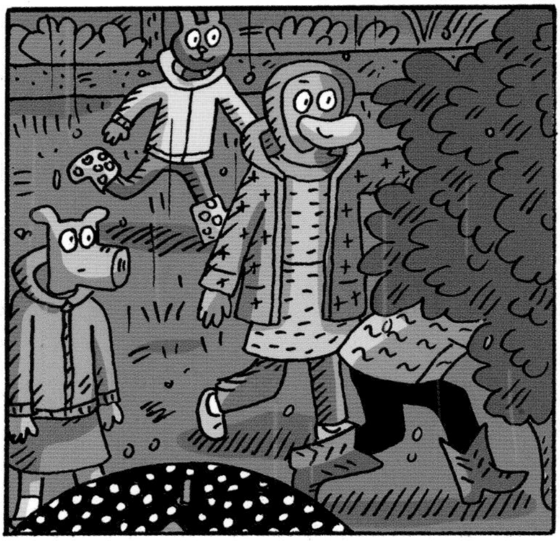
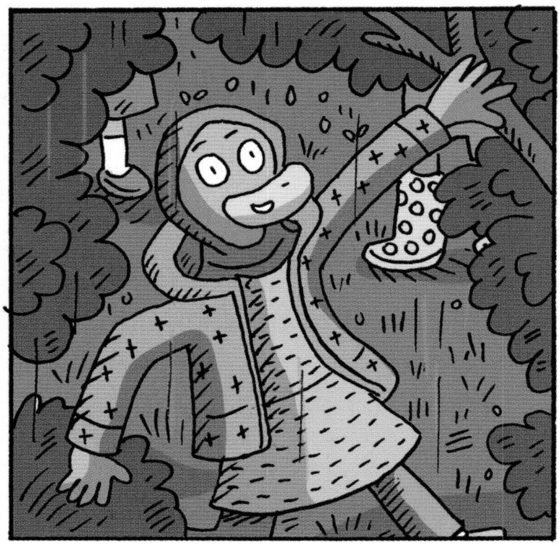
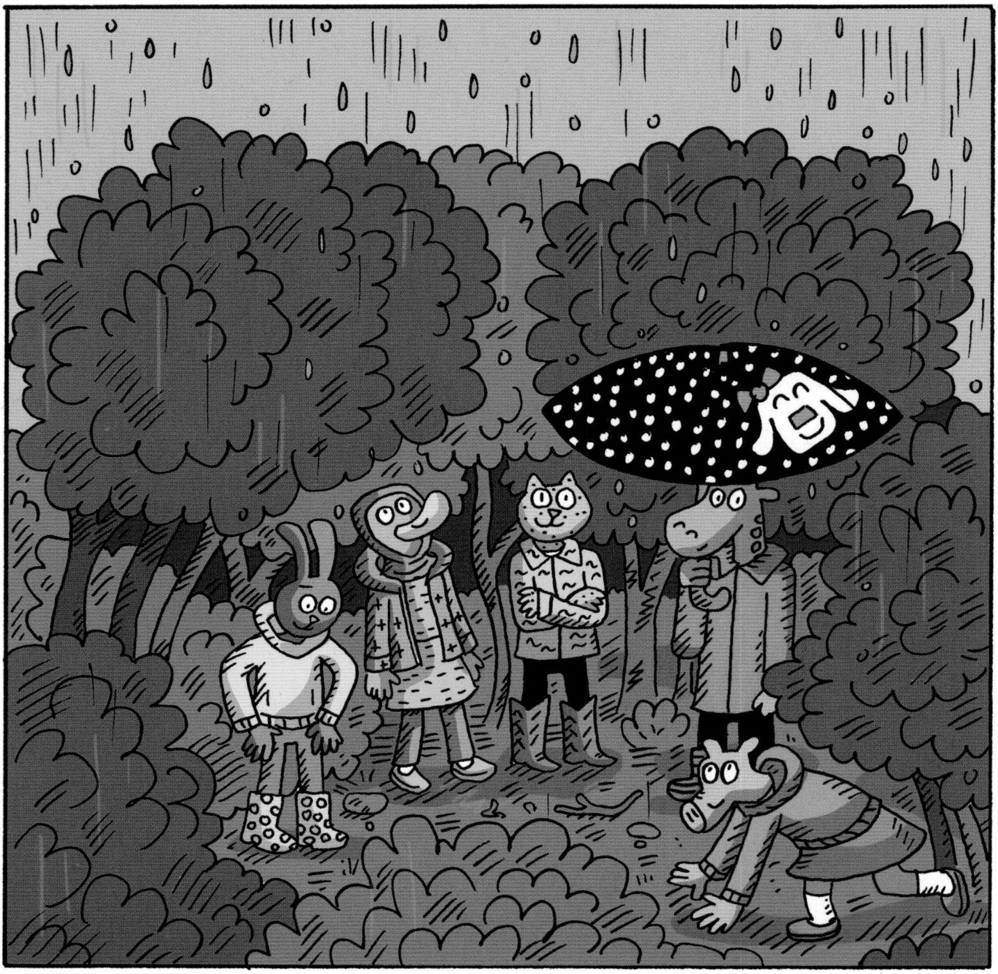

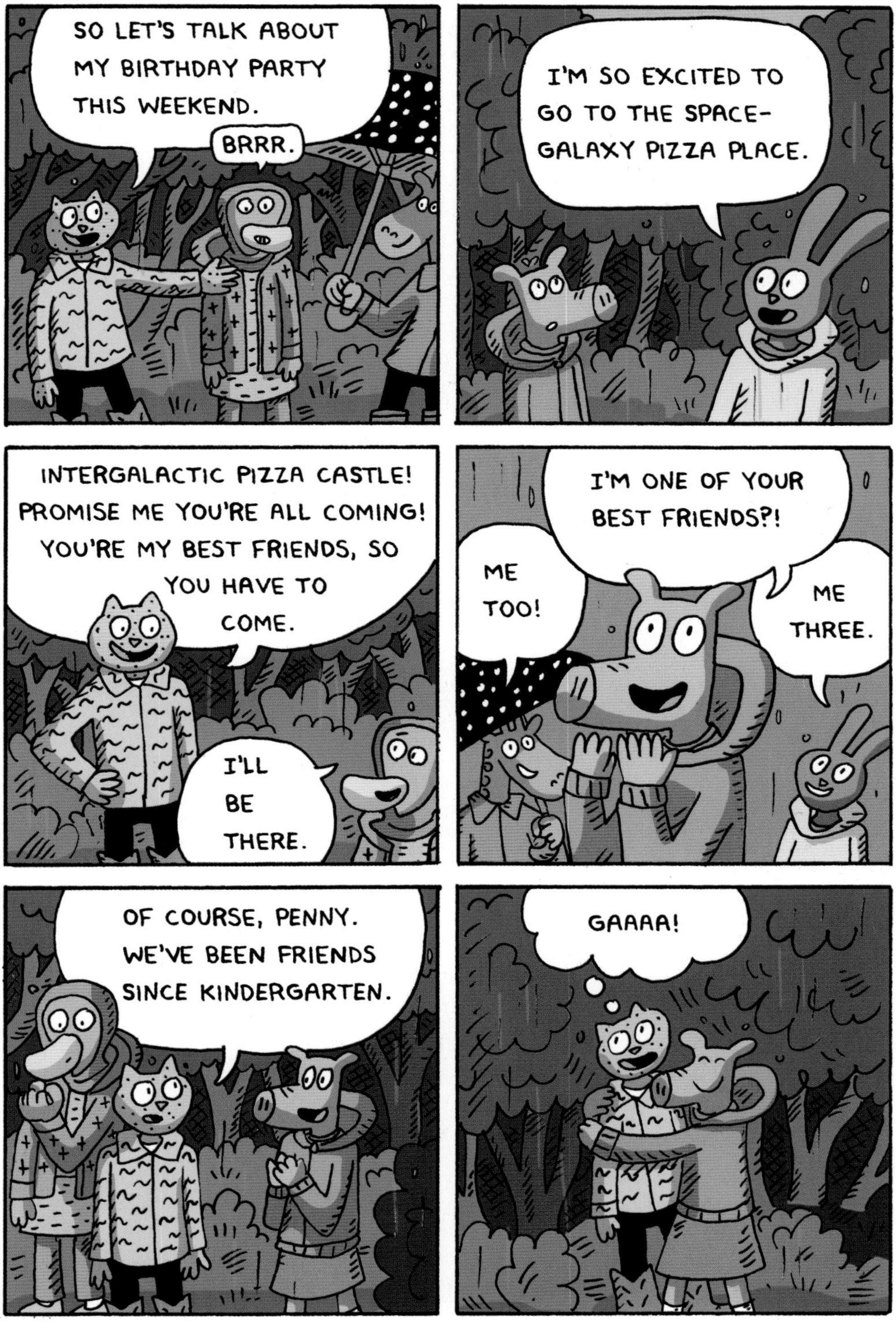
SO LET'S TALK ABOUT MY BIRTHDAY PARTY THIS WEEKEND.
BRRR.
I'M SO EXCITED TO GO TO THE SPACE-GALAXY PIZZA PLACE.
INTERGALACTIC PIZZA CASTLE! PROMISE ME YOU'RE ALL COMING! YOU'RE MY BEST FRIENDS, SO YOU HAVE TO COME.
I'LL BE THERE.
I'M ONE OF YOUR BEST FRIENDS?!
ME TOO!
ME THREE.
OF COURSE, PENNY. WE'VE BEEN FRIENDS SINCE KINDERGARTEN.
GAAAA!

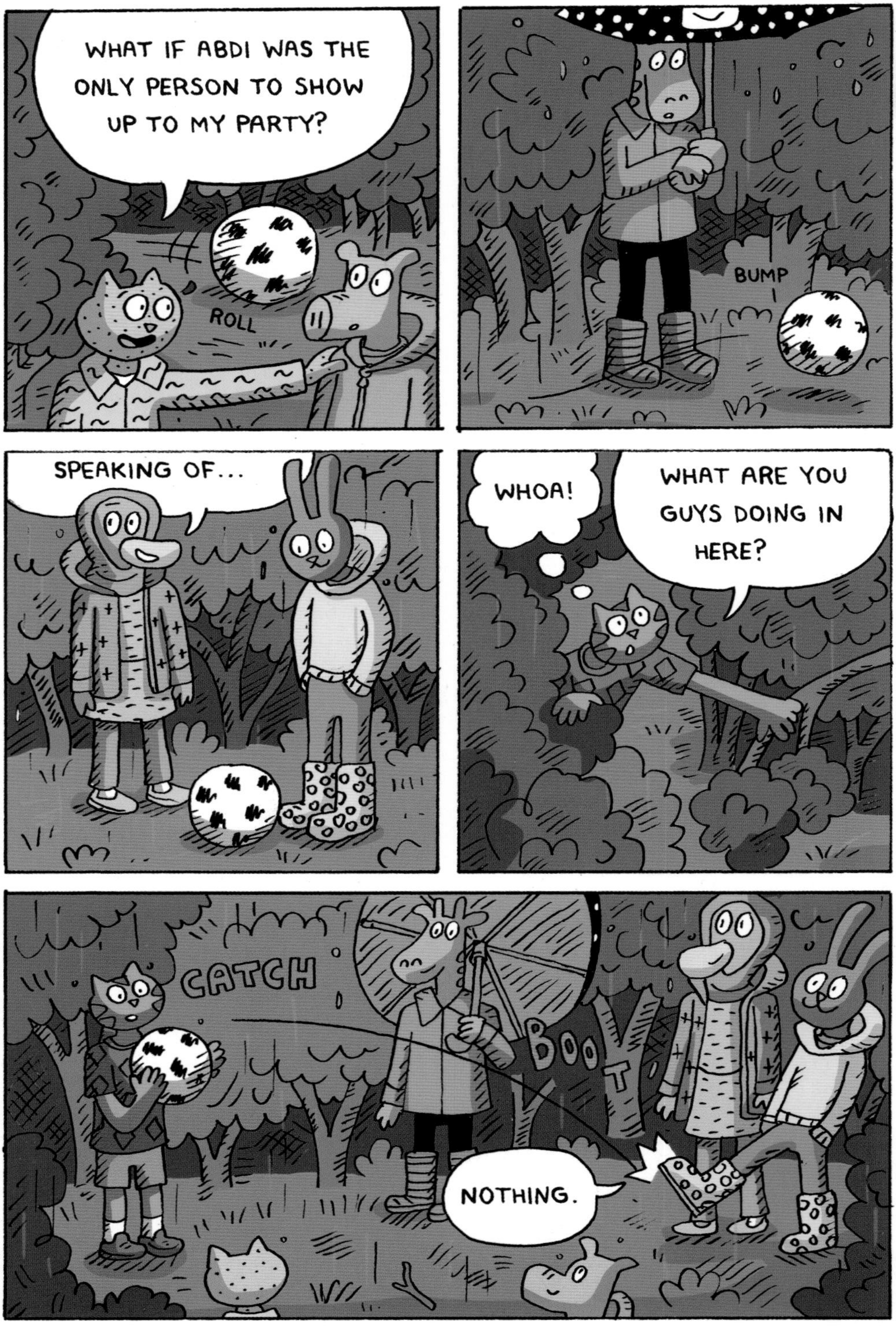

WHAT IF ABDI WAS THE ONLY PERSON TO SHOW UP TO MY PARTY?
ROLL
BUMP
SPEAKING OF...
WHOA!
WHAT ARE YOU GUYS DOING IN HERE?
CATCH
BOOT
NOTHING.

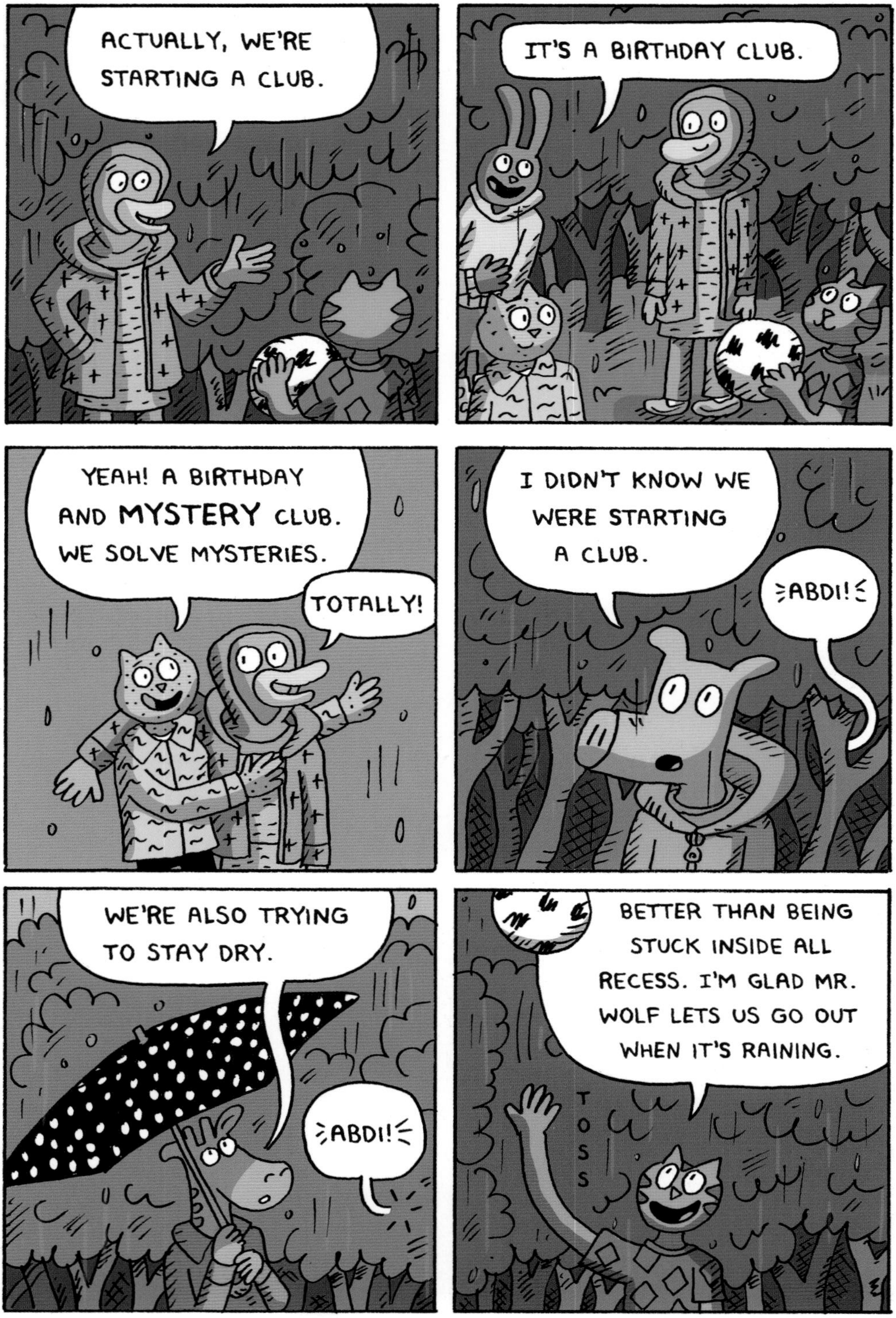
ACTUALLY, WE'RE STARTING A CLUB.
IT'S A BIRTHDAY CLUB.
YEAH! A BIRTHDAY AND MYSTERY CLUB. WE SOLVE MYSTERIES.
TOTALLY!
I DIDN'T KNOW WE WERE STARTING A CLUB.
ABDI!
WE'RE ALSO TRYING TO STAY DRY.
ABDI!
BETTER THAN BEING STUCK INSIDE ALL RECESS. I'M GLAD MR. WOLF LETS US GO OUT WHEN IT'S RAINING.
TOSS

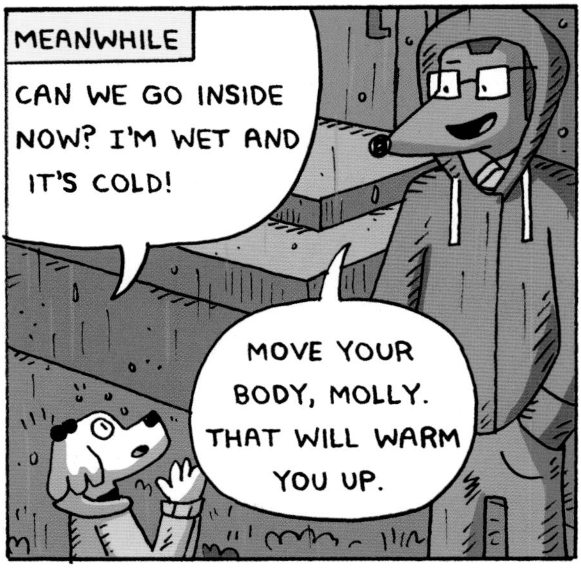
MEANWHILE
CAN WE GO INSIDE NOW? I'M WET AND IT'S COLD!
MOVE YOUR BODY, MOLLY. THAT WILL WARM YOU UP.

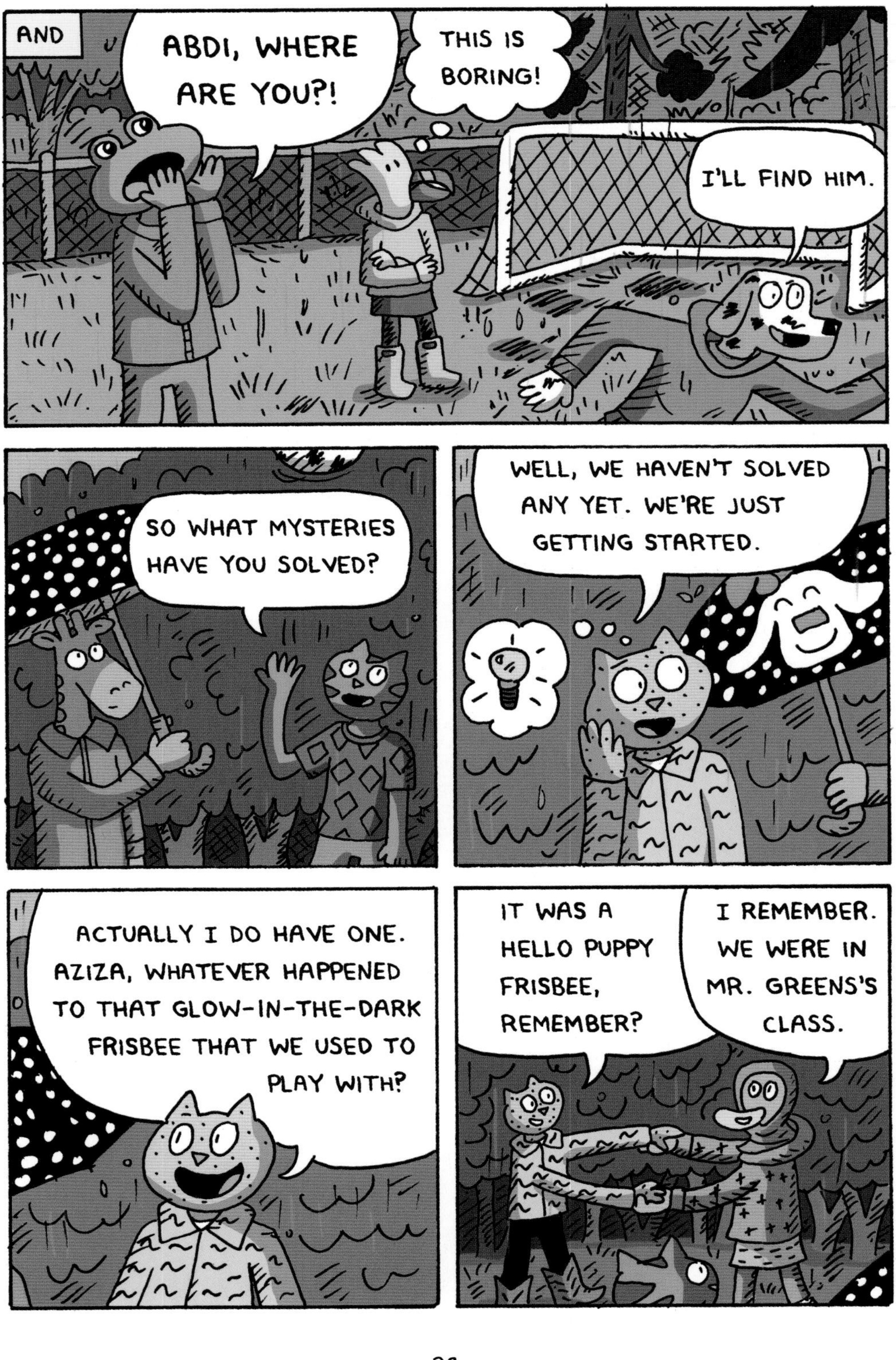
AND
ABDI, WHERE ARE YOU?!
THIS IS BORING!
I'LL FIND HIM.
SO WHAT MYSTERIES HAVE YOU SOLVED?
WELL, WE HAVEN'T SOLVED ANY YET. WE'RE JUST GETTING STARTED.
ACTUALLY I DO HAVE ONE. AZIZA, WHATEVER HAPPENED TO THAT GLOW-IN-THE-DARK FRISBEE THAT WE USED TO PLAY WITH?
IT WAS A HELLO PUPPY FRISBEE, REMEMBER?
I REMEMBER. WE WERE IN MR. GREENS'S CLASS.

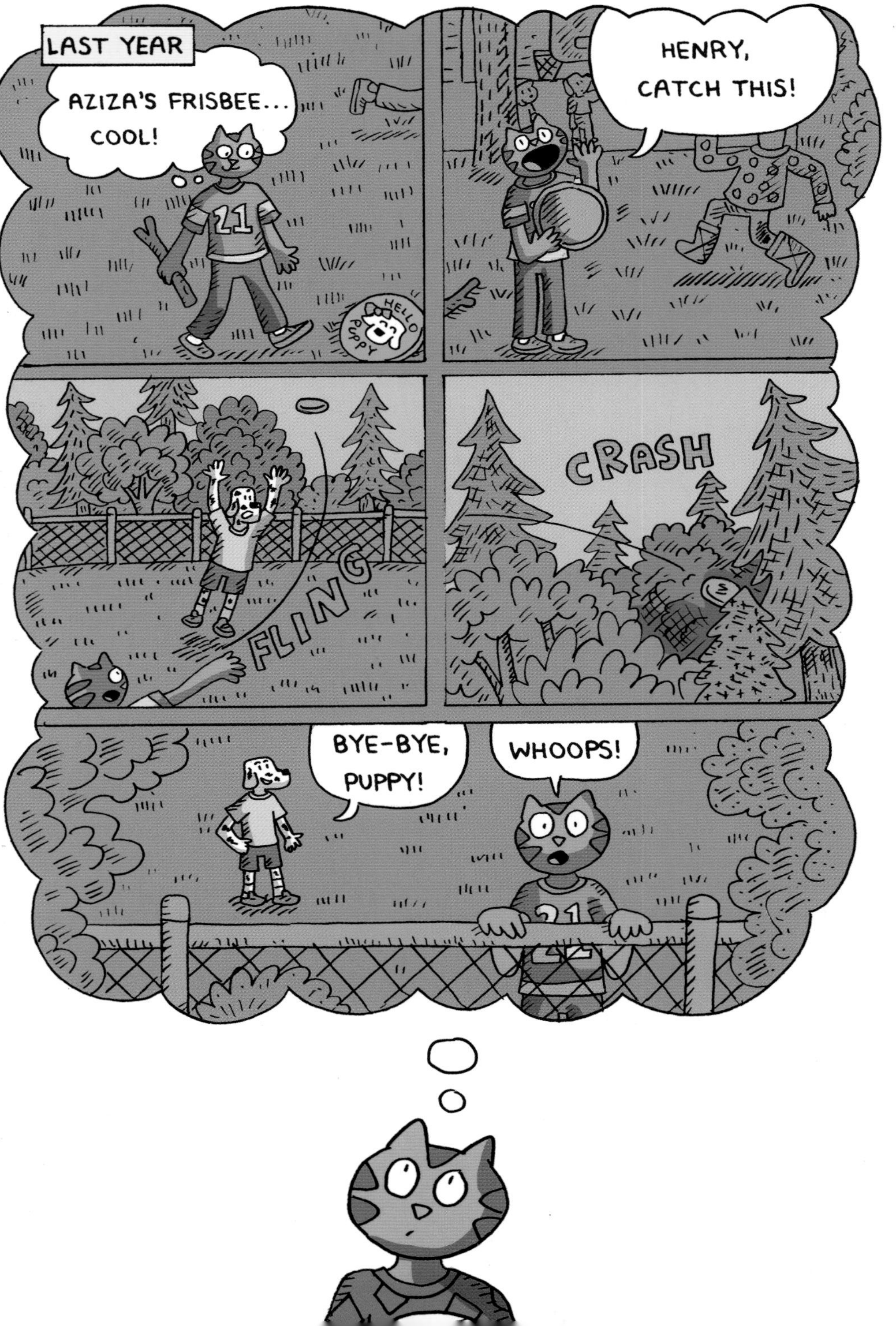
LAST YEAR
AZIZA'S FRISBEE... COOL!
HELLO PUPPY
HENRY, CATCH THIS!
FLING
CRASH
BYE-BYE, PUPPY!
WHOOPS!
21

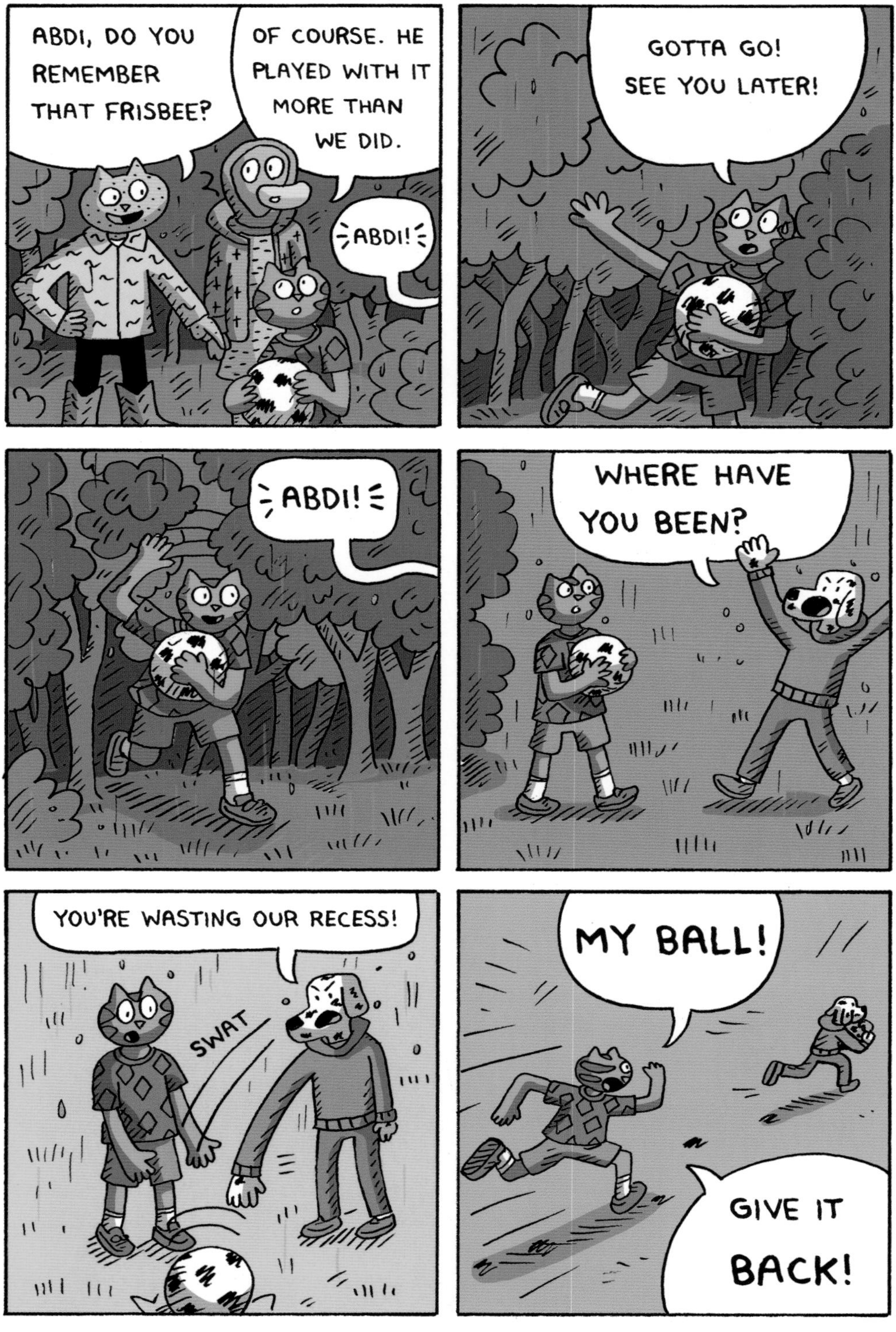
ABDI, DO YOU REMEMBER THAT FRISBEE?
OF COURSE. HE PLAYED WITH IT MORE THAN WE DID.
ABDI!
GOTTA GO! SEE YOU LATER!
ABDI!
WHERE HAVE YOU BEEN?
YOU'RE WASTING OUR RECESS!
SWAT
MY BALL!
GIVE IT BACK!

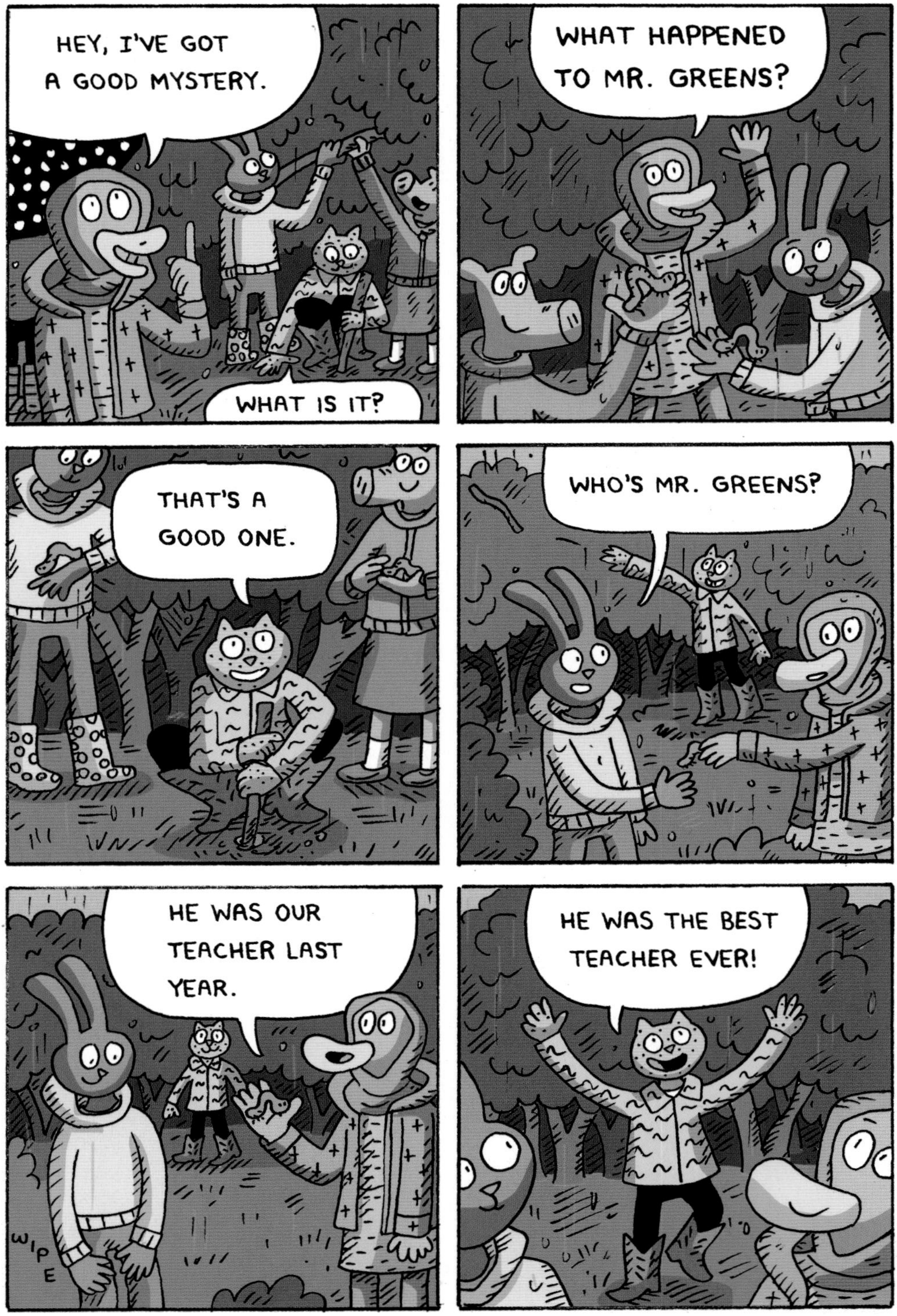
HEY, I'VE GOT A GOOD MYSTERY.
WHAT IS IT?
WHAT HAPPENED TO MR. GREENS?
THAT'S A GOOD ONE.
WHO'S MR. GREENS?
HE WAS OUR TEACHER LAST YEAR.
WIPE
HE WAS THE BEST TEACHER EVER!

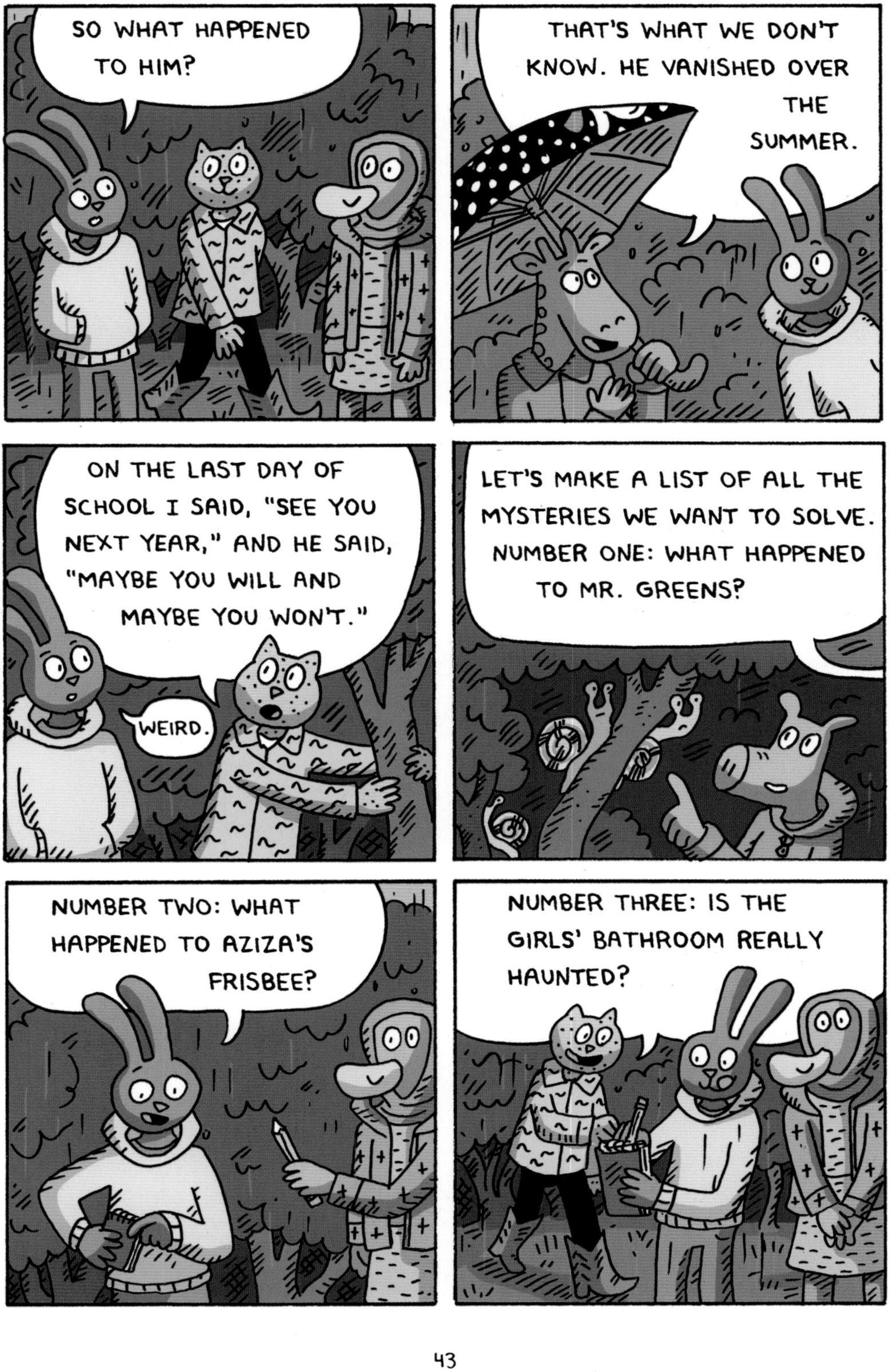
SO WHAT HAPPENED TO HIM?
THAT'S WHAT WE DON'T KNOW. HE VANISHED OVER THE SUMMER.
ON THE LAST DAY OF SCHOOL I SAID, "SEE YOU NEXT YEAR," AND HE SAID, "MAYBE YOU WILL AND MAYBE YOU WON'T."
WEIRD.
LET'S MAKE A LIST OF ALL THE MYSTERIES WE WANT TO SOLVE. NUMBER ONE: WHAT HAPPENED TO MR. GREENS?
NUMBER TWO: WHAT HAPPENED TO AZIZA'S FRISBEE?
NUMBER THREE: IS THE GIRLS' BATHROOM REALLY HAUNTED?

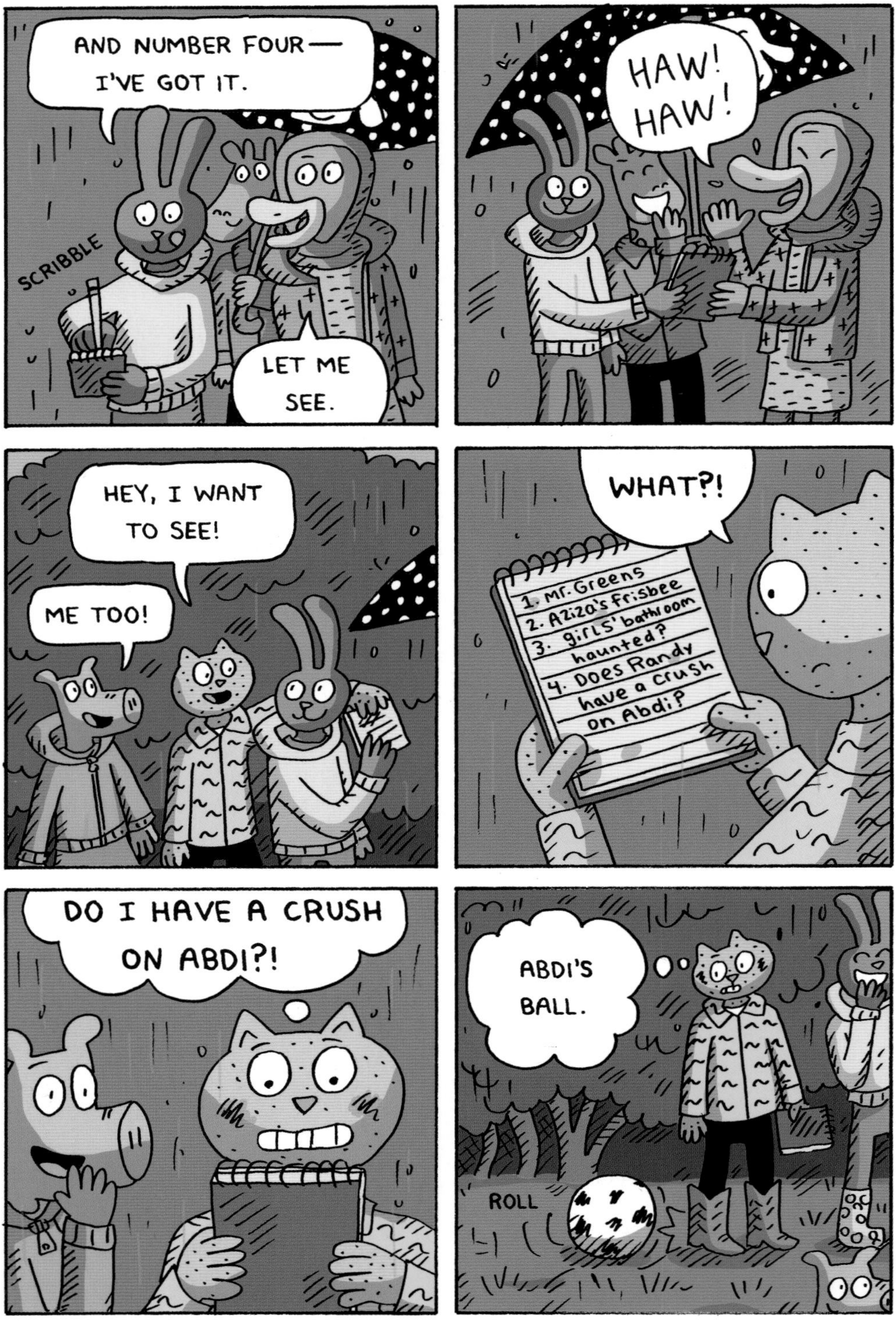
AND NUMBER FOUR—
I'VE GOT IT.
SCRIBBLE
LET ME SEE.
HAW! HAW!
HEY, I WANT TO SEE!
ME TOO!
WHAT?!
1. Mr. Greens
2. Aziza's Frisbee
3. girls' bathroom haunted?
4. Does Randy have a crush on Abdi?
DO I HAVE A CRUSH ON ABDI?!
ABDI'S BALL.
ROLL

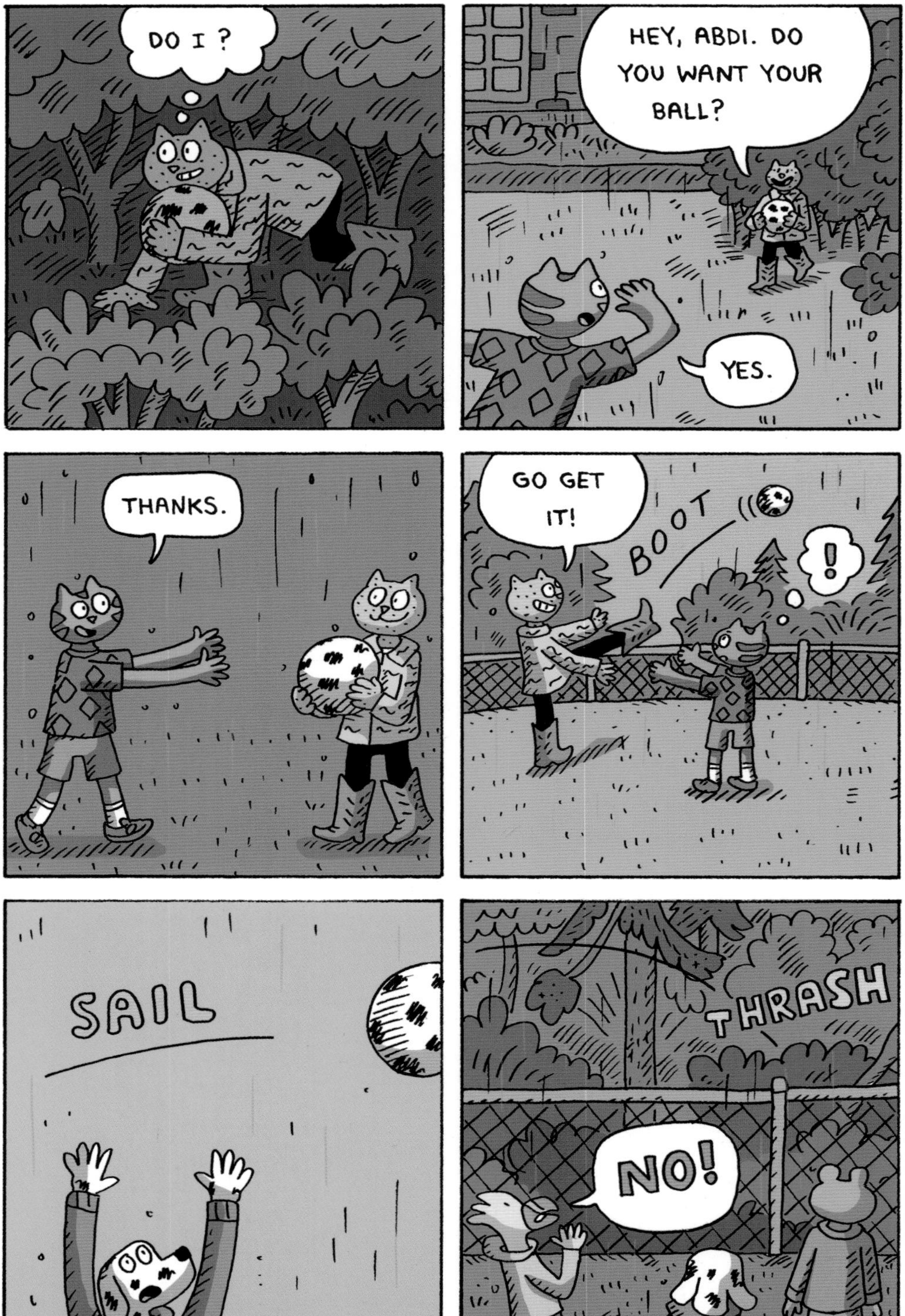
DO I ?
HEY, ABDI. DO YOU WANT YOUR BALL?
YES.
THANKS.
GO GET IT!
BOOT
!
SAIL
THRASH
NO!

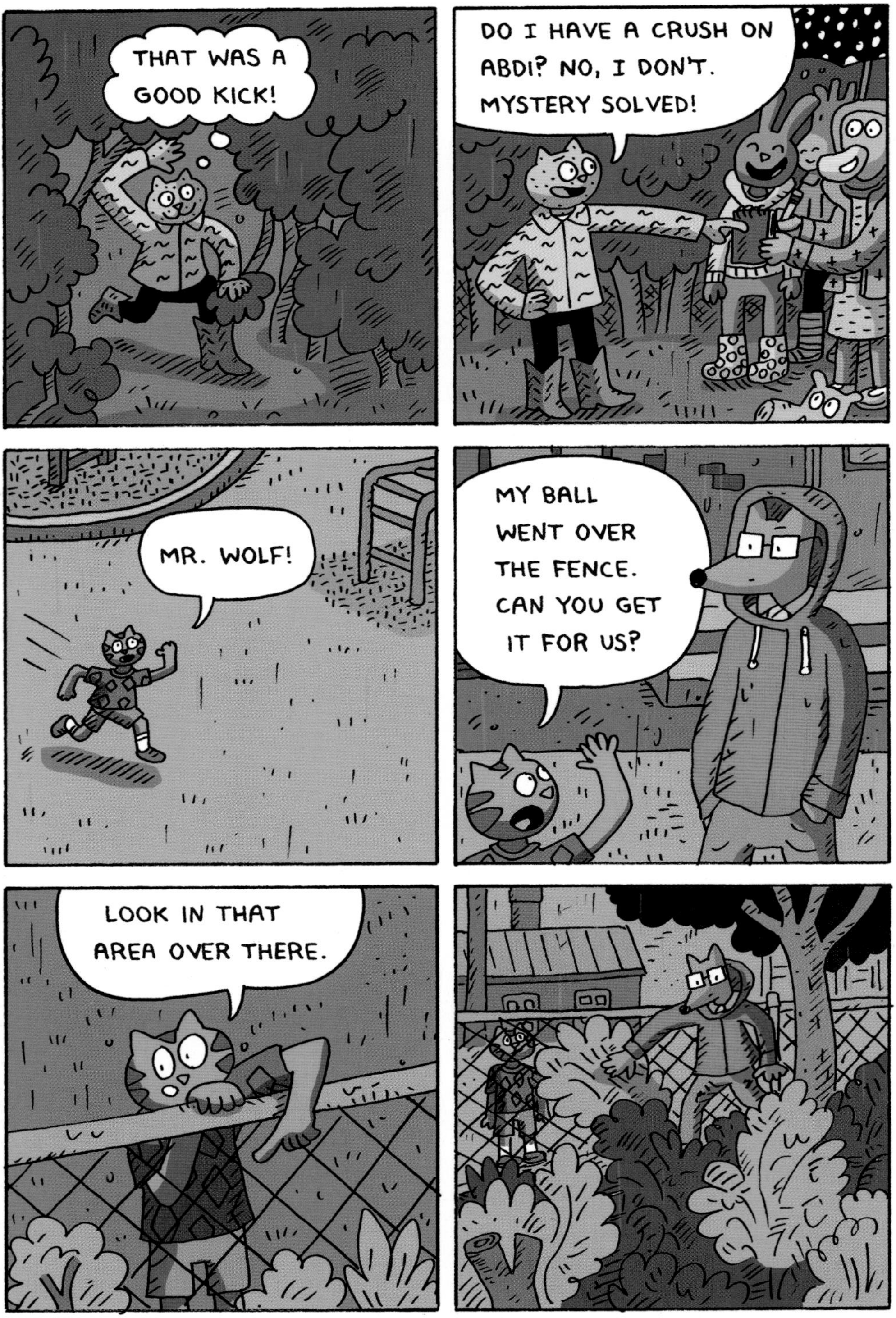
THAT WAS A GOOD KICK!
DO I HAVE A CRUSH ON ABDI? NO, I DON'T. MYSTERY SOLVED!
MR. WOLF!
MY BALL WENT OVER THE FENCE. CAN YOU GET IT FOR US?
LOOK IN THAT AREA OVER THERE.

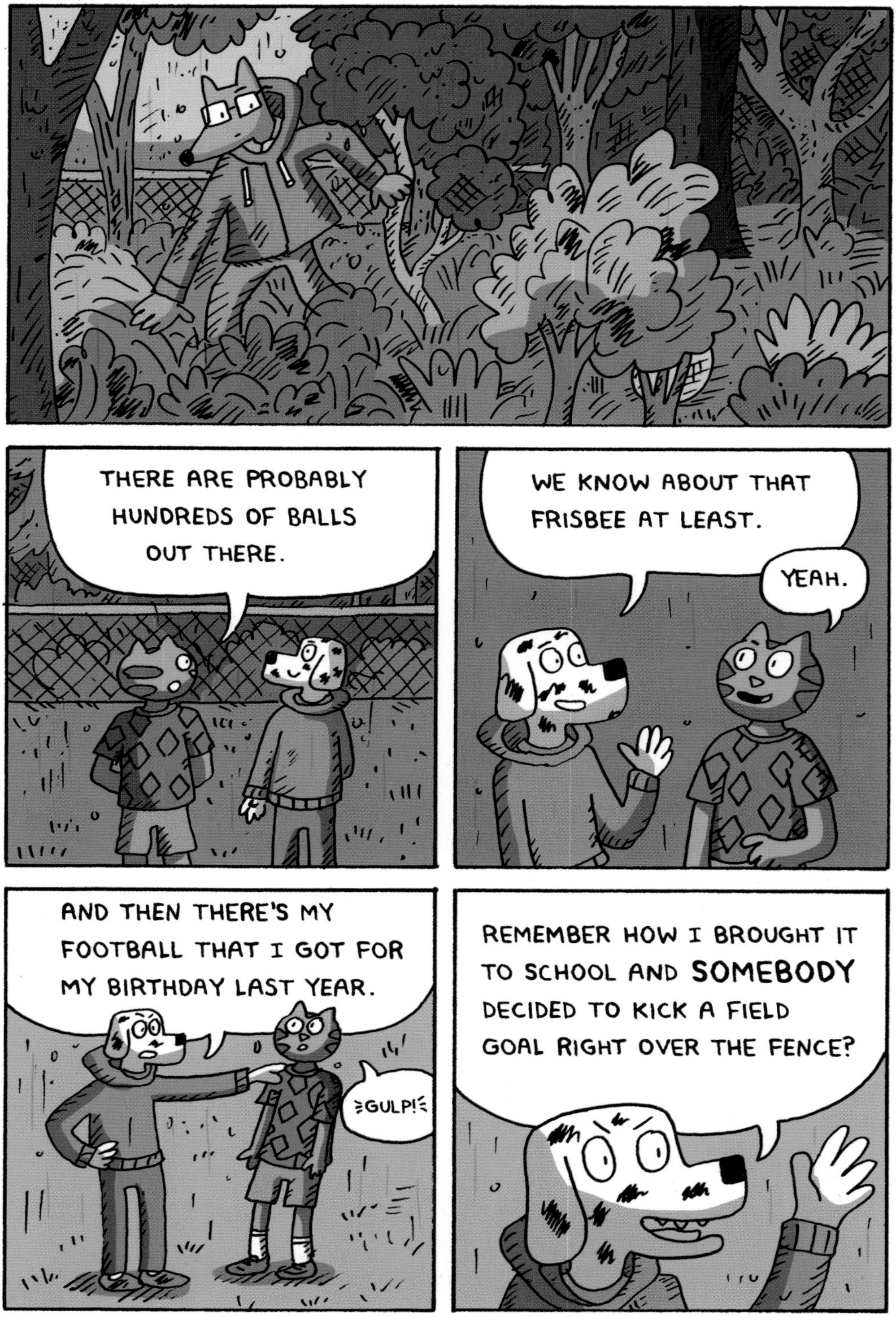
THERE ARE PROBABLY HUNDREDS OF BALLS OUT THERE.
WE KNOW ABOUT THAT FRISBEE AT LEAST.
YEAH.
AND THEN THERE'S MY FOOTBALL THAT I GOT FOR MY BIRTHDAY LAST YEAR.
GULP!
REMEMBER HOW I BROUGHT IT TO SCHOOL AND SOMEBODY DECIDED TO KICK A FIELD GOAL RIGHT OVER THE FENCE?

TOSS

≳GRUNT!≲

THANK YOU!

C A T C H

BOUNCE

I'M NOT DOING THAT AGAIN TODAY.

WE SHOULD RIDE OUR BIKES HERE AFTER SCHOOL ONE DAY SO WE CAN LOOK IN THE WOODS.

SURE, BUT MY MOM PROBABLY WON'T LET ME.

DRIBBLE

PASS! I'M GOING TO SCORE ON SAMPSON.

KICK

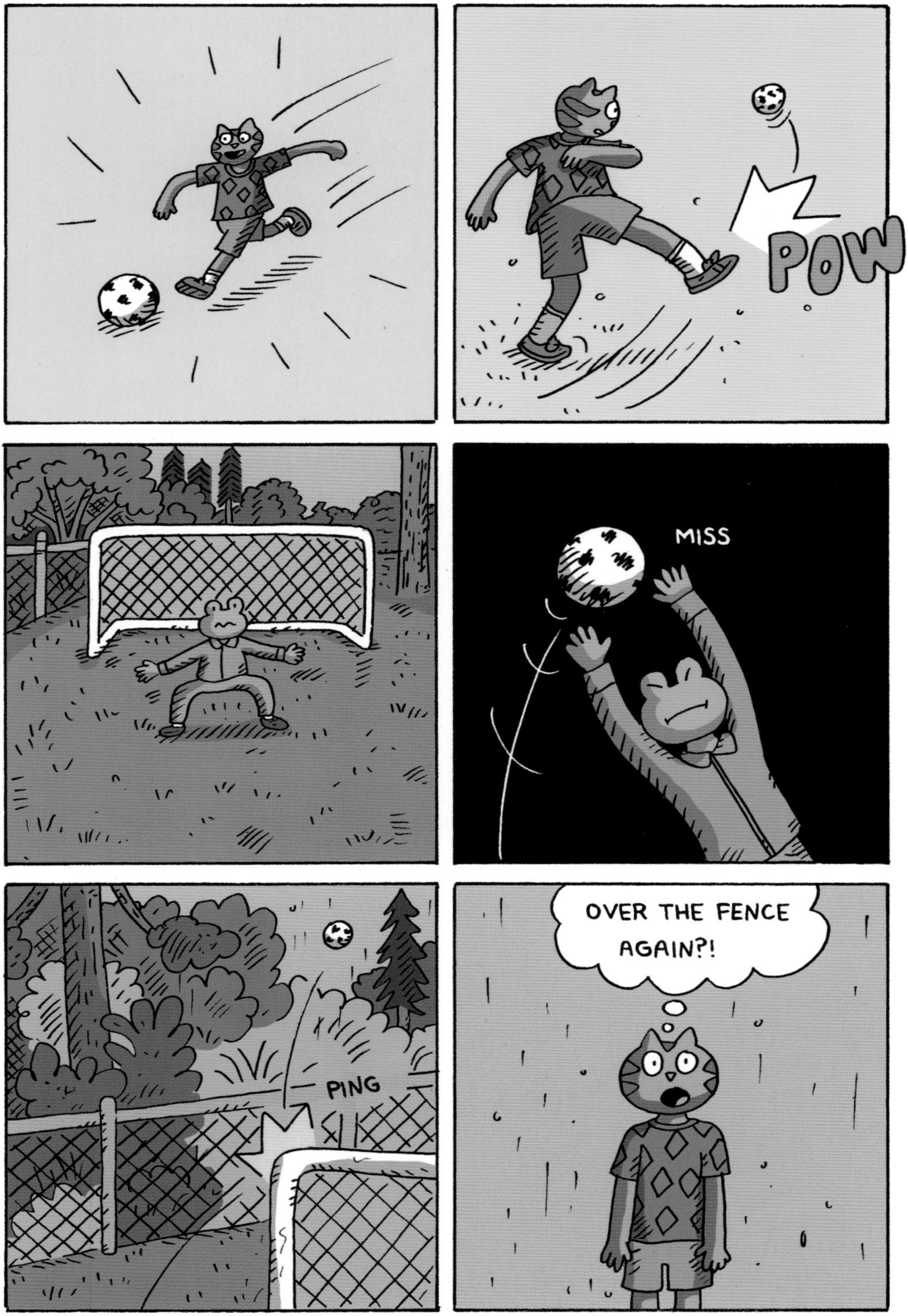

POW
MISS
PING
OVER THE FENCE AGAIN?!

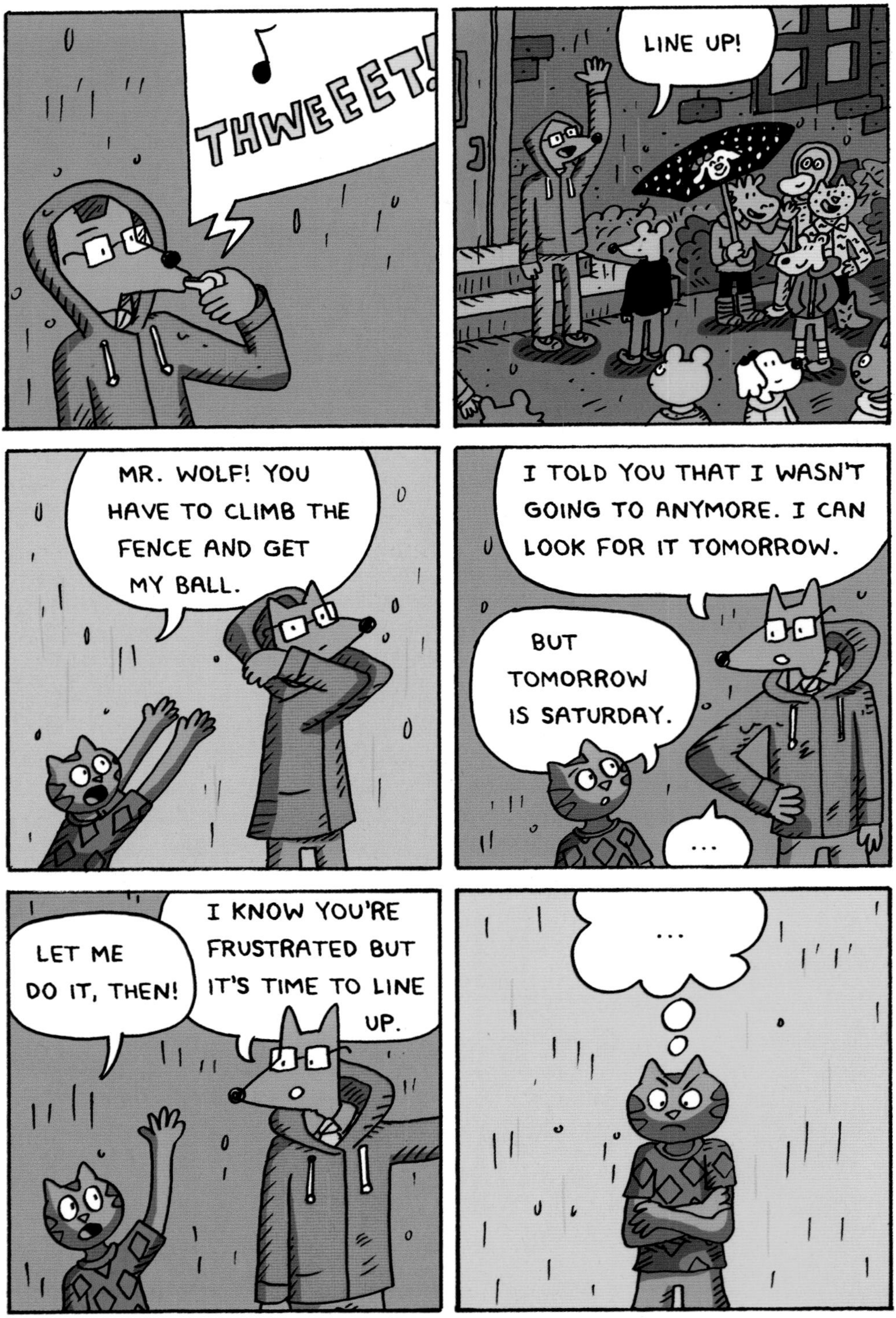
THWEEET!
LINE UP!
MR. WOLF! YOU HAVE TO CLIMB THE FENCE AND GET MY BALL.
I TOLD YOU THAT I WASN'T GOING TO ANYMORE. I CAN LOOK FOR IT TOMORROW.
BUT TOMORROW IS SATURDAY.
...
LET ME DO IT, THEN!
I KNOW YOU'RE FRUSTRATED BUT IT'S TIME TO LINE UP.
...

CHAPTER THREE
Anything Is Possible

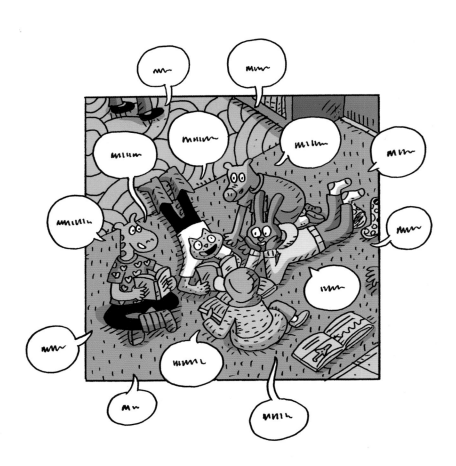

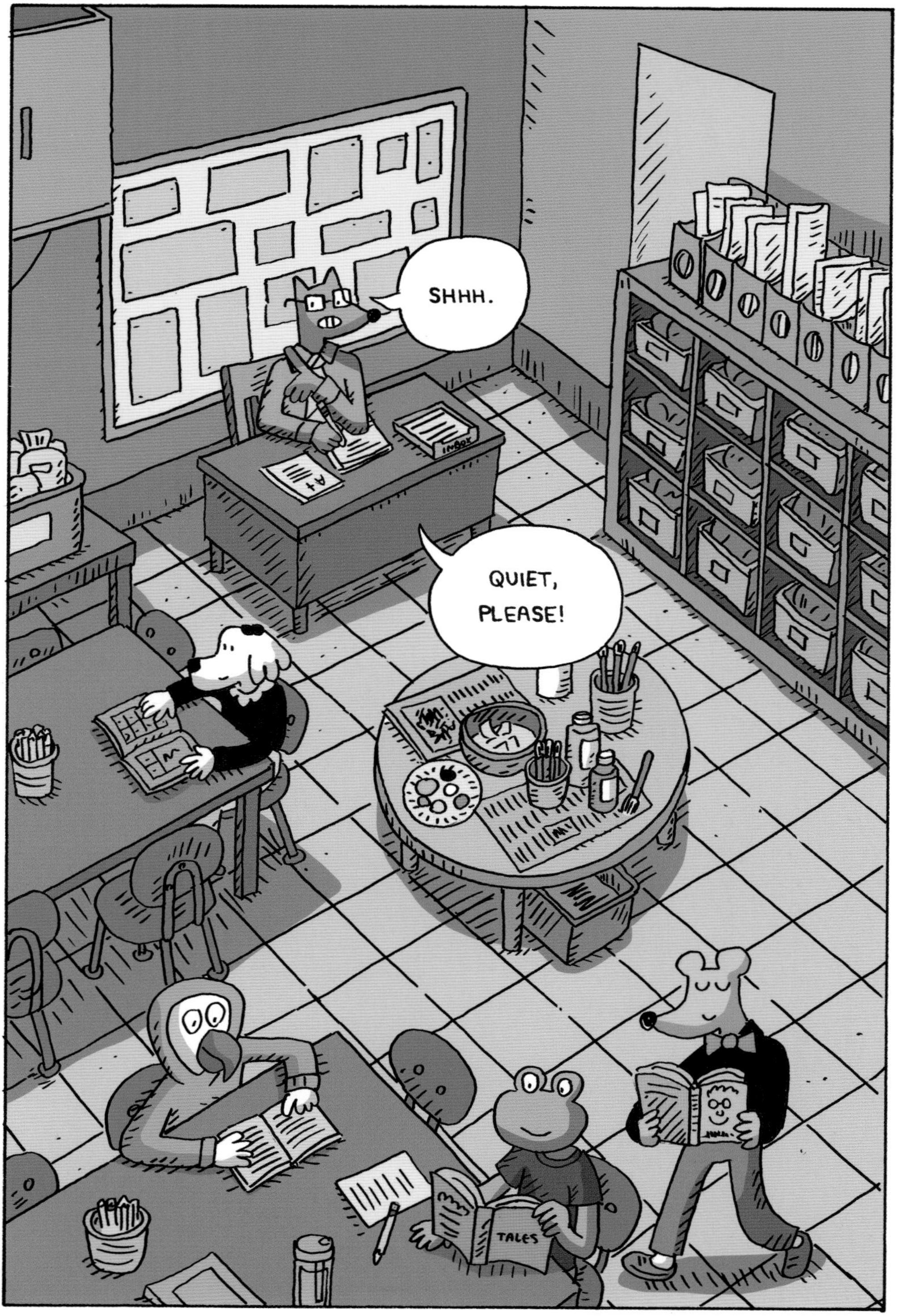
SHHH.
QUIET, PLEASE!
INBOX
A+
TALES

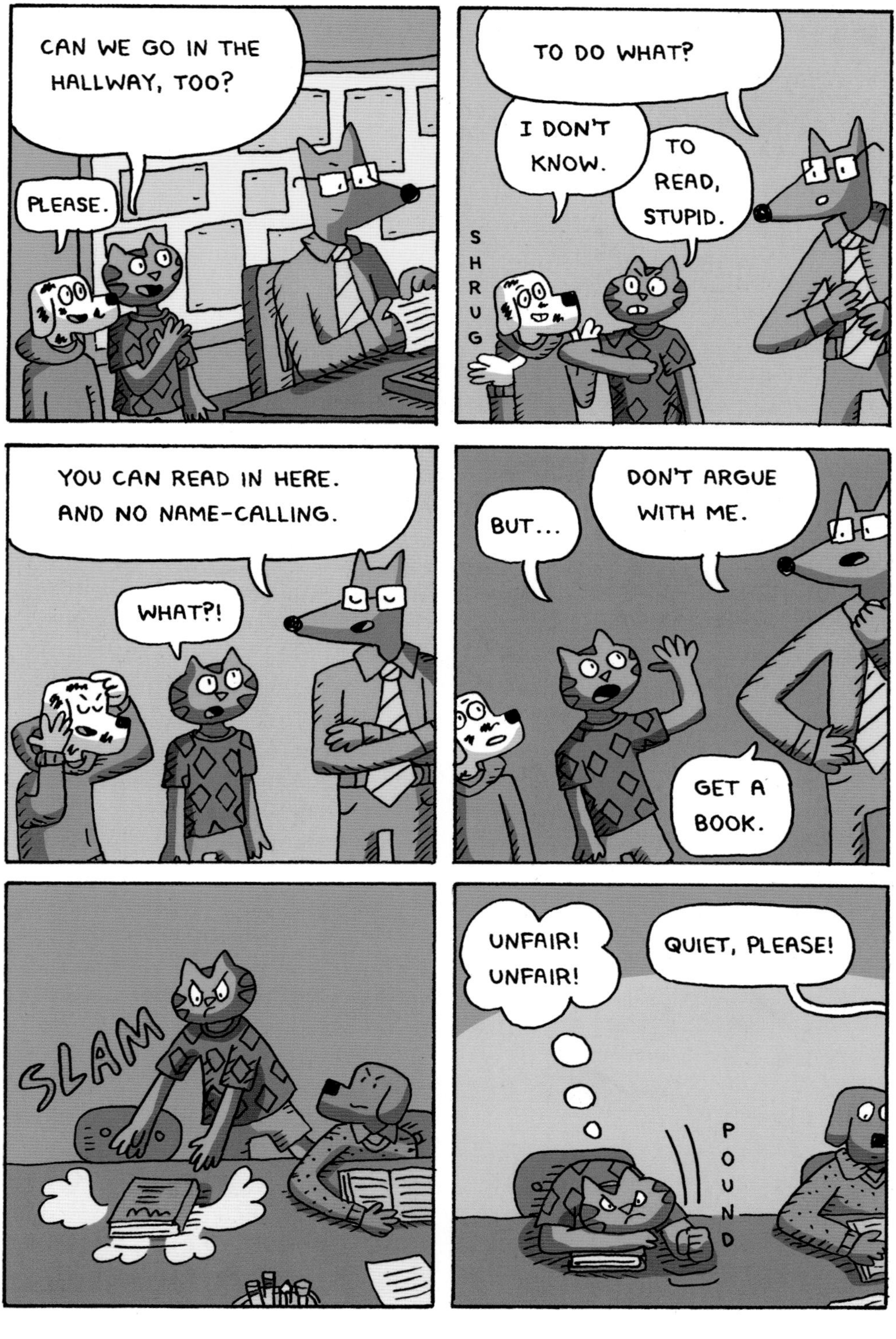
CAN WE GO IN THE HALLWAY, TOO?
PLEASE.
TO DO WHAT?
I DON'T KNOW.
SHRUG
TO READ, STUPID.
YOU CAN READ IN HERE. AND NO NAME-CALLING.
WHAT?!
BUT...
DON'T ARGUE WITH ME.
GET A BOOK.
SLAM
UNFAIR! UNFAIR!
QUIET, PLEASE!
POUND

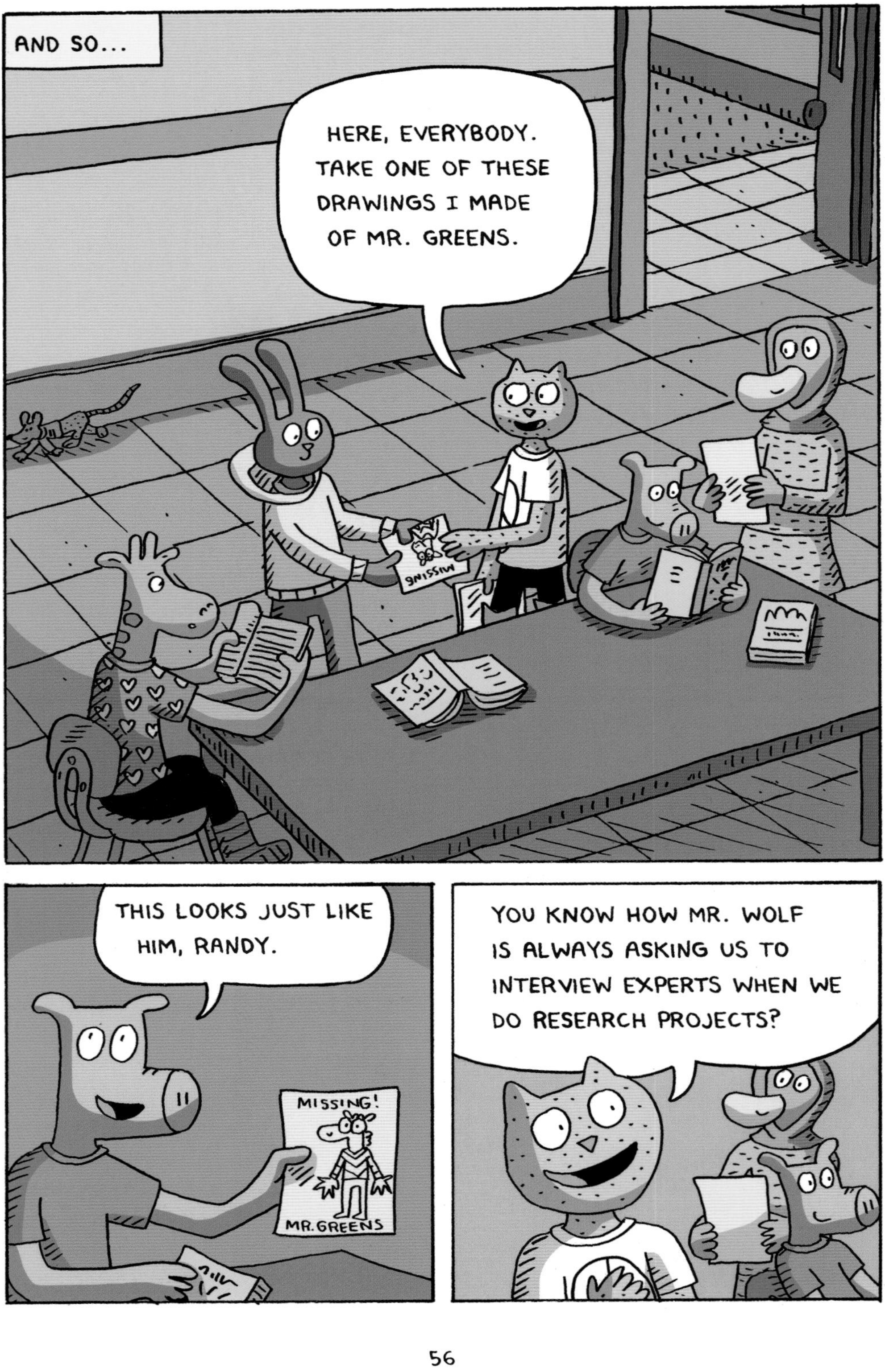
AND SO...
HERE, EVERYBODY. TAKE ONE OF THESE DRAWINGS I MADE OF MR. GREENS.
THIS LOOKS JUST LIKE HIM, RANDY.
MISSING!
MR. GREENS
YOU KNOW HOW MR. WOLF IS ALWAYS ASKING US TO INTERVIEW EXPERTS WHEN WE DO RESEARCH PROJECTS?

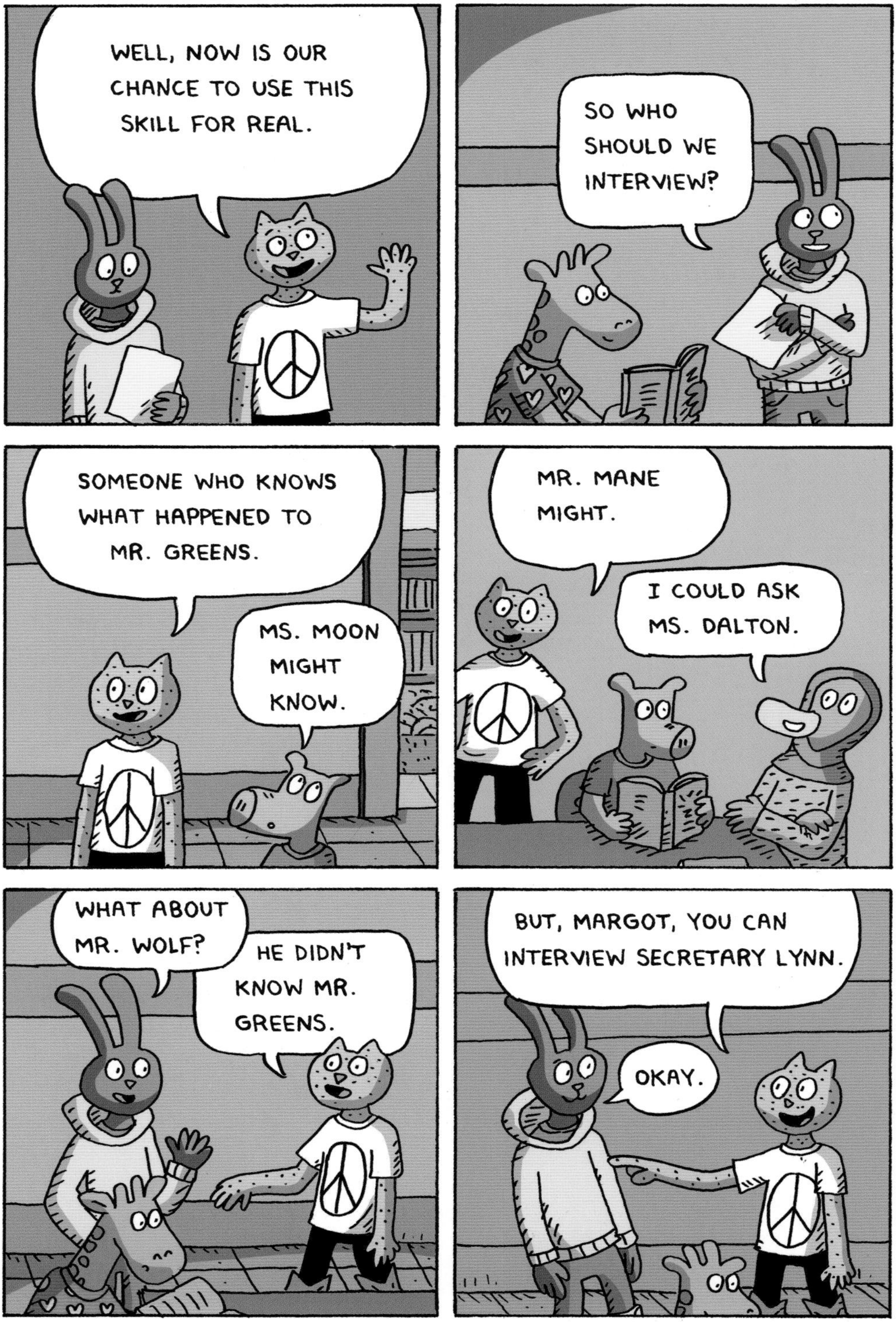
WELL, NOW IS OUR CHANCE TO USE THIS SKILL FOR REAL.
SO WHO SHOULD WE INTERVIEW?
SOMEONE WHO KNOWS WHAT HAPPENED TO MR. GREENS.
MS. MOON MIGHT KNOW.
MR. MANE MIGHT.
I COULD ASK MS. DALTON.
WHAT ABOUT MR. WOLF?
HE DIDN'T KNOW MR. GREENS.
BUT, MARGOT, YOU CAN INTERVIEW SECRETARY LYNN.
OKAY.

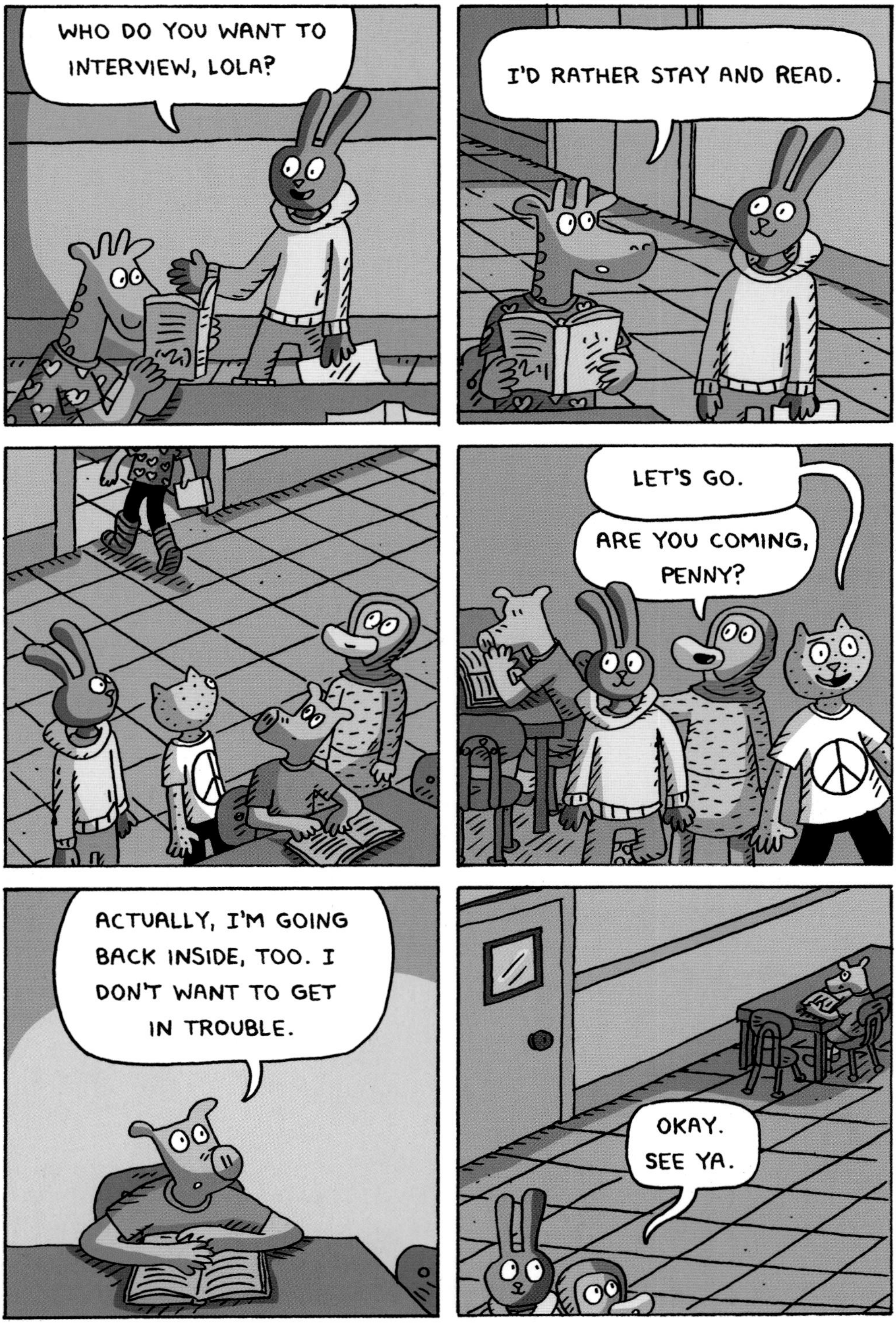
WHO DO YOU WANT TO INTERVIEW, LOLA?
I'D RATHER STAY AND READ.
LET'S GO.
ARE YOU COMING, PENNY?
ACTUALLY, I'M GOING BACK INSIDE, TOO. I DON'T WANT TO GET IN TROUBLE.
OKAY. SEE YA.

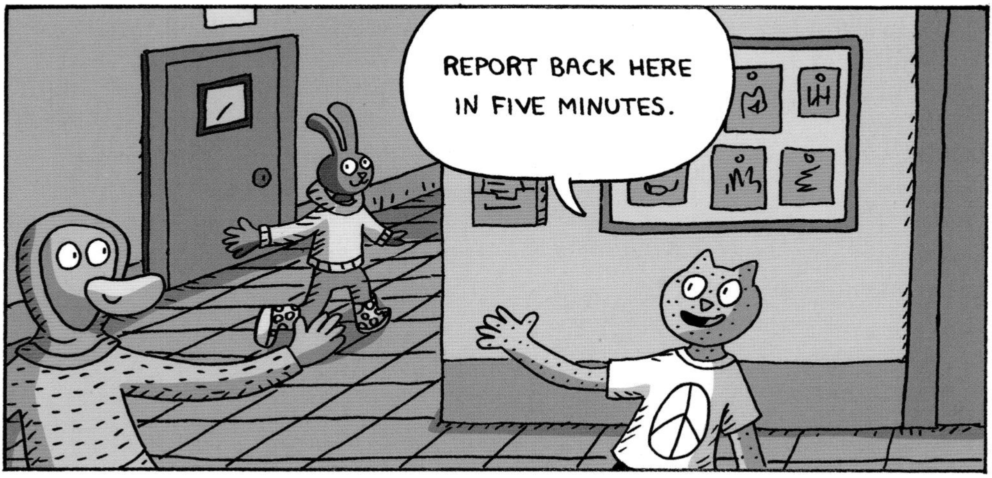
REPORT BACK HERE IN FIVE MINUTES.

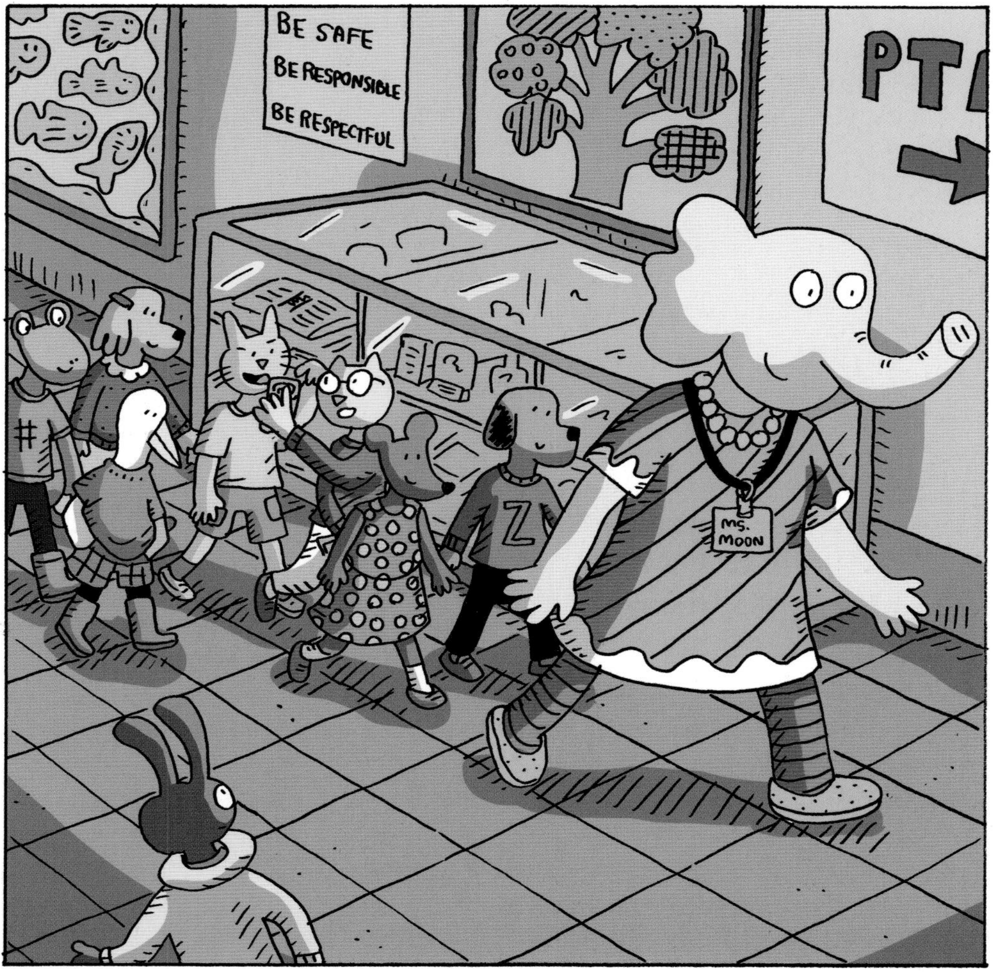
BE SAFE
BE RESPONSIBLE
BE RESPECTFUL
PT
MS. MOON

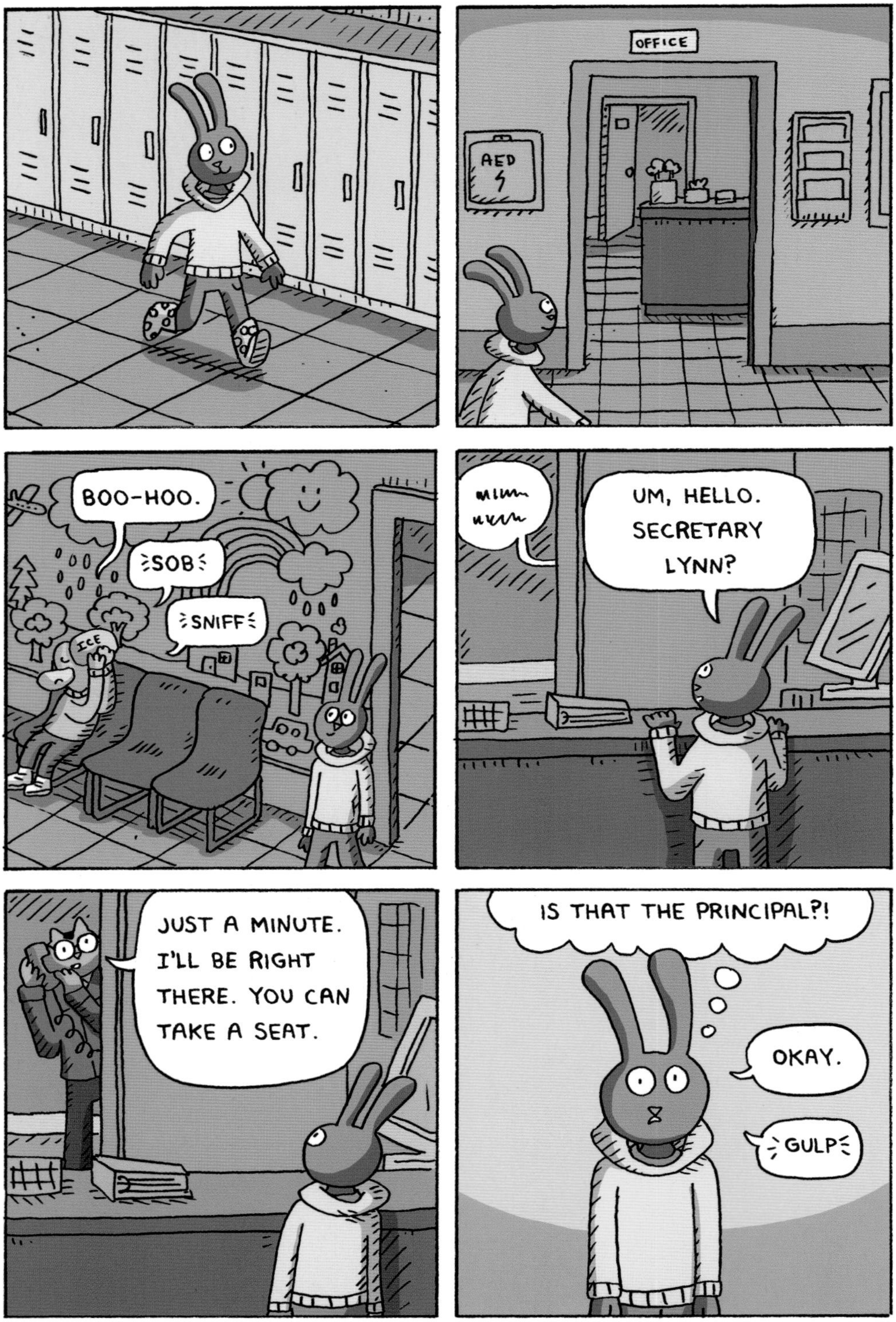
OFFICE
AED
BOO-HOO.
SOB
SNIFF
ICE
UM, HELLO. SECRETARY LYNN?
JUST A MINUTE. I'LL BE RIGHT THERE. YOU CAN TAKE A SEAT.
IS THAT THE PRINCIPAL?!
OKAY.
GULP

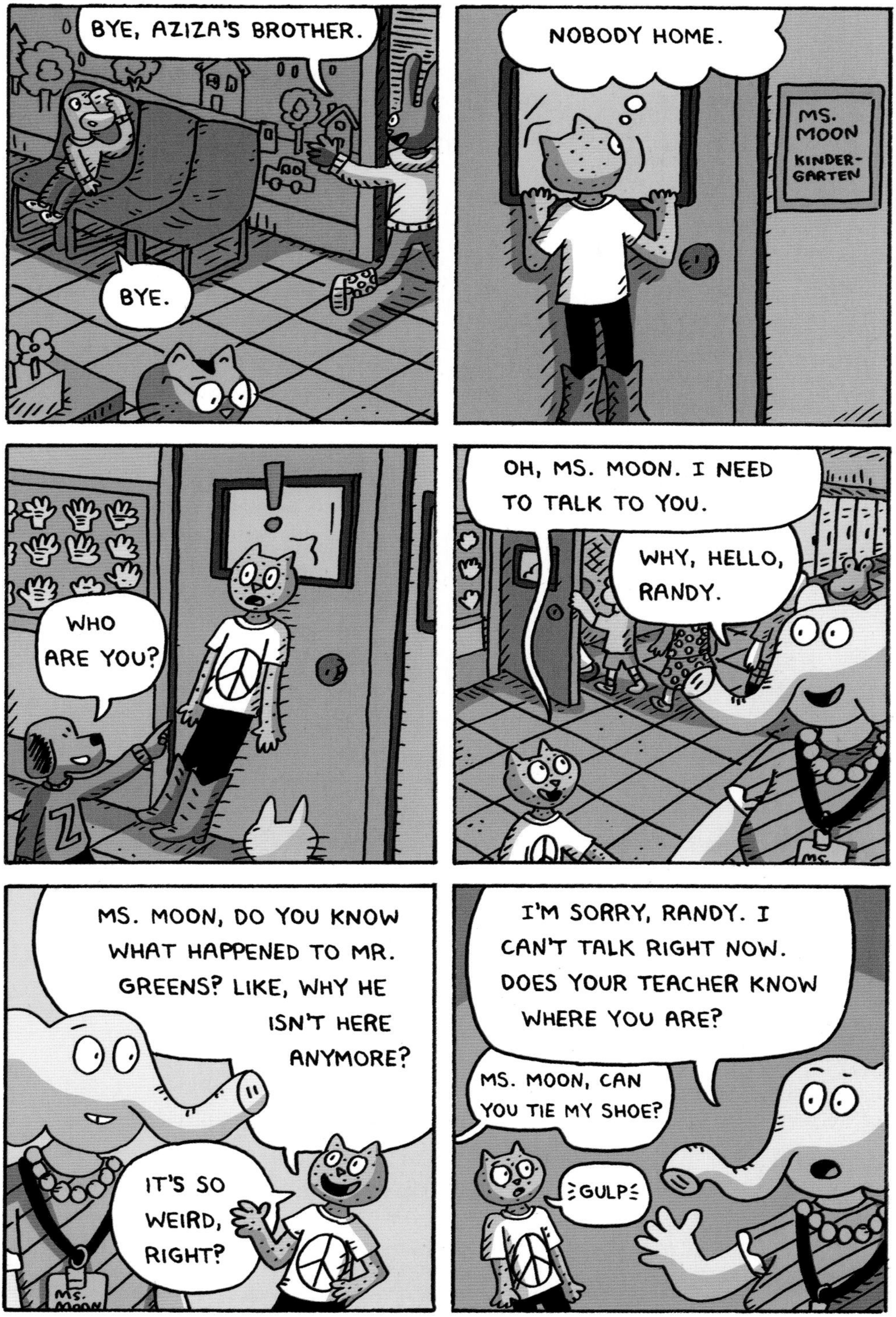
BYE, AZIZA'S BROTHER.
BYE.
NOBODY HOME.
MS. MOON KINDER-GARTEN
WHO ARE YOU?
OH, MS. MOON. I NEED TO TALK TO YOU.
WHY, HELLO, RANDY.
MS. MOON, DO YOU KNOW WHAT HAPPENED TO MR. GREENS? LIKE, WHY HE ISN'T HERE ANYMORE?
IT'S SO WEIRD, RIGHT?
MS. MOON
I'M SORRY, RANDY. I CAN'T TALK RIGHT NOW. DOES YOUR TEACHER KNOW WHERE YOU ARE?
MS. MOON, CAN YOU TIE MY SHOE?
GULP

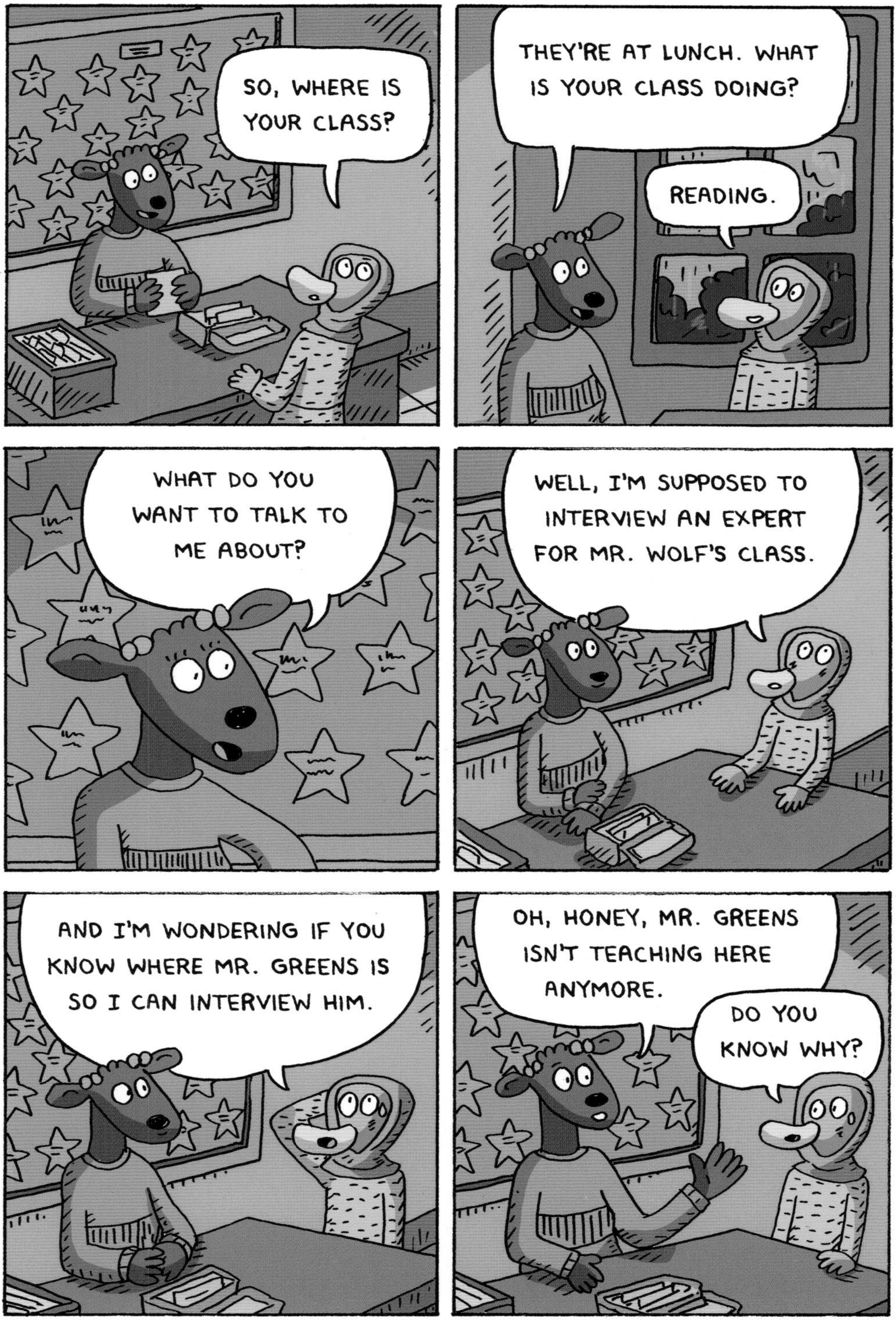
SO, WHERE IS YOUR CLASS?
THEY'RE AT LUNCH. WHAT IS YOUR CLASS DOING?
READING.
WHAT DO YOU WANT TO TALK TO ME ABOUT?
WELL, I'M SUPPOSED TO INTERVIEW AN EXPERT FOR MR. WOLF'S CLASS.
AND I'M WONDERING IF YOU KNOW WHERE MR. GREENS IS SO I CAN INTERVIEW HIM.
OH, HONEY, MR. GREENS ISN'T TEACHING HERE ANYMORE.
DO YOU KNOW WHY?

*NATIONAL AERONAUTICS AND SPACE ADMINISTRATION

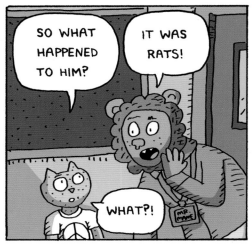

CHAPTER FOUR

The Truth about Mr. Greens

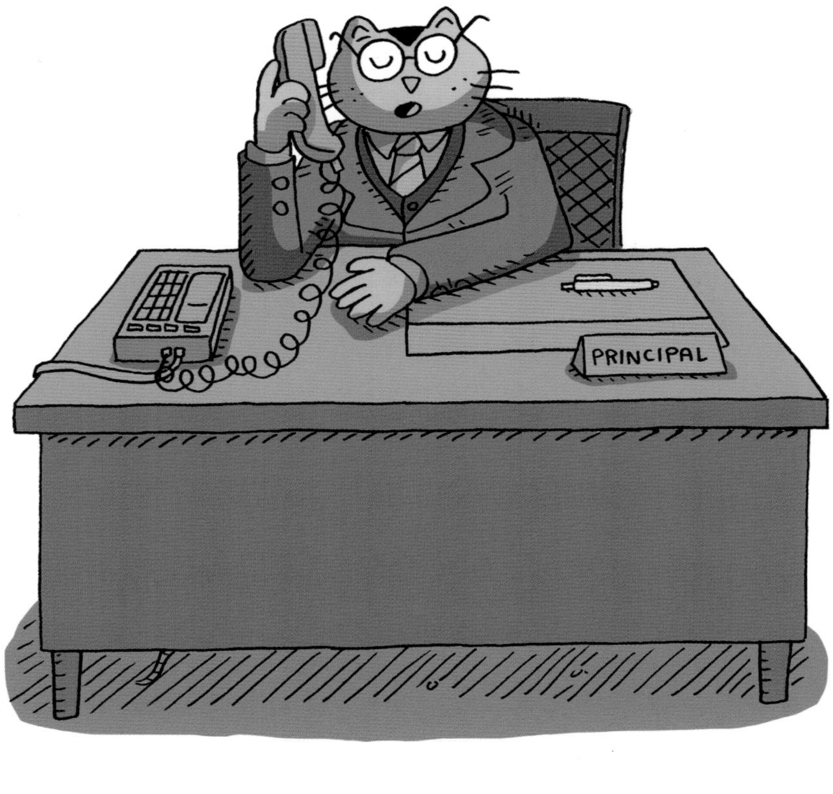
PRINCIPAL

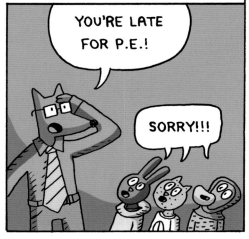

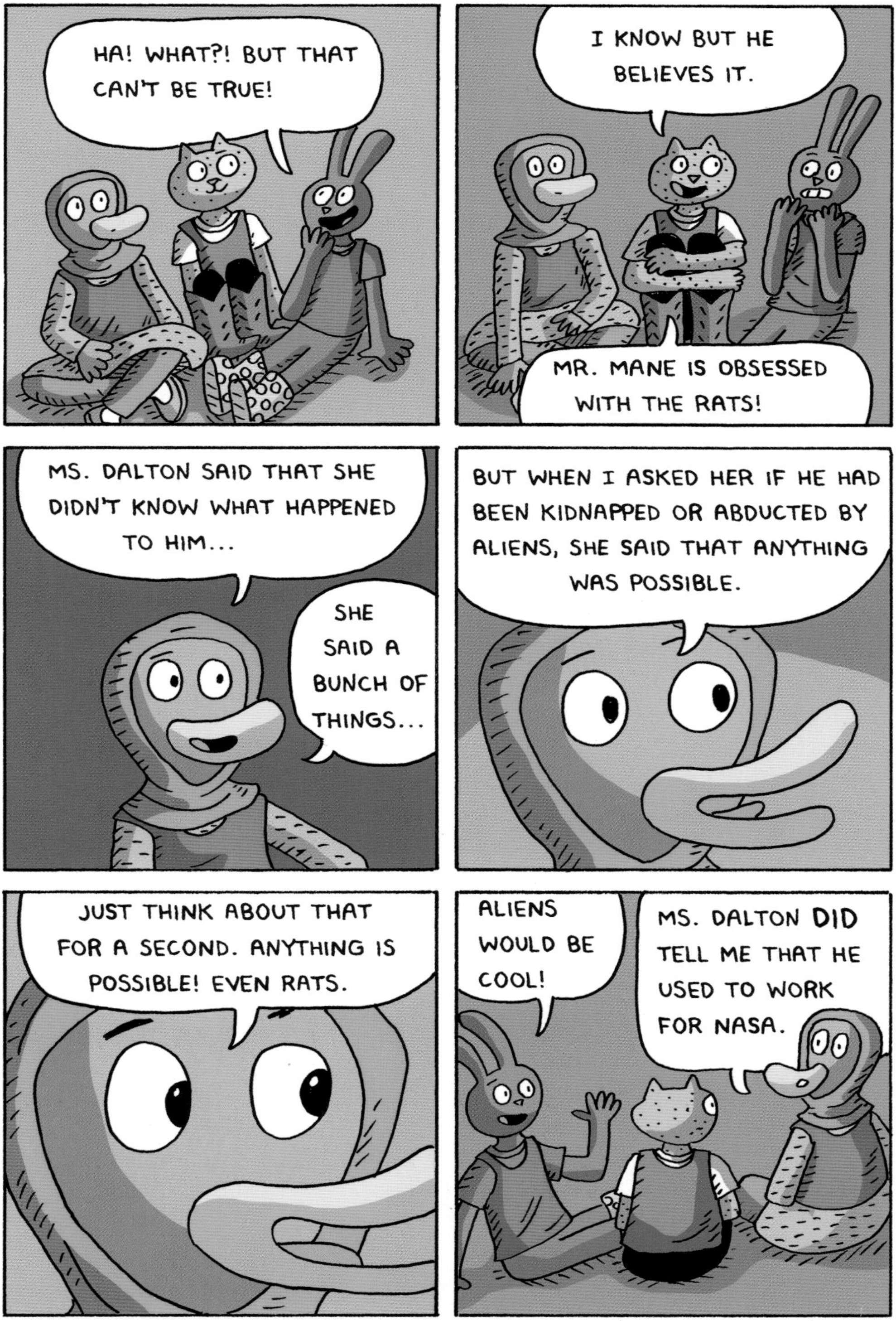
HA! WHAT?! BUT THAT CAN'T BE TRUE!
I KNOW BUT HE BELIEVES IT.
MR. MANE IS OBSESSED WITH THE RATS!
MS. DALTON SAID THAT SHE DIDN'T KNOW WHAT HAPPENED TO HIM...
SHE SAID A BUNCH OF THINGS...
BUT WHEN I ASKED HER IF HE HAD BEEN KIDNAPPED OR ABDUCTED BY ALIENS, SHE SAID THAT ANYTHING WAS POSSIBLE.
JUST THINK ABOUT THAT FOR A SECOND. ANYTHING IS POSSIBLE! EVEN RATS.
ALIENS WOULD BE COOL!
MS. DALTON **DID** TELL ME THAT HE USED TO WORK FOR NASA.

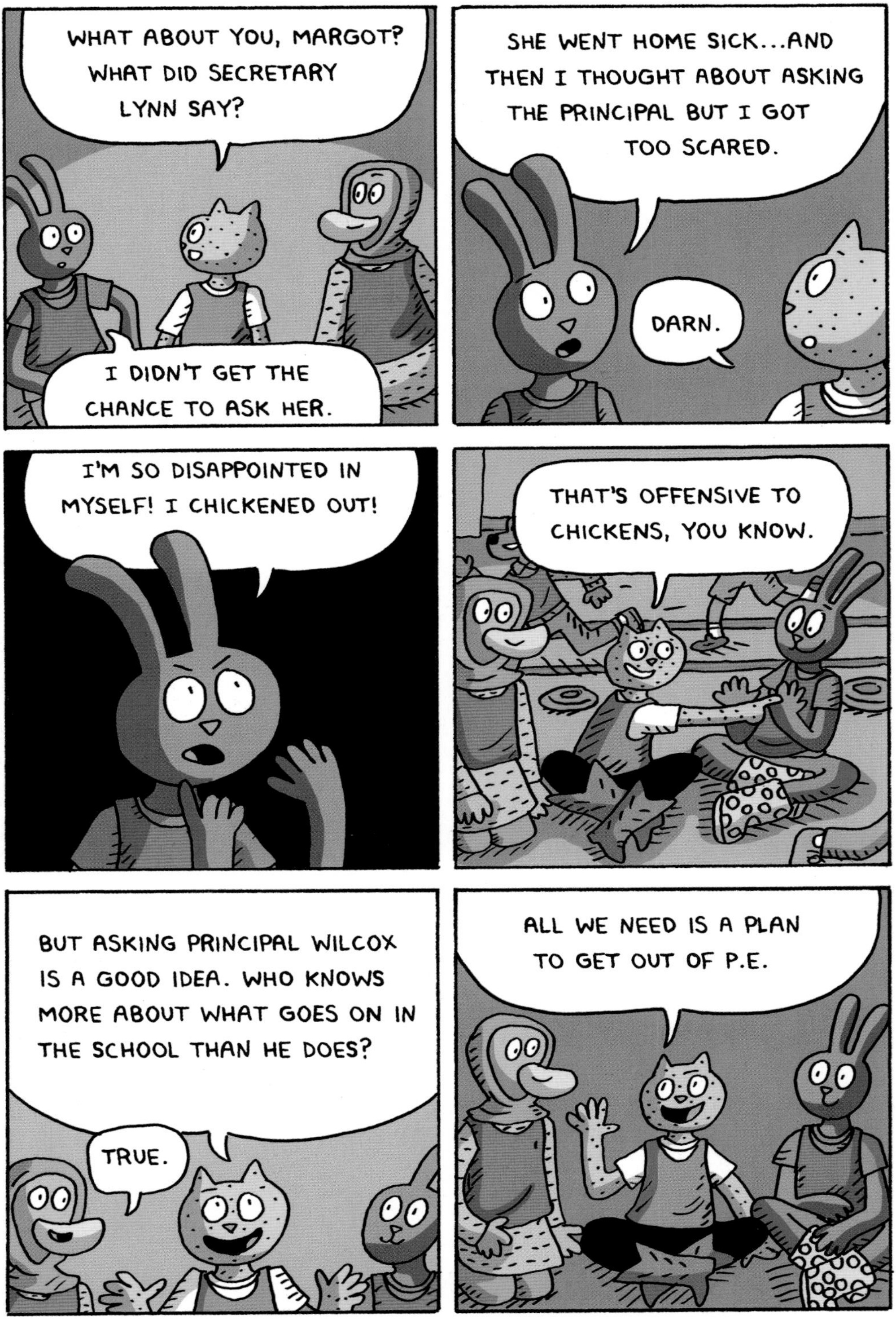

WHAT ABOUT YOU, MARGOT? WHAT DID SECRETARY LYNN SAY?
I DIDN'T GET THE CHANCE TO ASK HER.
SHE WENT HOME SICK...AND THEN I THOUGHT ABOUT ASKING THE PRINCIPAL BUT I GOT TOO SCARED.
DARN.
I'M SO DISAPPOINTED IN MYSELF! I CHICKENED OUT!
THAT'S OFFENSIVE TO CHICKENS, YOU KNOW.
BUT ASKING PRINCIPAL WILCOX IS A GOOD IDEA. WHO KNOWS MORE ABOUT WHAT GOES ON IN THE SCHOOL THAN HE DOES?
TRUE.
ALL WE NEED IS A PLAN TO GET OUT OF P.E.

75

YAWN

EXCUSE ME...

MR. GREENS WAS A GOOD TEACHER AND HE'LL BE MISSED.

SO...WHAT HAPPENED?

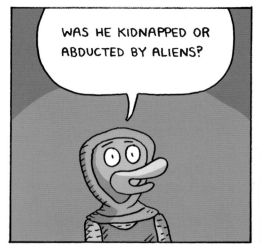

WAS HE KIDNAPPED OR ABDUCTED BY ALIENS?

WAS HE EATEN BY RATS?

CHAPTER FIVE

Locker Surprise

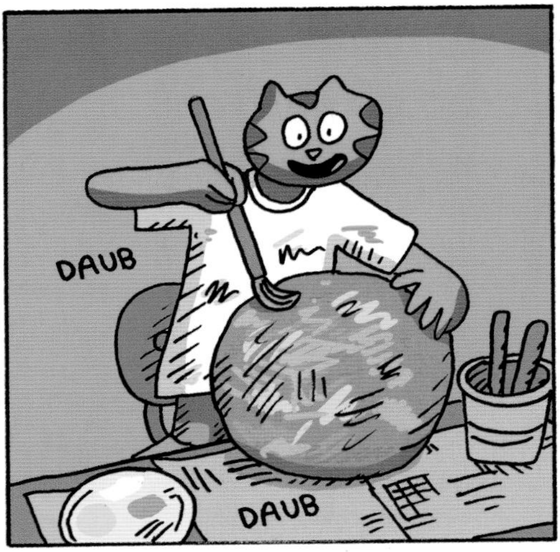
DAUB
DAUB

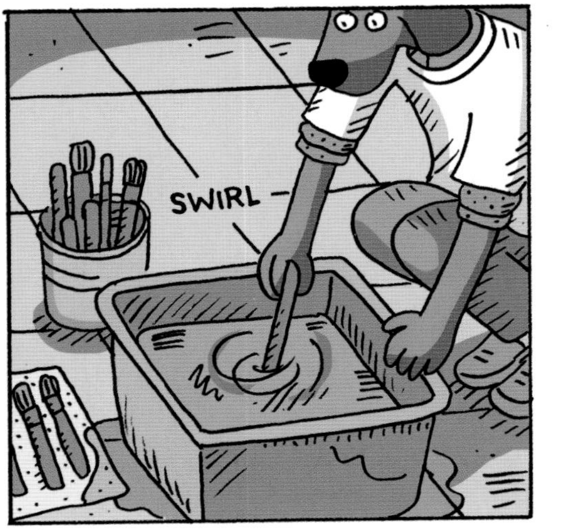
SWIRL

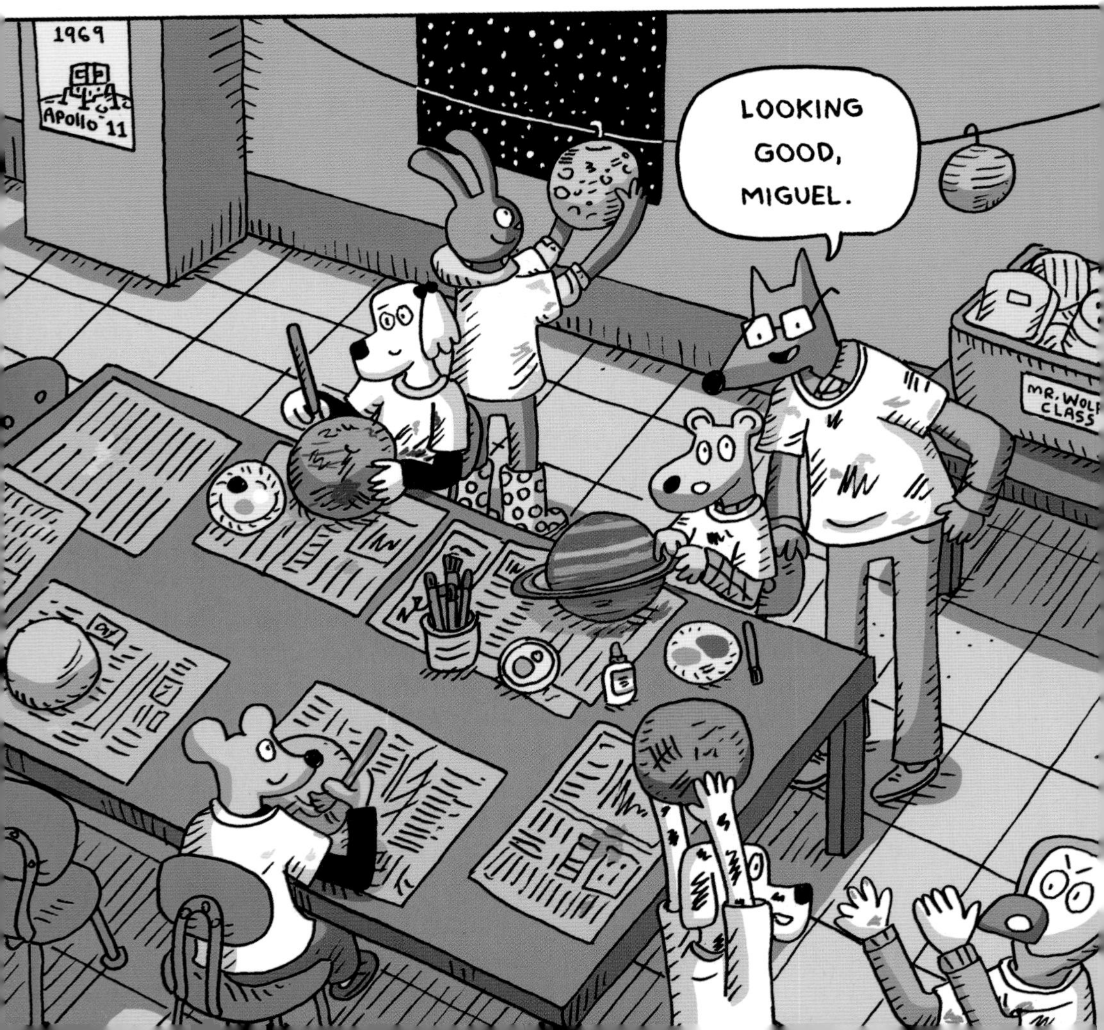
1969
APOLLO 11
LOOKING GOOD, MIGUEL.
MR. WOLF CLASS

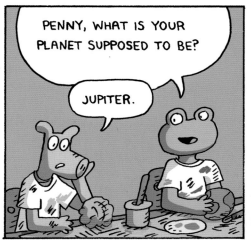

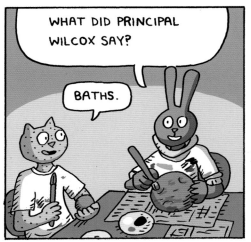

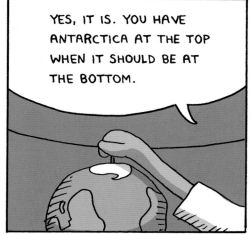

NORTH'S ALWAYS AT THE TOP. THIS IS WHAT I SAY TO REMEMBER IT—"NEVER EAT SOGGY WAFFLES."

BUT WHAT IF THE WAFFLES WERE SOGGY FROM MAPLE SYRUP? I WOULD EAT THAT.

LET ME EXPLAIN WHAT I MEAN. NORTH CAN BE AT THE TOP OR IT CAN BE AT THE BOTTOM.

HOW?

IN SPACE THERE IS NO UP OR DOWN— THINK ABOUT THAT FOR A SECOND.

WE ARE SPINNING AT AROUND 1,000 MILES PER HOUR ON THE EARTH'S AXIS. WE ARE SPINNING THROUGH SPACE.

PUTTING NORTH AT THE TOP IS JUST A STANDARD. IT COULD ALSO BE AT THE BOTTOM. AND NOW I'VE GOT PAINT ON MY HANDS.

HA!

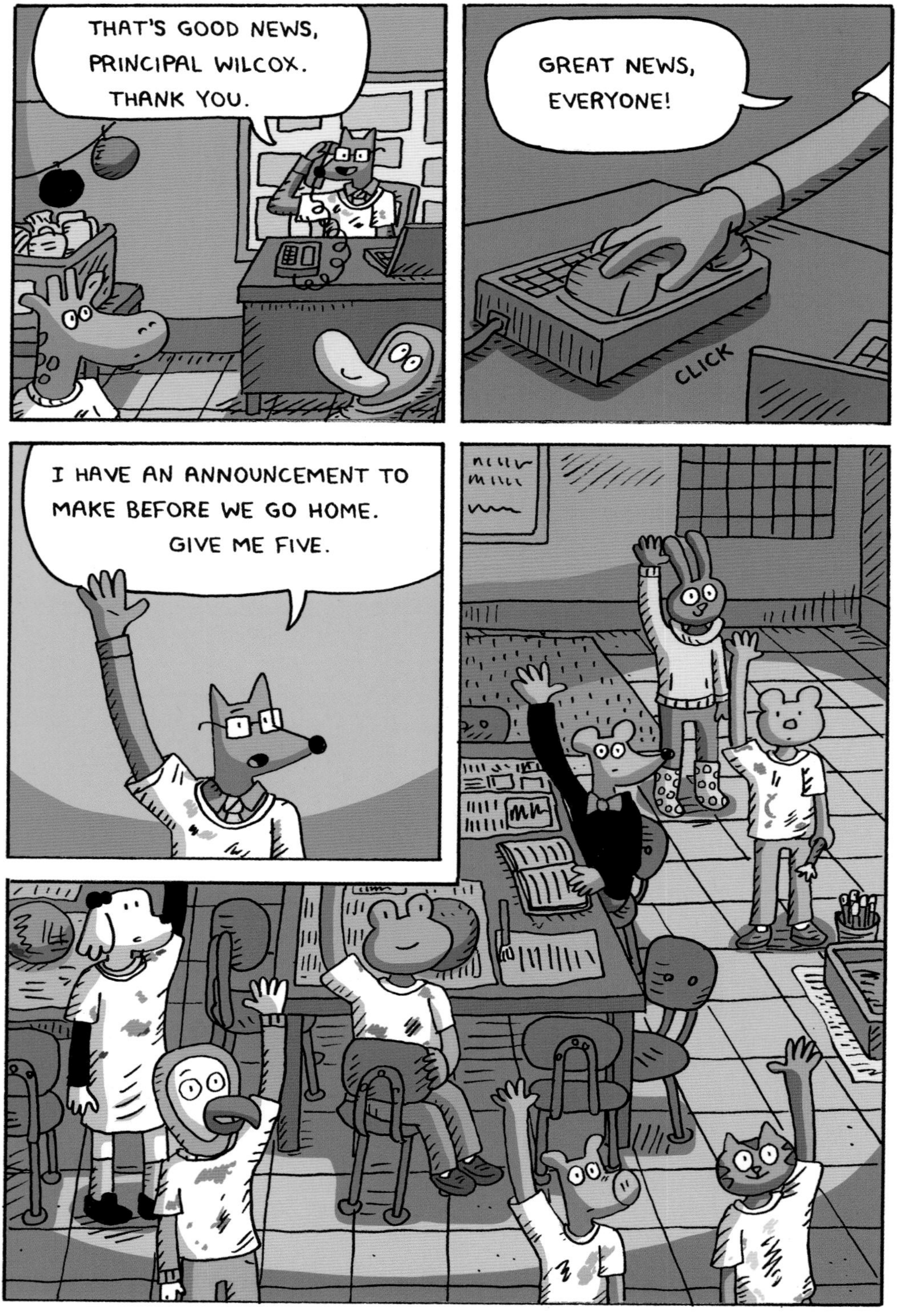
THAT'S GOOD NEWS, PRINCIPAL WILCOX. THANK YOU.
GREAT NEWS, EVERYONE!
CLICK
I HAVE AN ANNOUNCEMENT TO MAKE BEFORE WE GO HOME. GIVE ME FIVE.

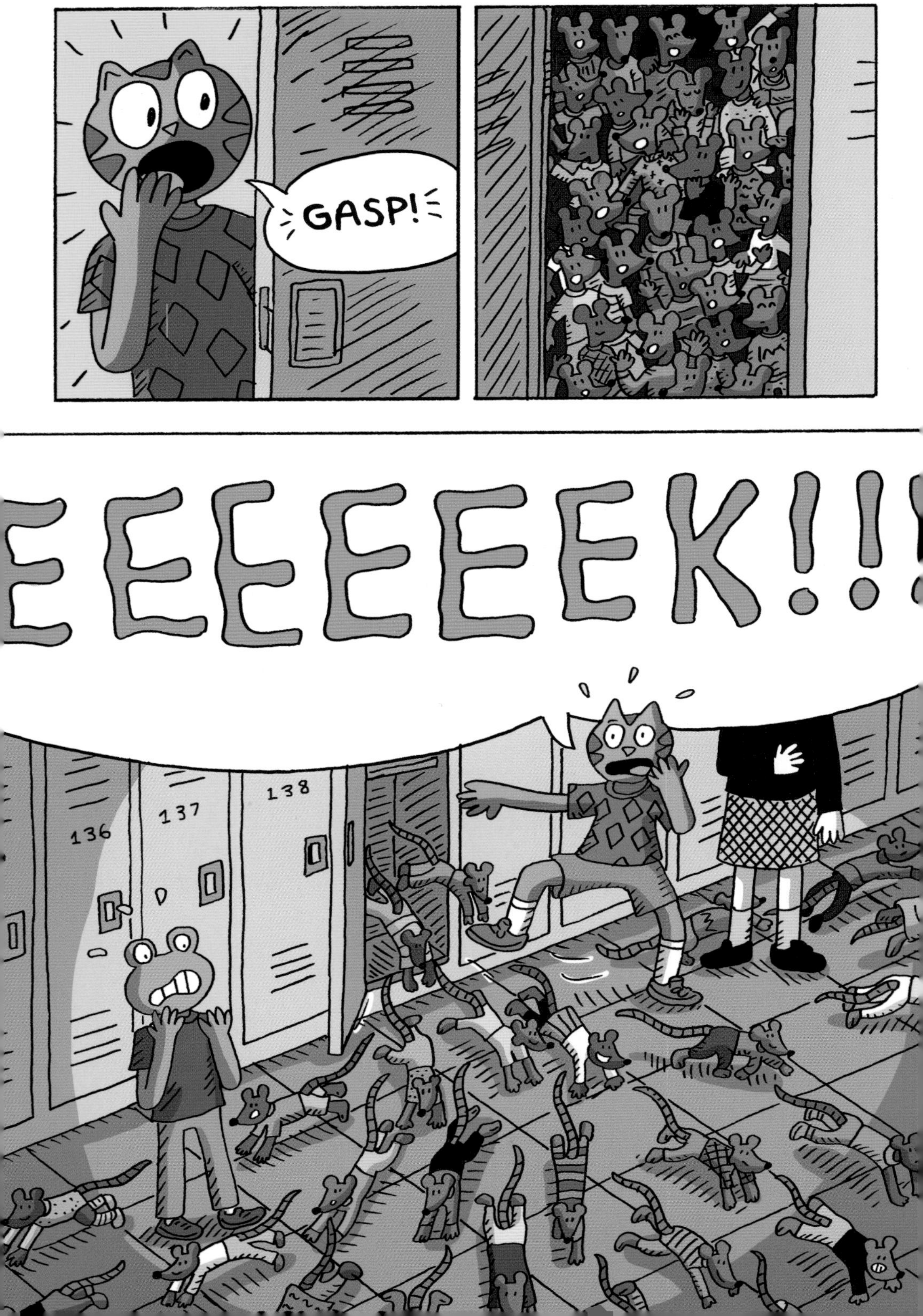
GASP!
EEEEEEK!!!
136
137
138

CHAPTER SIX

The Mystery in the Woods

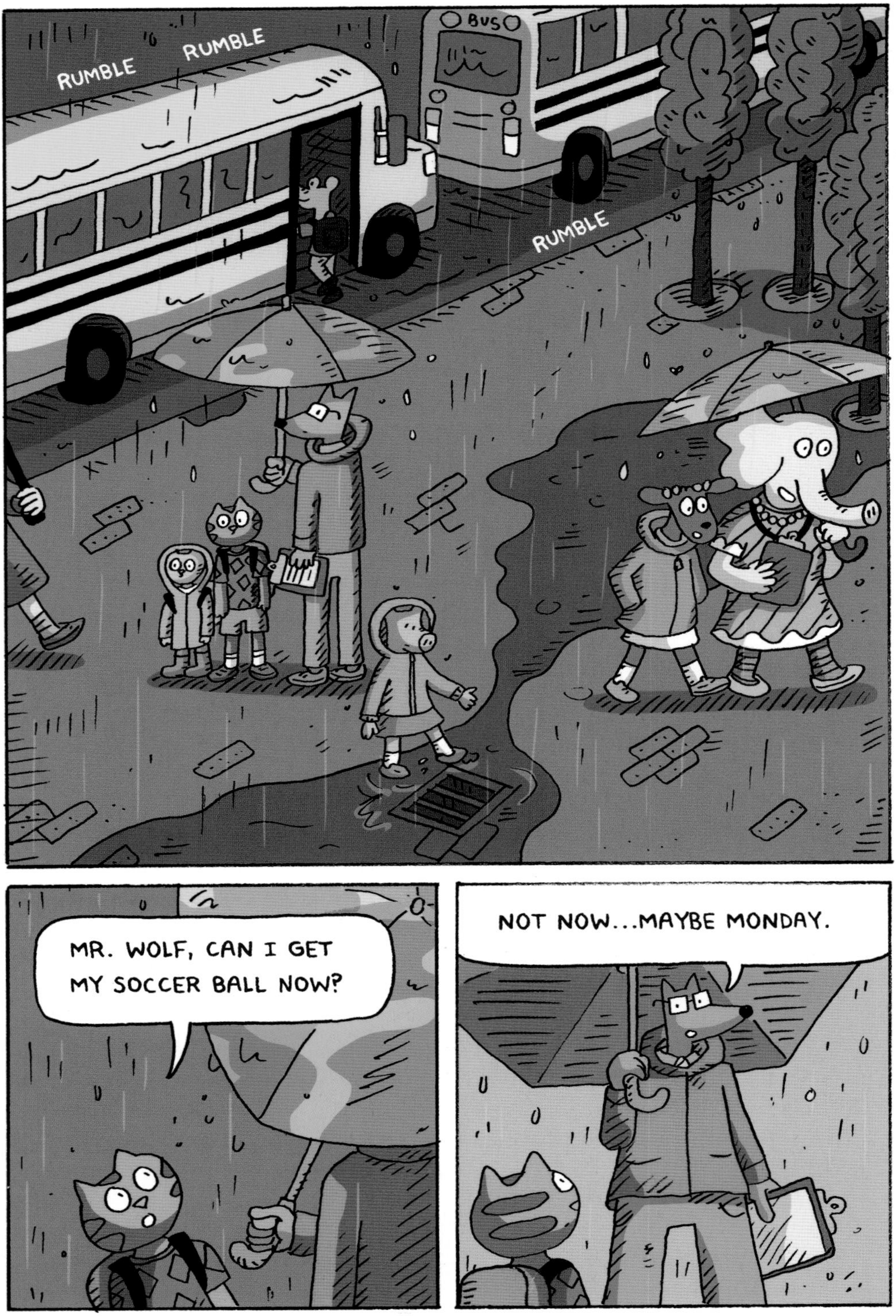
RUMBLE
RUMBLE
BUS
RUMBLE
MR. WOLF, CAN I GET MY SOCCER BALL NOW?
NOT NOW...MAYBE MONDAY.

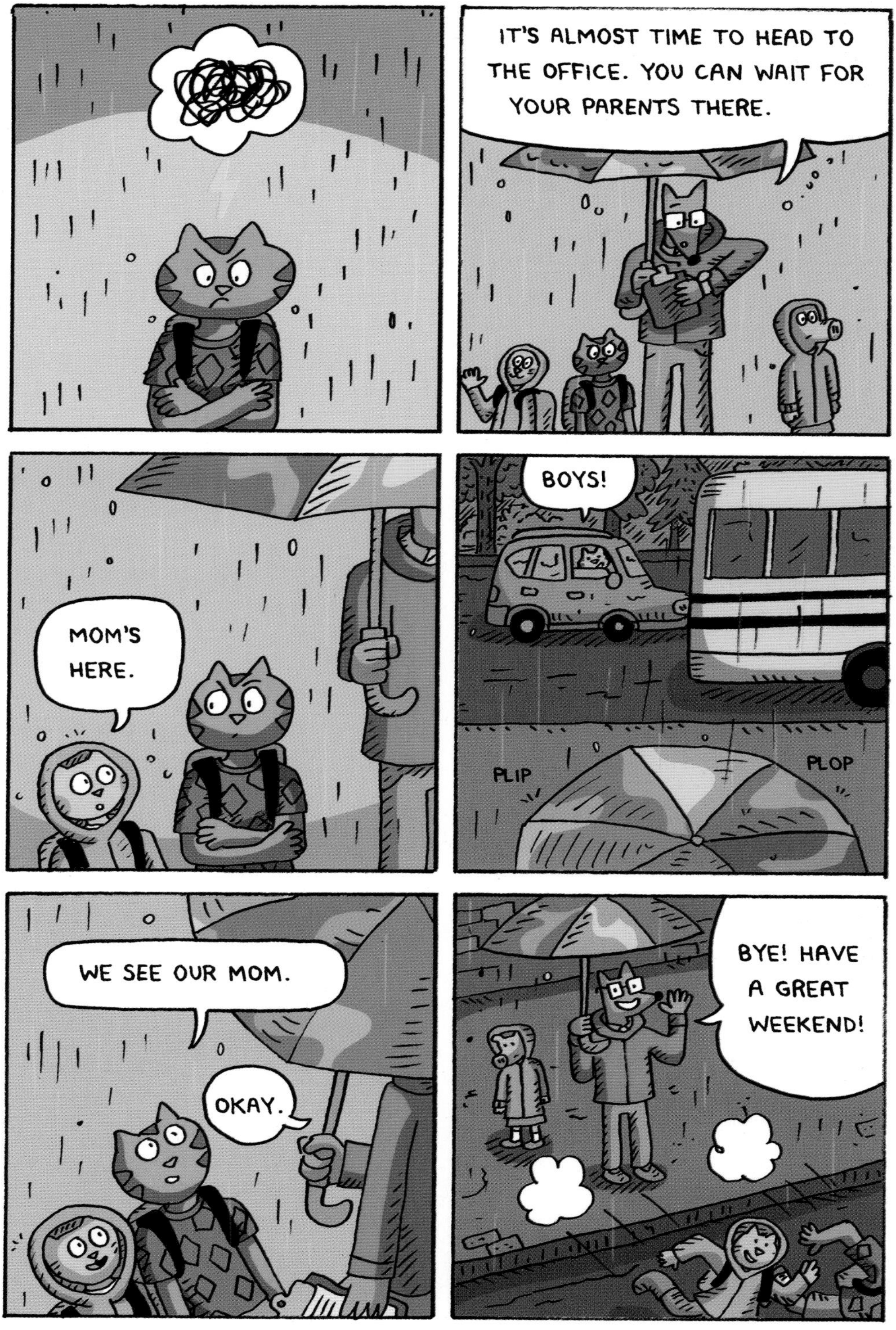
IT'S ALMOST TIME TO HEAD TO THE OFFICE. YOU CAN WAIT FOR YOUR PARENTS THERE.
MOM'S HERE.
BOYS!
PLIP
PLOP
WE SEE OUR MOM.
OKAY.
BYE! HAVE A GREAT WEEKEND!

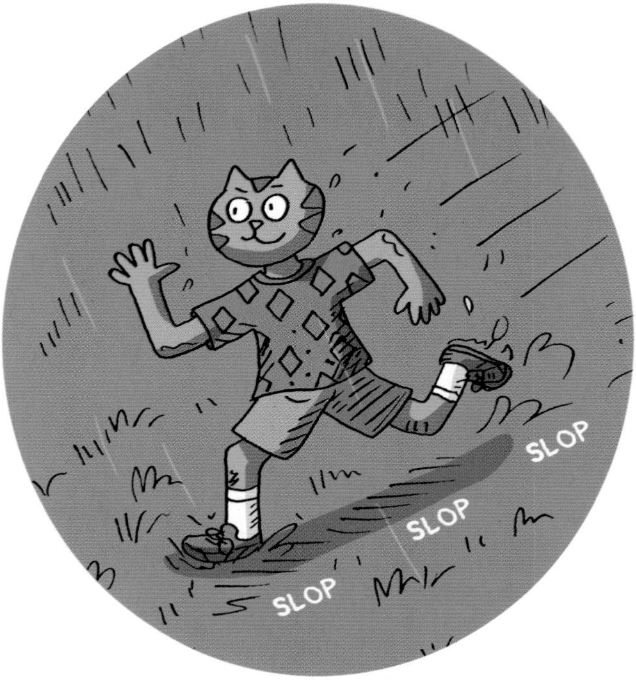
SLOP
SLOP
SLOP

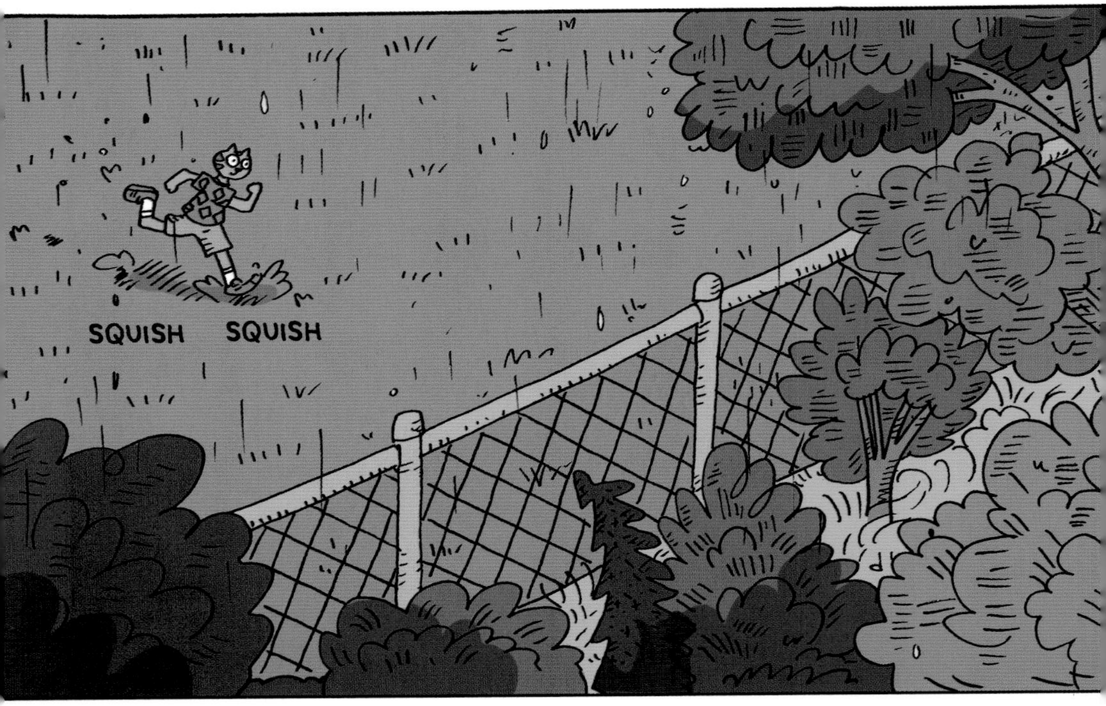
SQUISH SQUISH

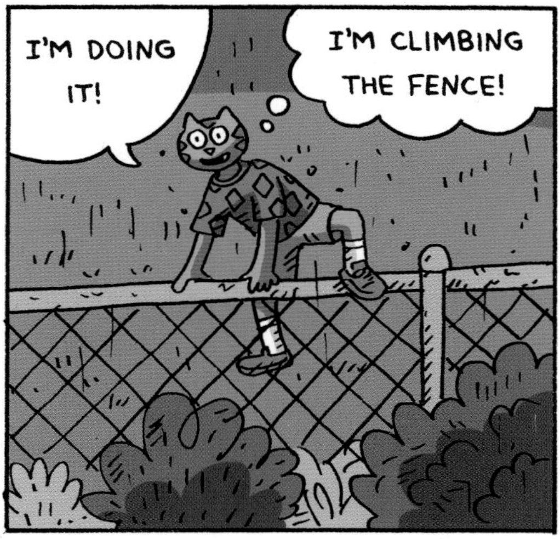
I'M DOING IT!
I'M CLIMBING THE FENCE!

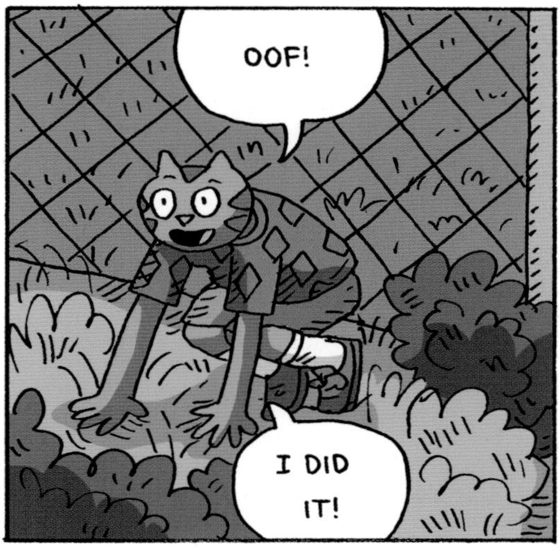
OOF!
I DID IT!

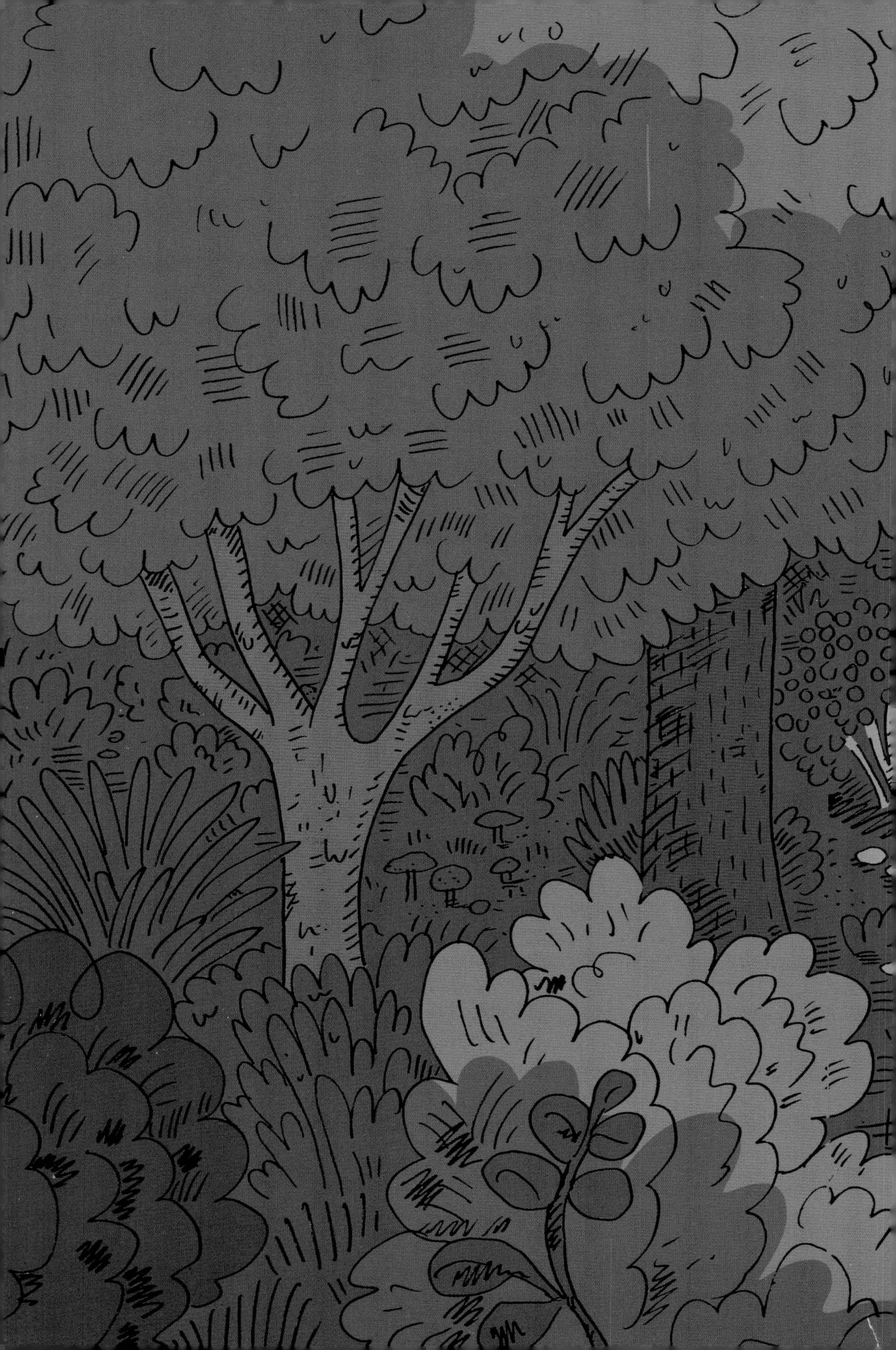

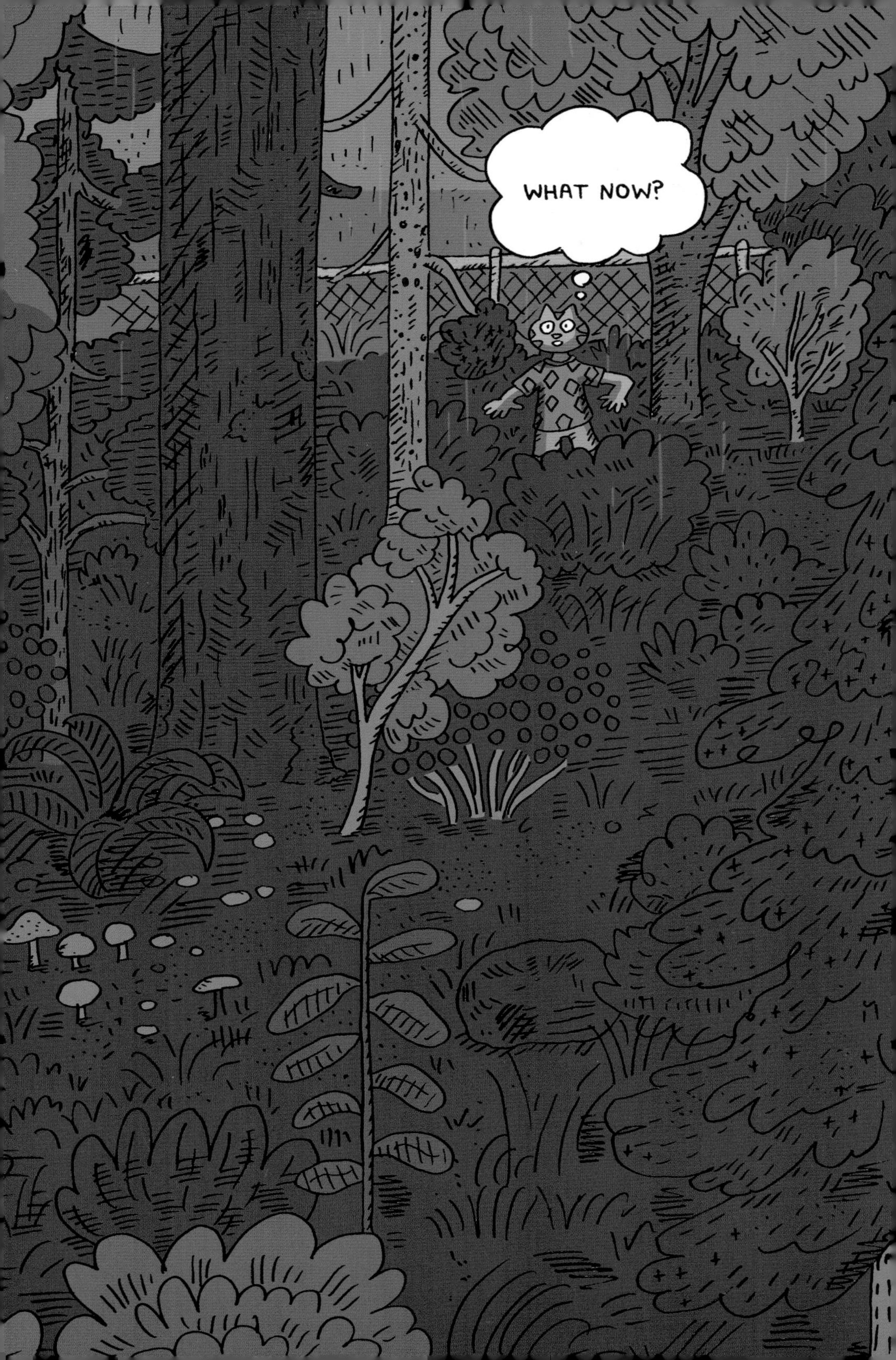
WHAT NOW?

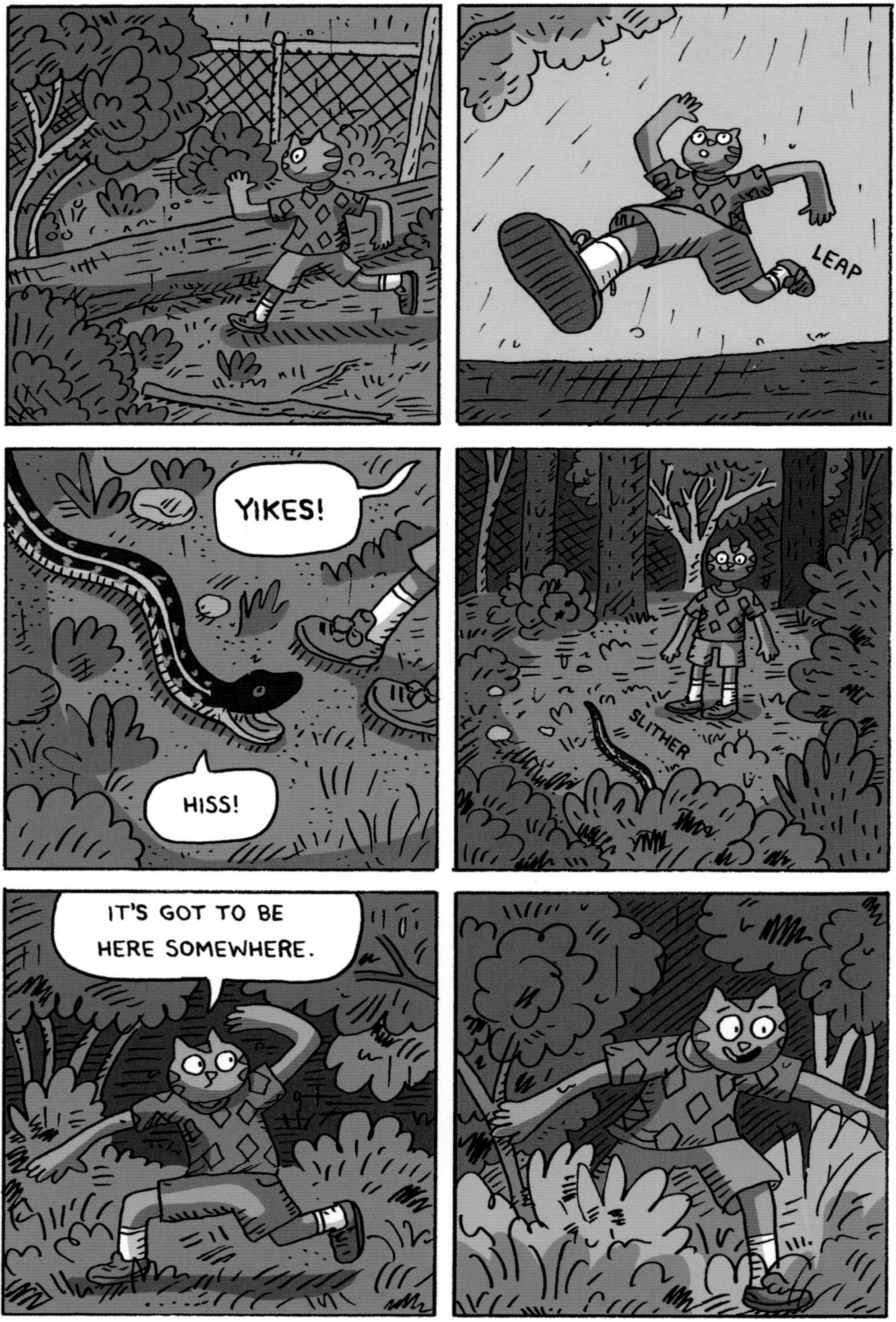
LEAP
YIKES!
HISS!
SLITHER
IT'S GOT TO BE HERE SOMEWHERE.

*ABDI'S MEMORY MAY OR MAY NOT BE 100% ACCURATE.

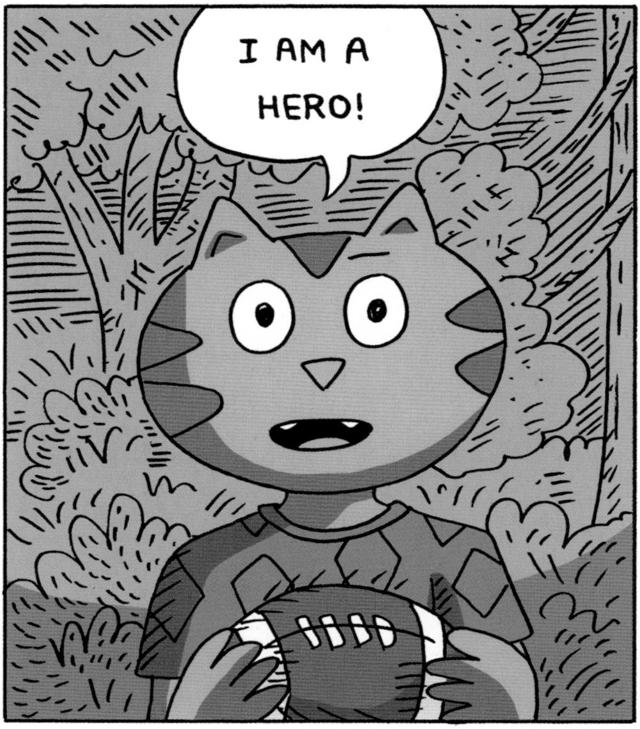
I AM A HERO!

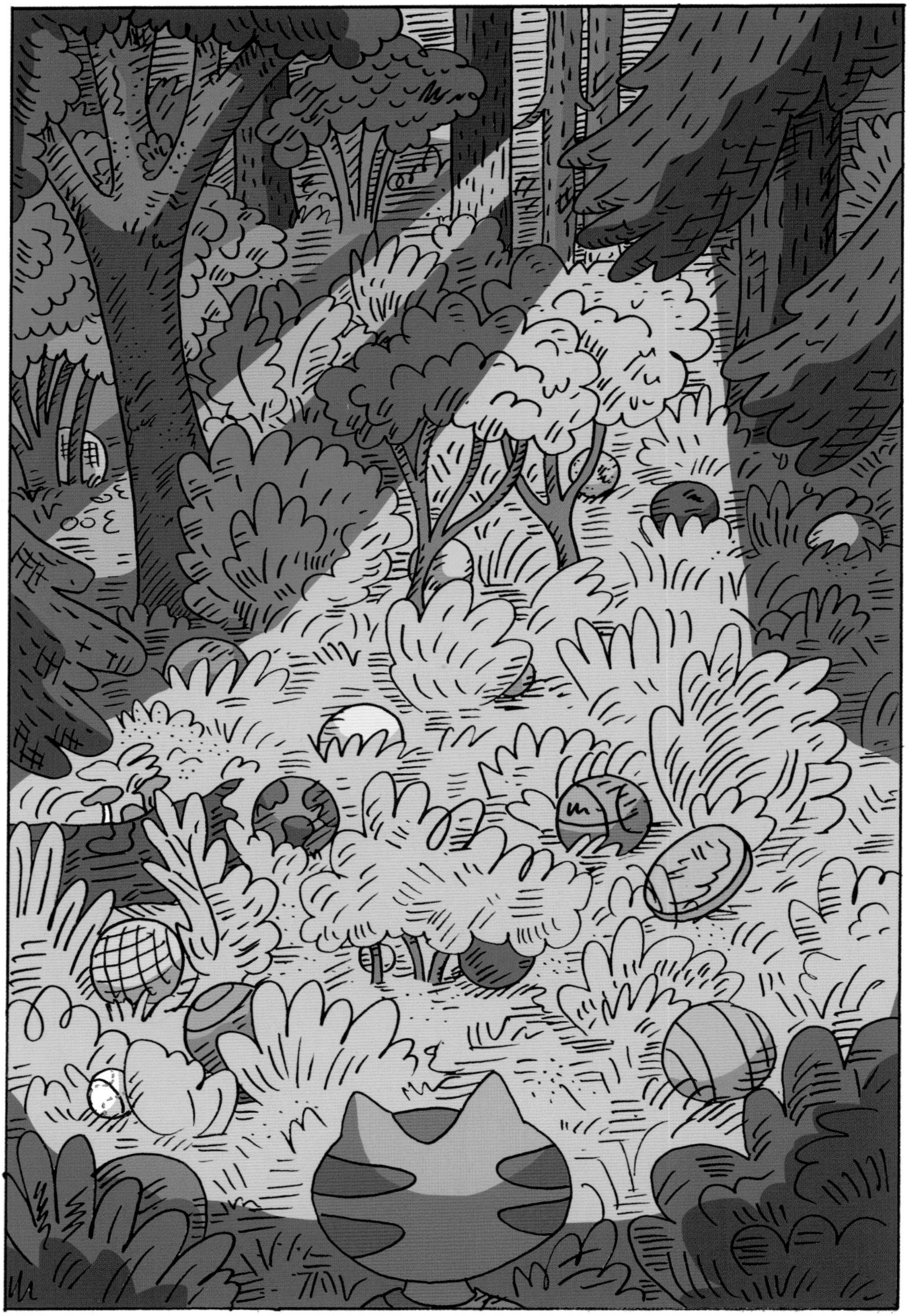

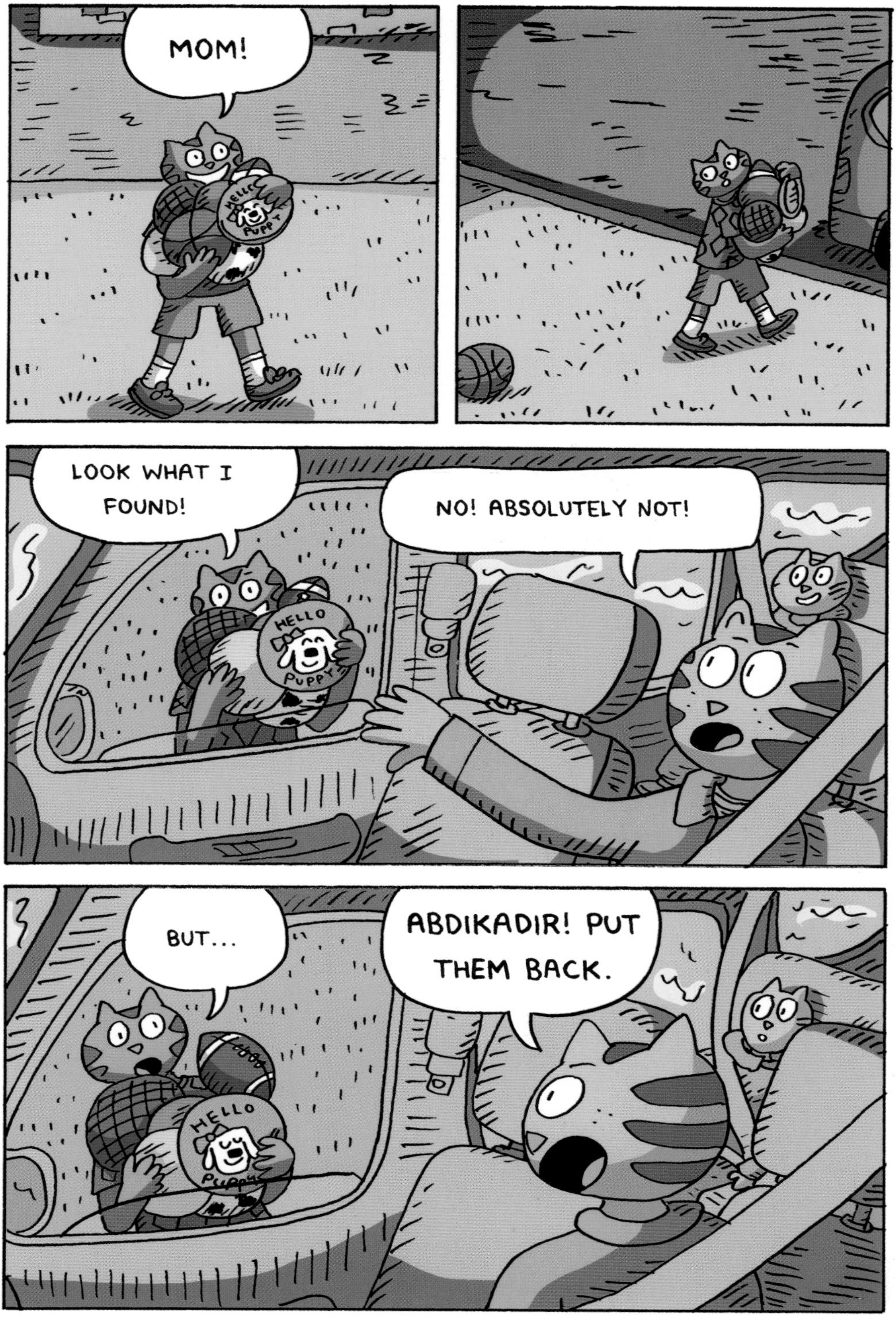
MOM!
LOOK WHAT I FOUND!
HELLO PUPPY
NO! ABSOLUTELY NOT!
BUT...
ABDIKADIR! PUT THEM BACK.

110

CHAPTER SEVEN

Party Time

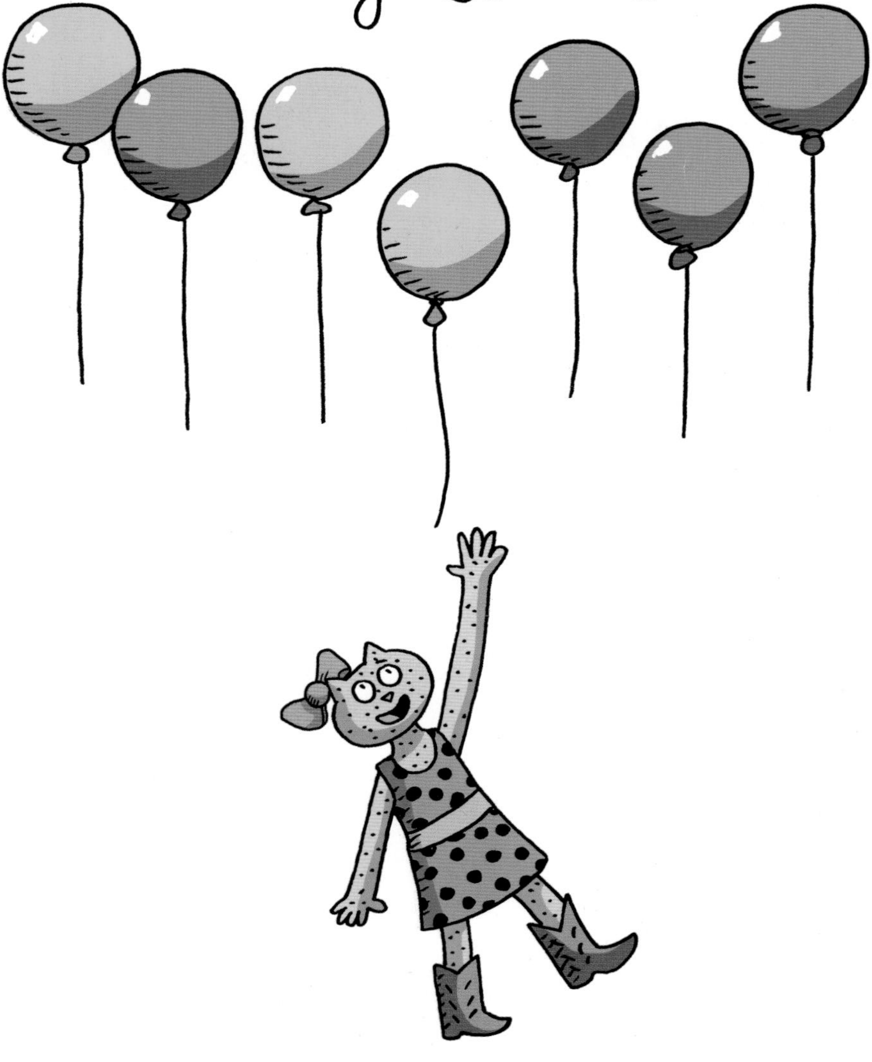

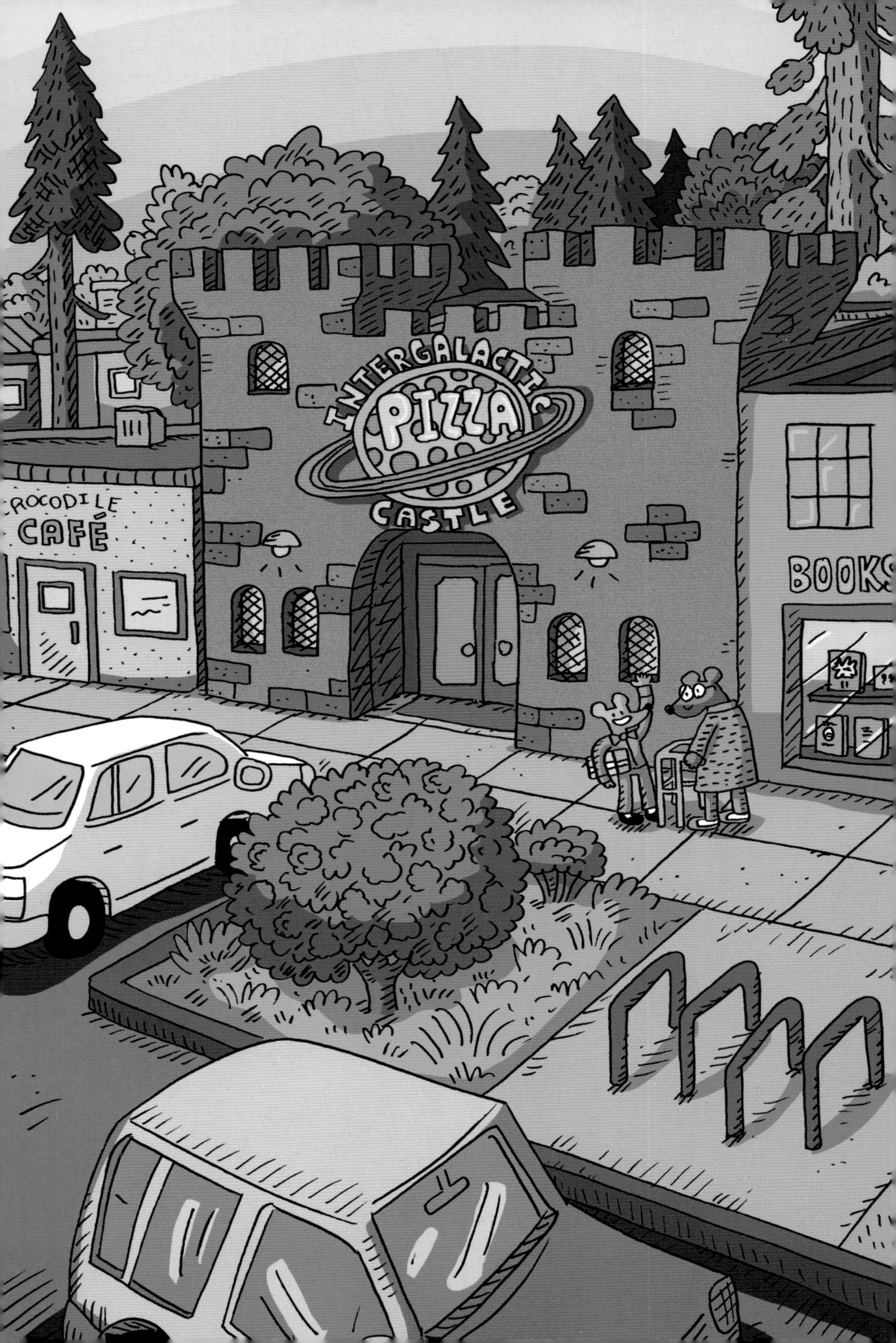
INTERGALACTIC
PIZZA
CASTLE
CROCODILE
CAFÉ
BOOKS

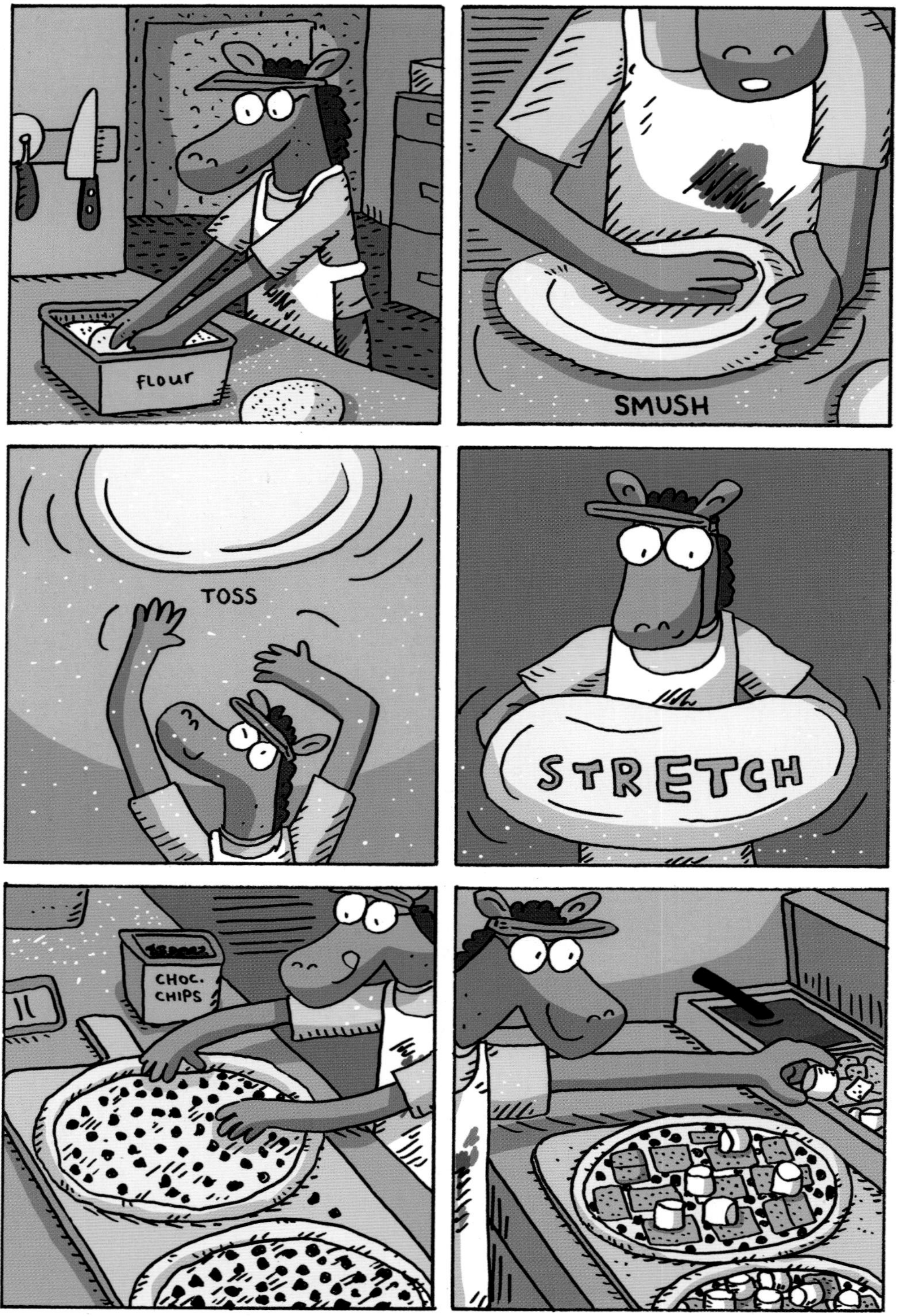
FLOUR
SMUSH
TOSS
STRETCH
CHOC.
CHIPS

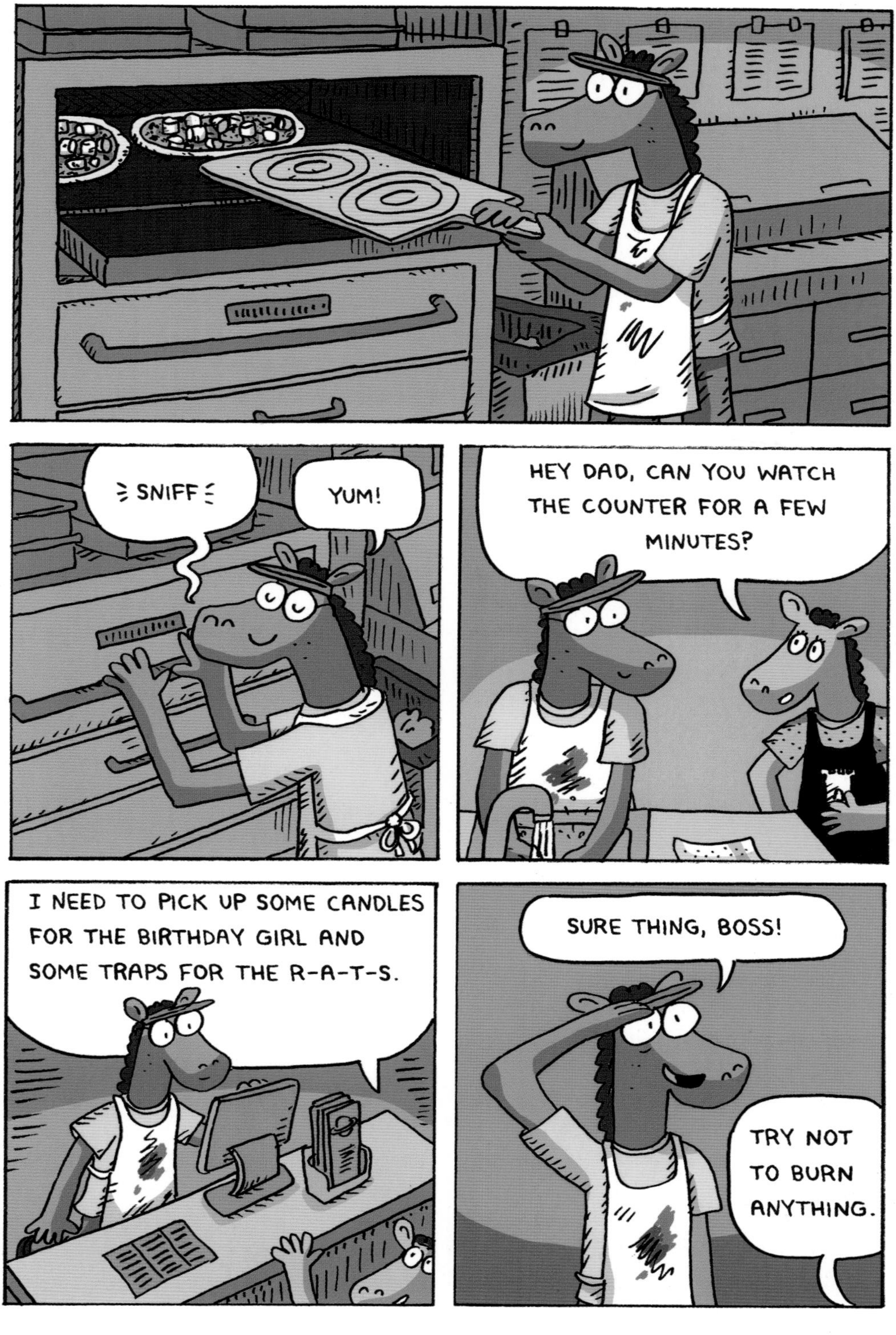
SNIFF
YUM!
HEY DAD, CAN YOU WATCH THE COUNTER FOR A FEW MINUTES?
I NEED TO PICK UP SOME CANDLES FOR THE BIRTHDAY GIRL AND SOME TRAPS FOR THE R-A-T-S.
SURE THING, BOSS!
TRY NOT TO BURN ANYTHING.

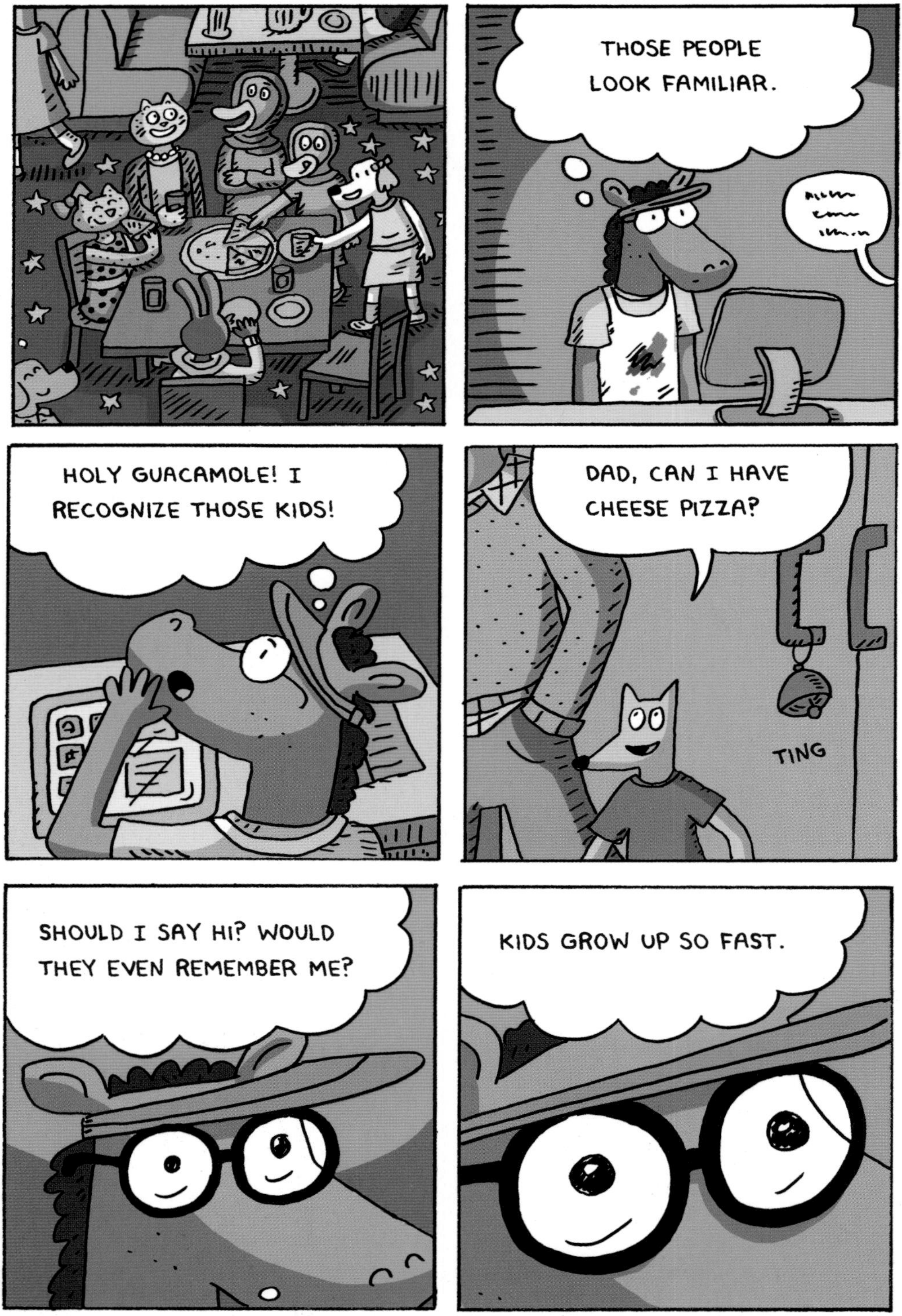
THOSE PEOPLE LOOK FAMILIAR.
HOLY GUACAMOLE! I RECOGNIZE THOSE KIDS!
DAD, CAN I HAVE CHEESE PIZZA?
TING
SHOULD I SAY HI? WOULD THEY EVEN REMEMBER ME?
KIDS GROW UP SO FAST.

121

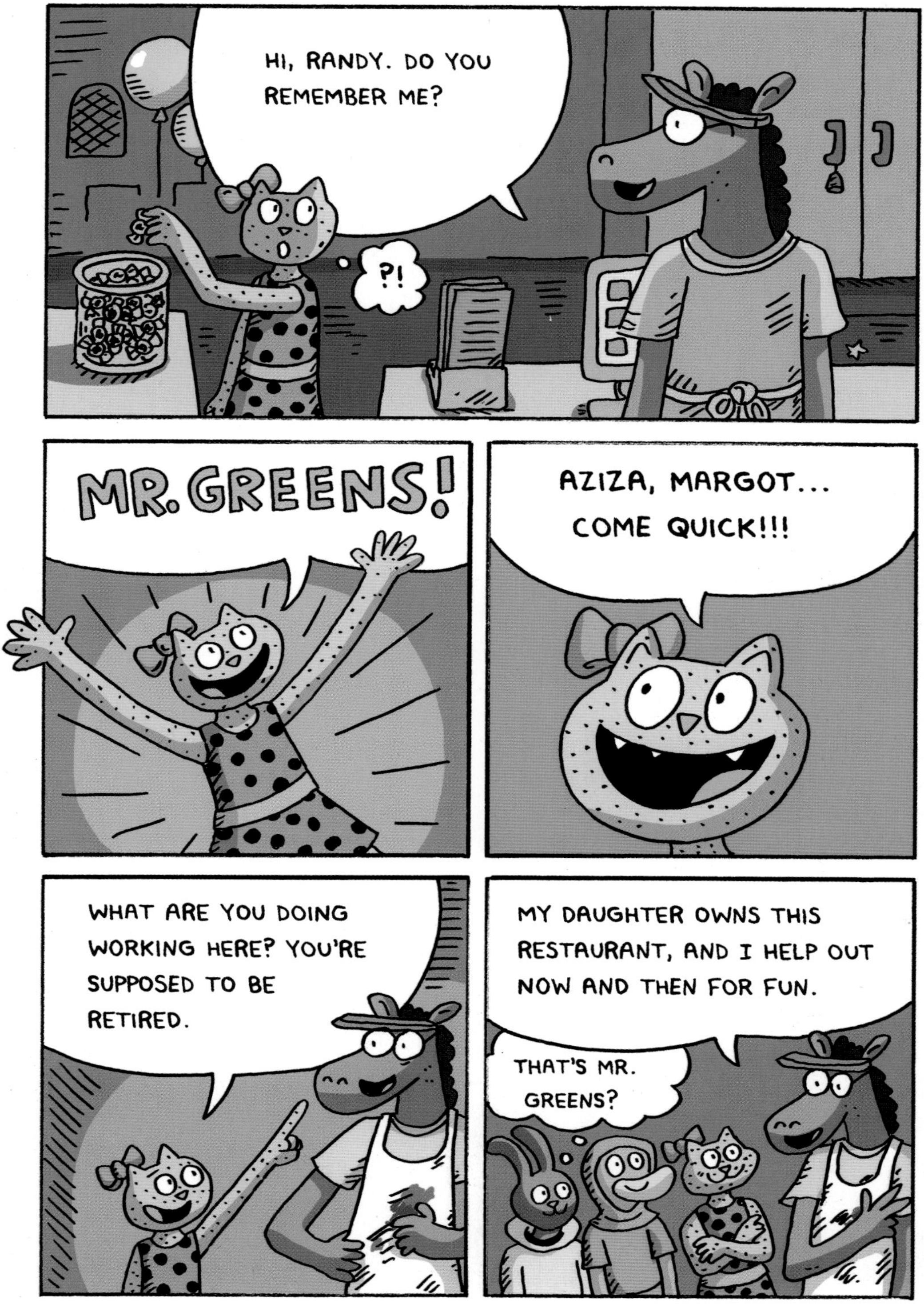
HI, RANDY. DO YOU REMEMBER ME?
?!
MR. GREENS!
AZIZA, MARGOT... COME QUICK!!!
WHAT ARE YOU DOING WORKING HERE? YOU'RE SUPPOSED TO BE RETIRED.
MY DAUGHTER OWNS THIS RESTAURANT, AND I HELP OUT NOW AND THEN FOR FUN.
THAT'S MR. GREENS?

WORKING HERE MEANS I GET TO EAT ALL THE FREE PIZZA I COULD EVER WANT!

PLUS, I GET TO MAKE MY OWN PIZZA IDEAS AND THEN PUT THEM ON THE MENU.

JUST TODAY I'VE CREATED A TOASTED PEANUT BUTTER AND STRAWBERRY JELLY PIZZA.

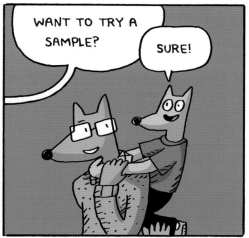

WANT TO TRY A SAMPLE?

SURE!

THANK YOU.

TOSS

CHOMP CHEW

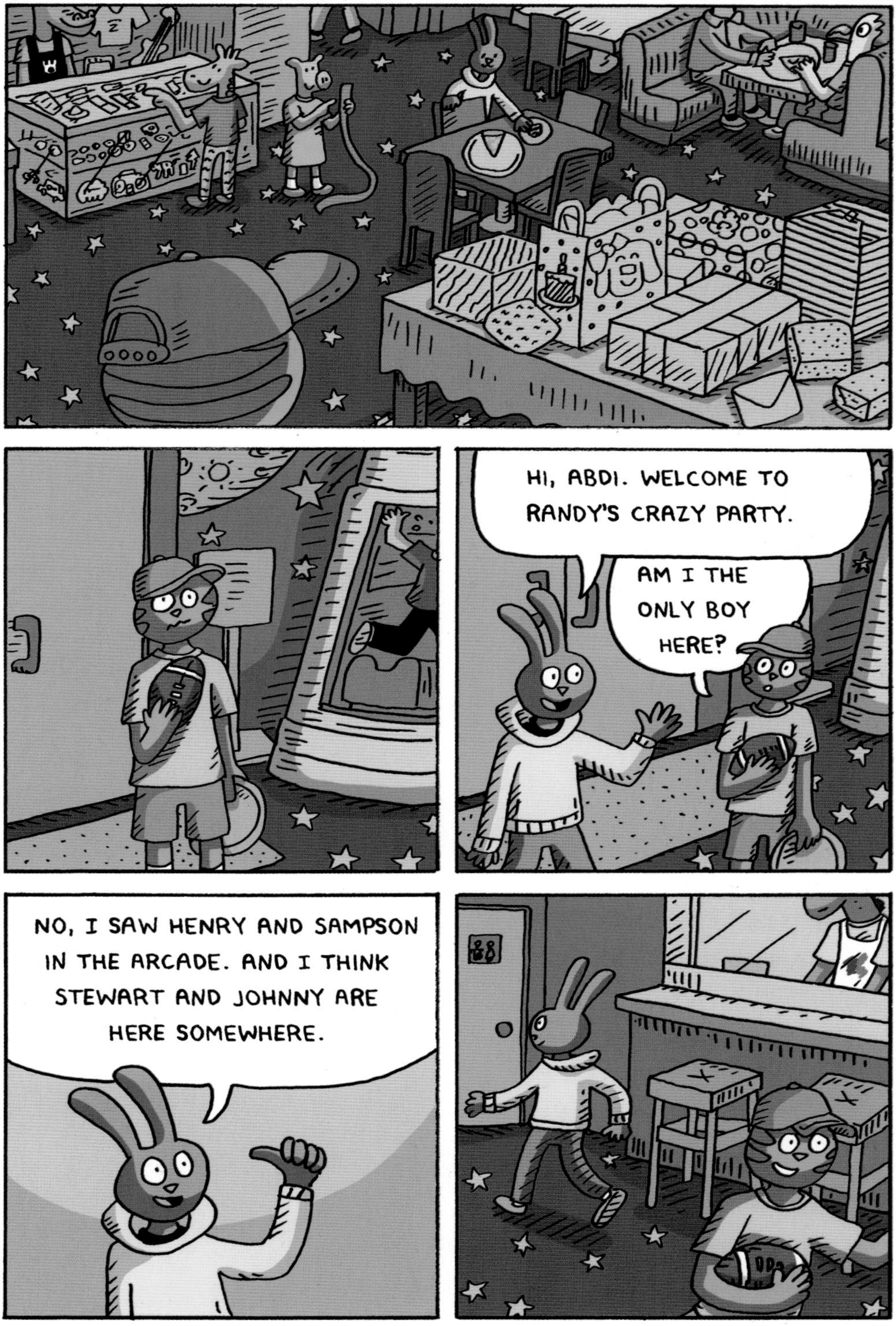
HI, ABDI. WELCOME TO RANDY'S CRAZY PARTY.
AM I THE ONLY BOY HERE?
NO, I SAW HENRY AND SAMPSON IN THE ARCADE. AND I THINK STEWART AND JOHNNY ARE HERE SOMEWHERE.

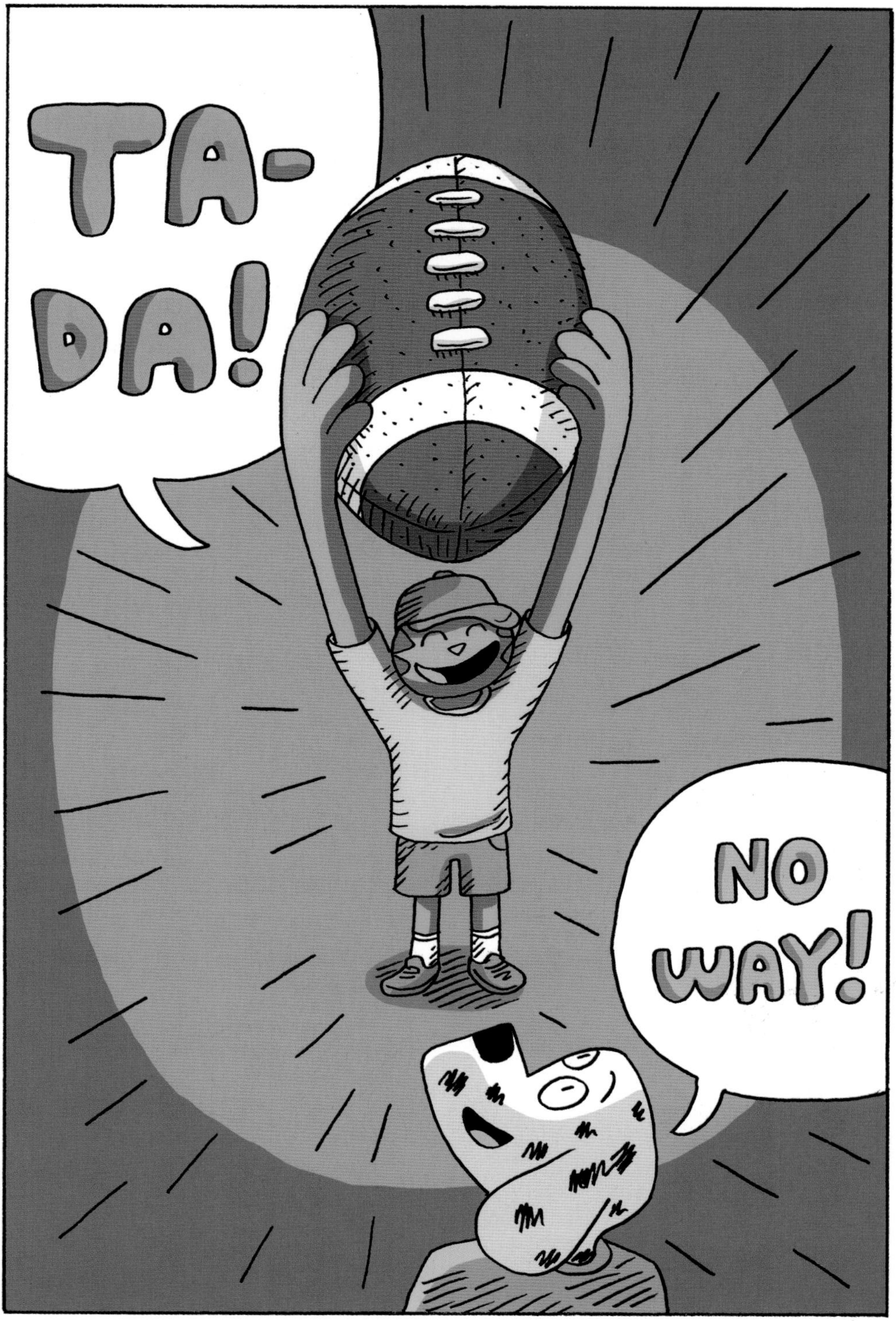
TA-DA!
NO WAY!

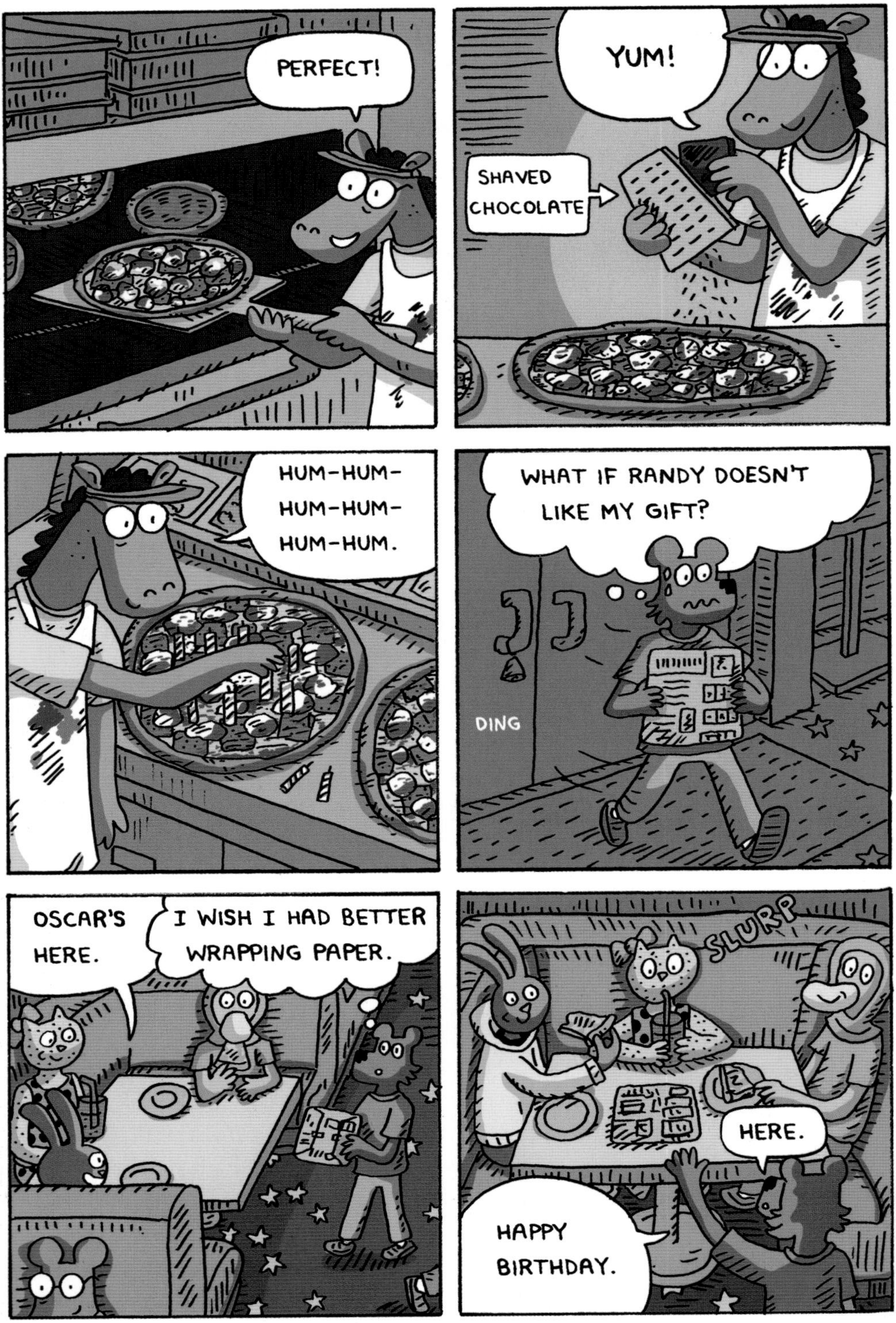
PERFECT!
YUM!
SHAVED CHOCOLATE
HUM-HUM-
HUM-HUM-
HUM-HUM.
WHAT IF RANDY DOESN'T LIKE MY GIFT?
DING
OSCAR'S HERE.
I WISH I HAD BETTER WRAPPING PAPER.
SLURP
HERE.
HAPPY BIRTHDAY.

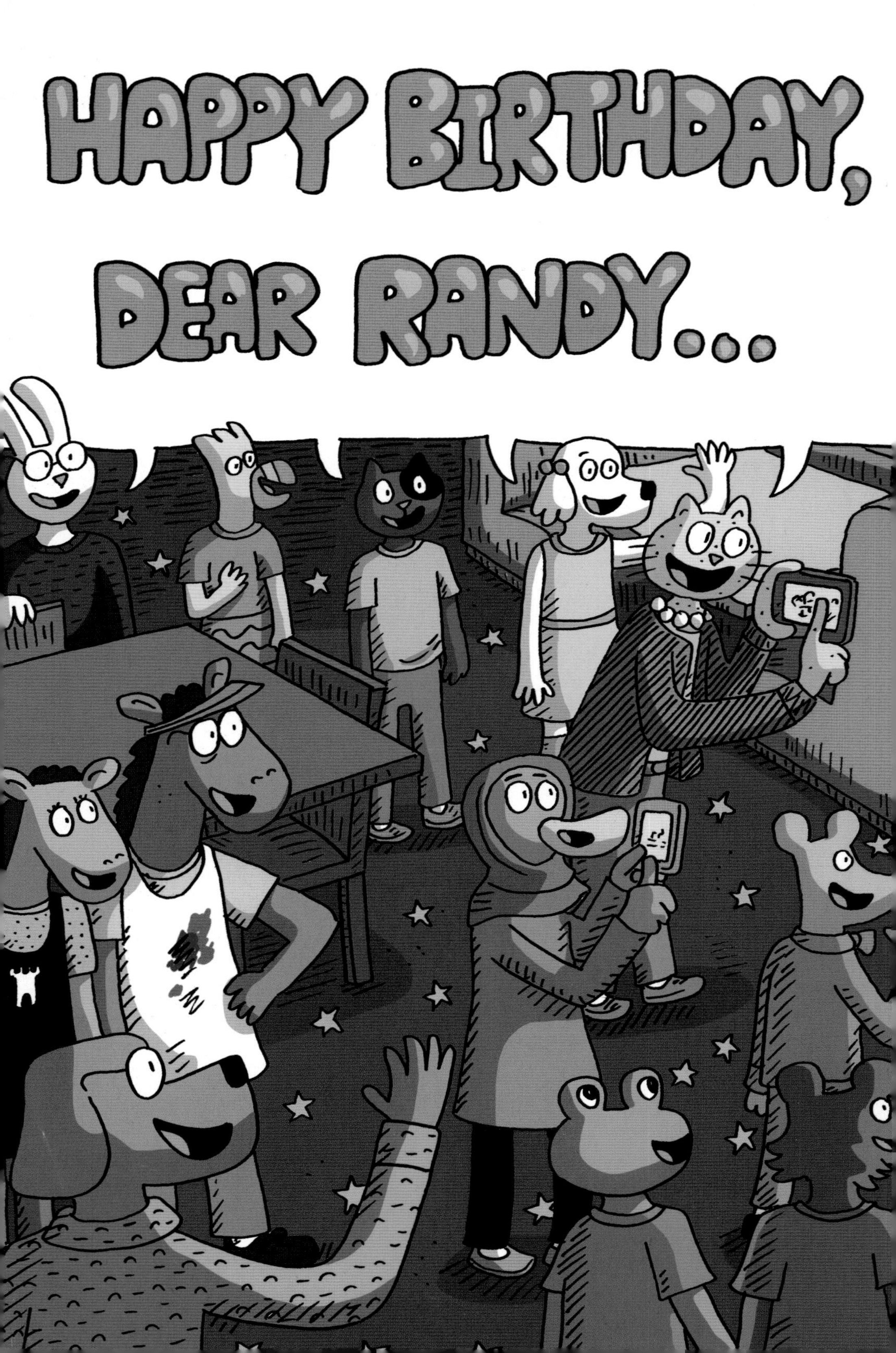
HAPPY BIRTHDAY,
DEAR RANDY...

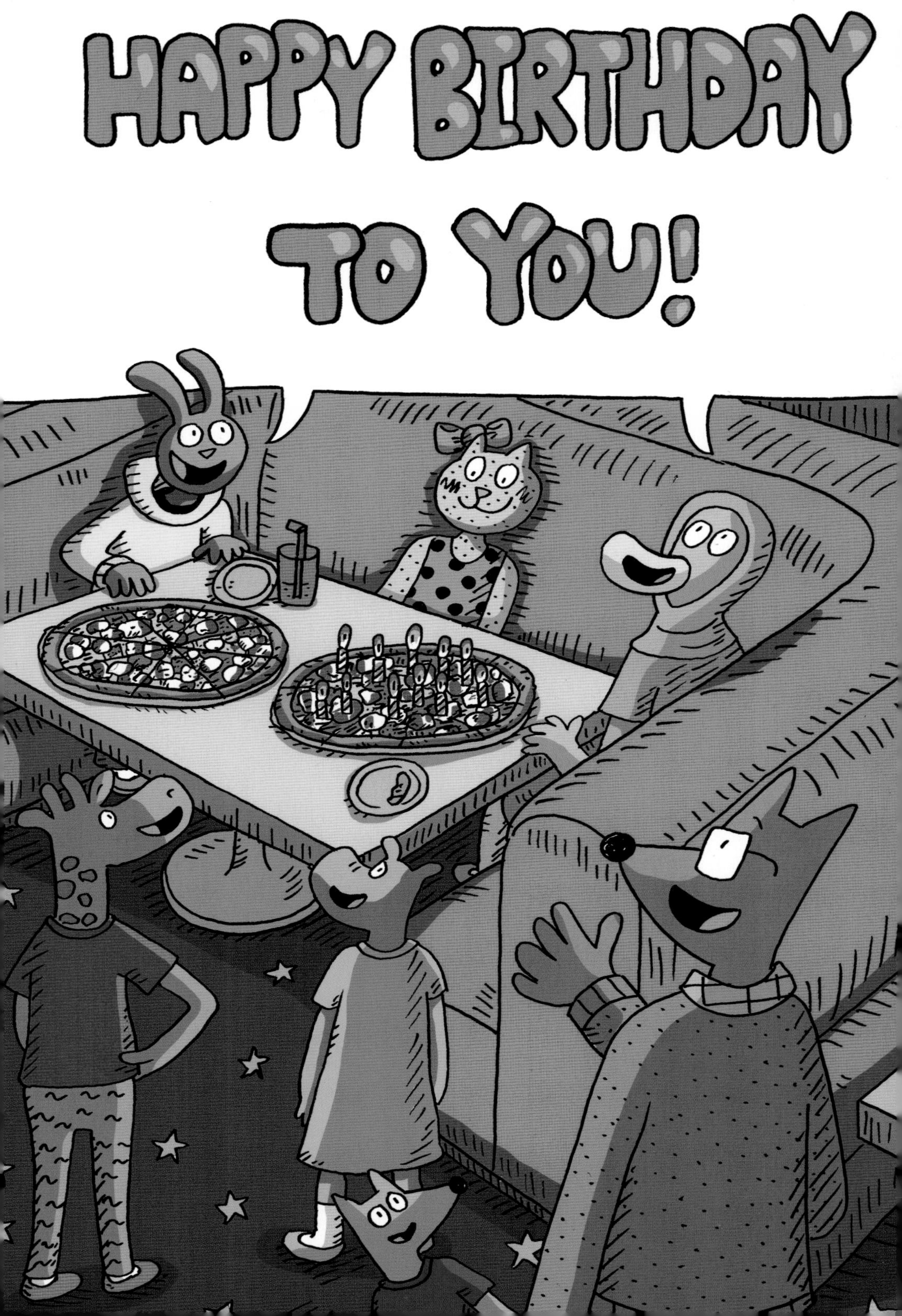
HAPPY BIRTHDAY TO YOU!

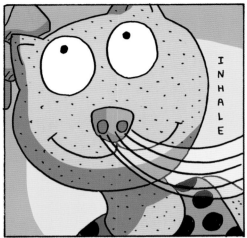

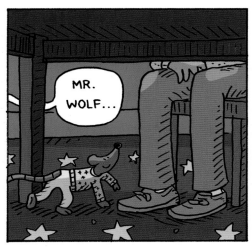

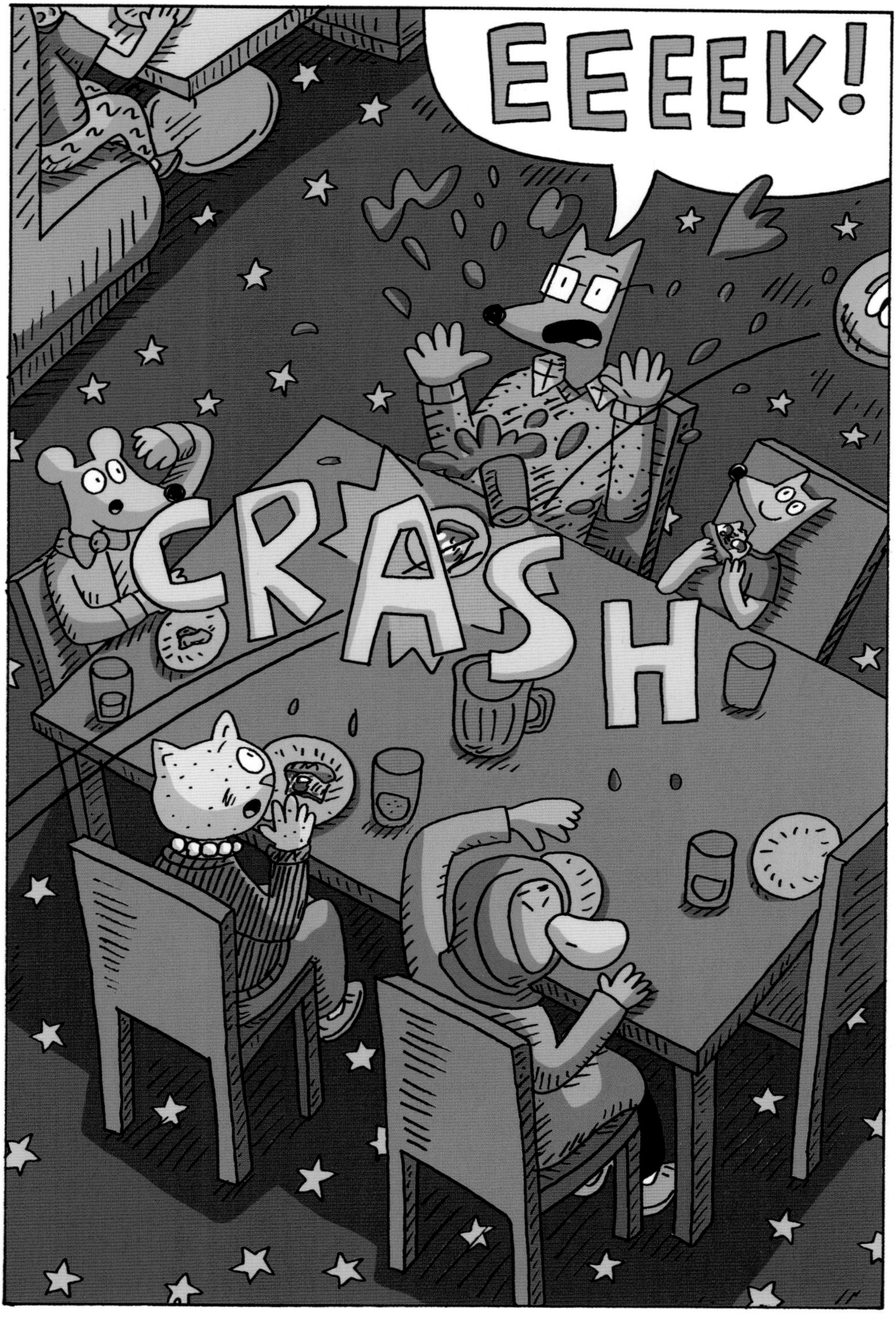
EEEEK!
CRASH

GASP!
OH NO!

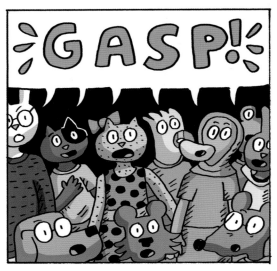

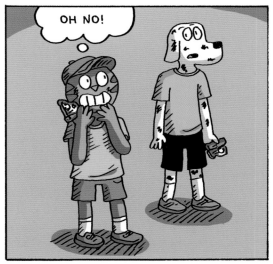

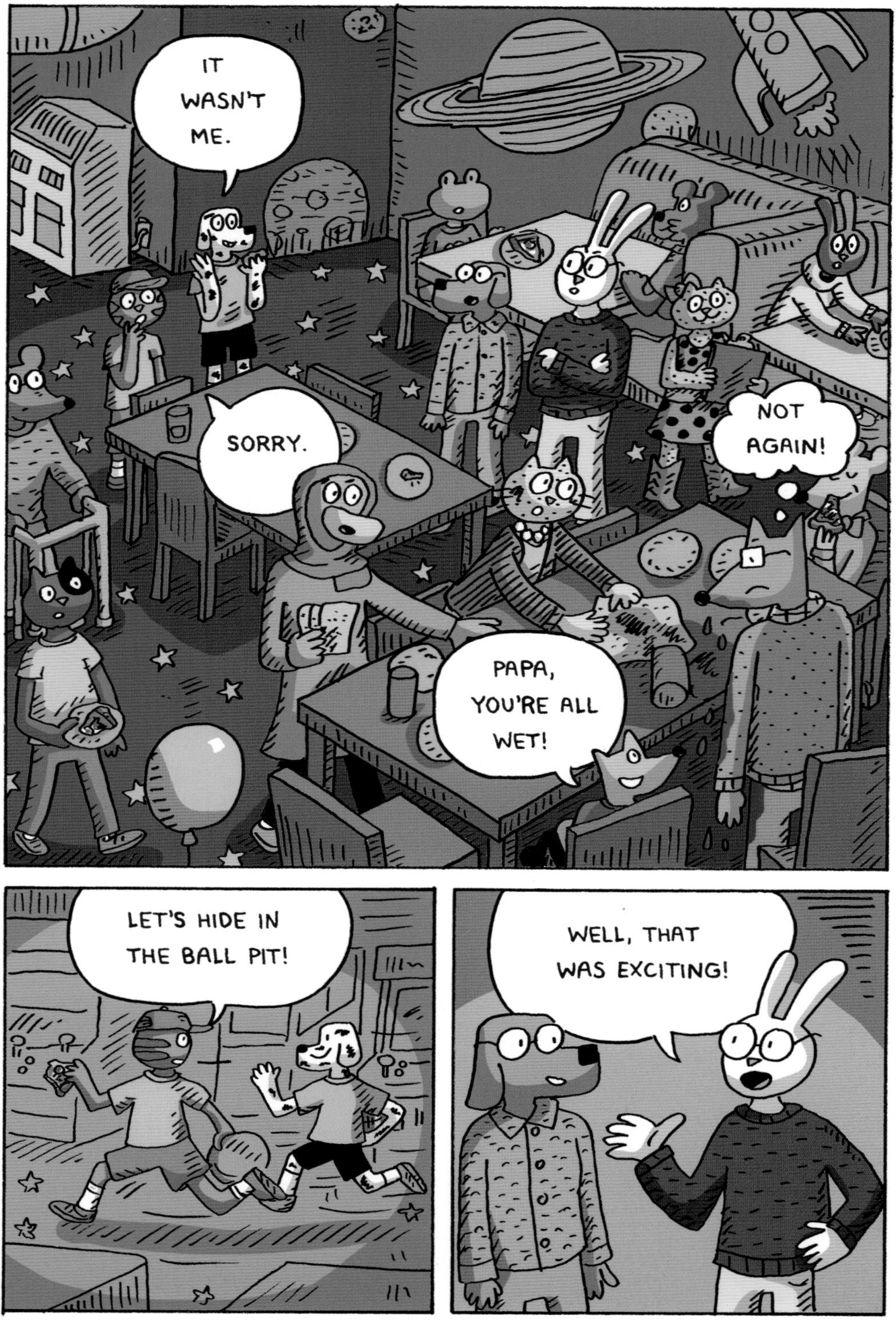
IT WASN'T ME.
NOT AGAIN!
SORRY.
PAPA, YOU'RE ALL WET!
LET'S HIDE IN THE BALL PIT!
WELL, THAT WAS EXCITING!

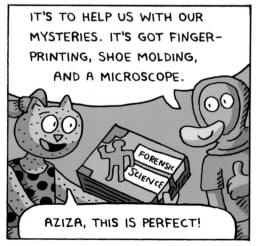

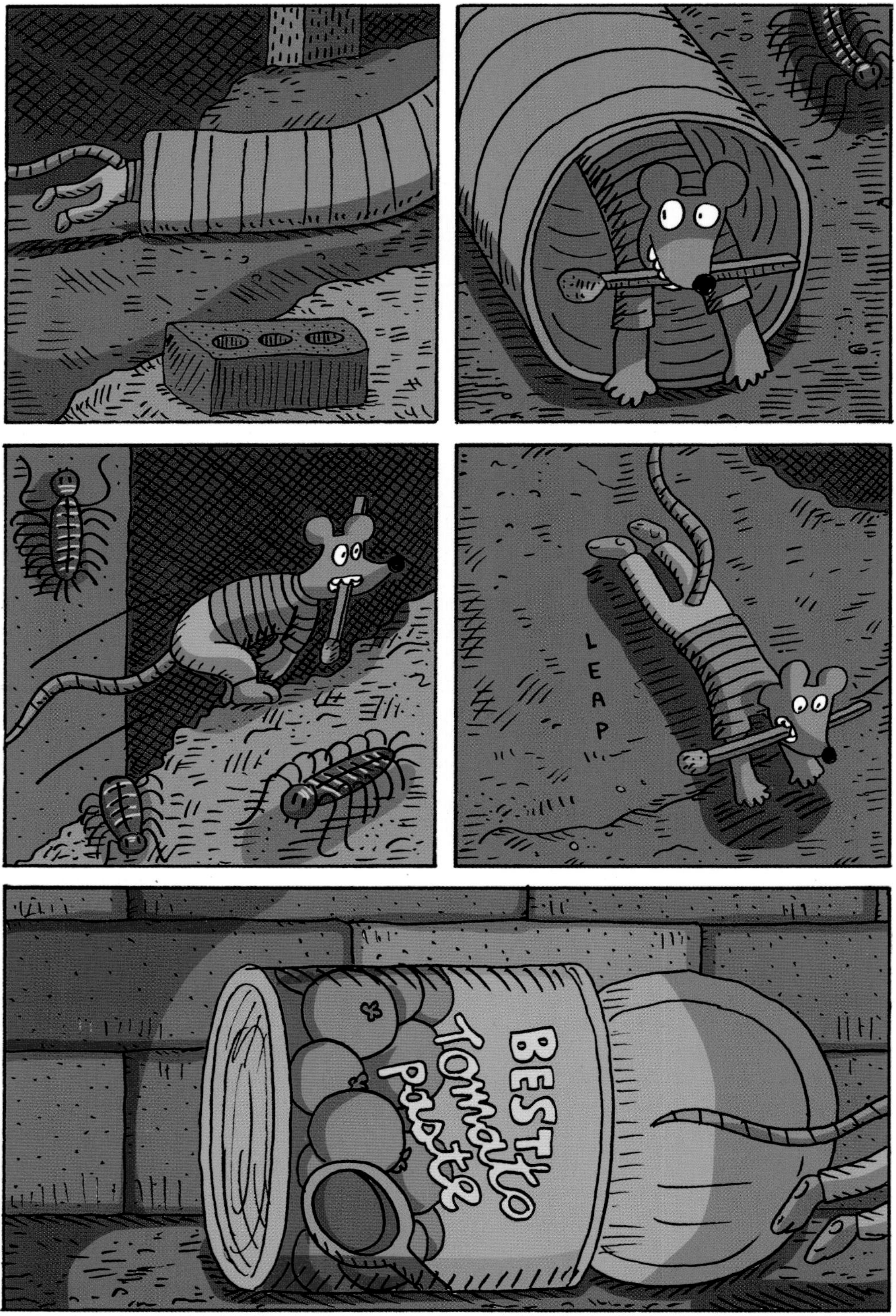
LEAP
BESTto
Tomato Paste

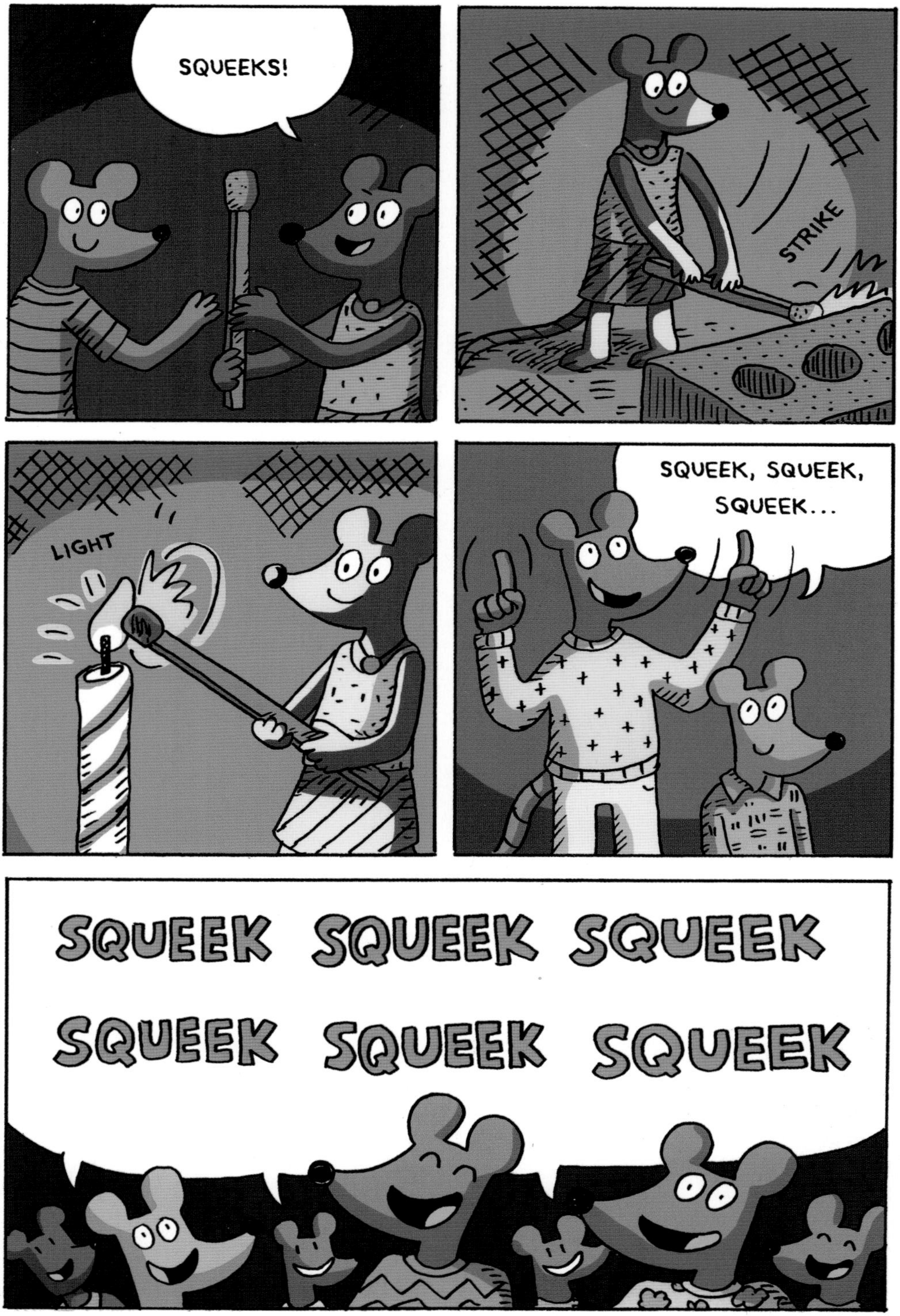
SQUEEKS!
STRIKE
LIGHT
SQUEEK, SQUEEK, SQUEEK...
SQUEEK SQUEEK SQUEEK
SQUEEK SQUEEK SQUEEK

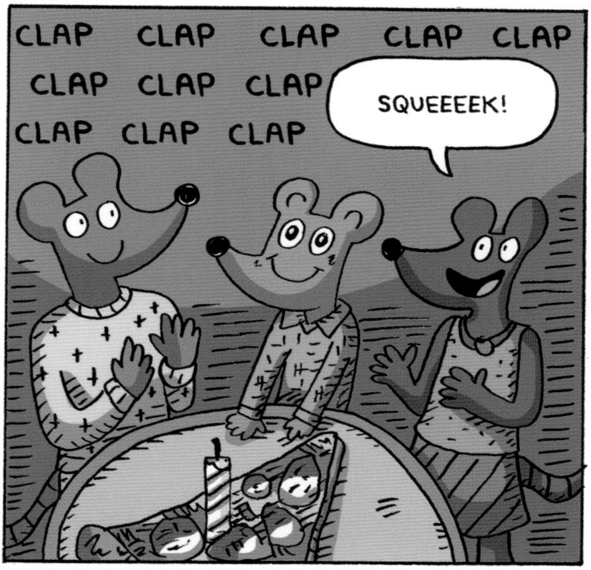
CLAP CLAP CLAP CLAP CLAP
CLAP CLAP CLAP
CLAP CLAP CLAP
SQUEEEEK!

Thank you to . . .

My amazing editor, Cassandra Pelham Fulton; art director, Phil Falco; creative director, David Saylor; and the whole team at Scholastic/Graphix who have helped make Mr. Wolf's Class a reality.

To my agent, Judy Hansen, who has superpowers.

To Tanya, my acupuncturist, who helped my poor arm heal so that I could keep drawing and writing this book.

To my family: As always, Ariel and Marlen, XOXO. And to my mom and dad, who always encouraged and supported my art.

To Calista Brill, who gave me valuable feedback early on. I should have thanked you sooner.

And of course, to all of my students, who give me hope for the future.

This book was made over the course of a year. Thank you, dear reader, for spending your time with these characters and stories, which were once just thoughts in my head.

Author photo by Renée Lopez

Aron Nels Steinke is the Eisner Award—winning illustrator and coauthor, with Ariel Cohn, of *The Zoo Box*. After graduating from Vancouver Film School with a specialization in hand-drawn animation, he discovered the magic of making comics and hasn't looked back since. He teaches fifth graders by day and draws comics by night in Portland, Oregon, where he lives with his wife, Ariel, and their Robin Hood—obsessed son, Marlen. In the summer, when he's not hunched over a drawing board, you might find him swimming the frigid rivers of the Cascade Mountains or possibly hugging a tree.

Don't miss the next adventure in Mr. Wolf's class!

LUCKY STARS

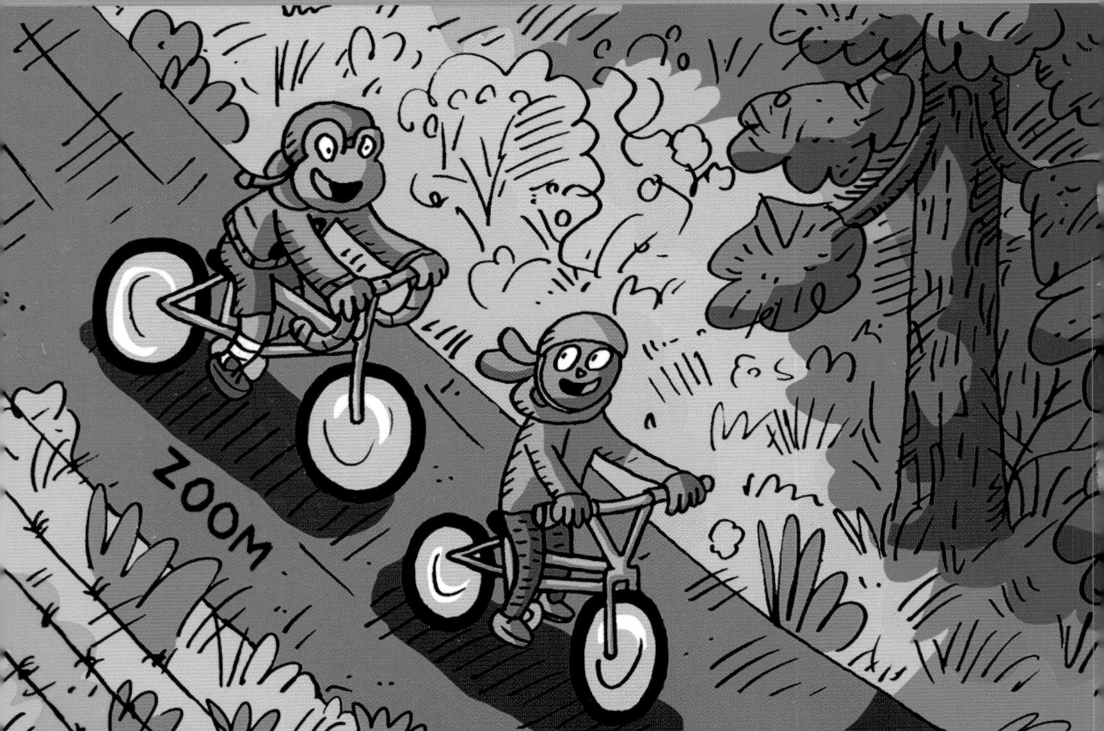
ZOOM